4

Known to millions as the agony aunt from Granada Television's *This Morning* programme, Denise Robertson has worked extensively on television and radio and as a national newspaper journalist. Beginning with *The Land of Lost Content* in 1984, which won the Constable Trophy for Fiction, she has published 18 successful novels. She lives near Sunderland with her husband and an assortment of dogs.

Other titles by Denise Robertson

The Bad Sister

The Beloved People trilogy:

The Beloved People
Strength for the Morning
Towards Jerusalem

DENISE ROBERTSON

Wait for the Day

This edition published in the United Kingdom in 2006 by Little Books Ltd,
48 Catherine Place, London SW1E 6HL

A CIP catalogue record for this book is available from the British Library.

ISBN: 1 904435 56 4

Printed by Bookmarque Limited, Croydon

For Bryan Thubron, who has made all things new.

Wait For The Day

Book One

1945

Prologue

Spring 1945

It is 9 p.m. on an April evening. The world is still at war but the Western Allies and their Russian comrades-in-arms are swarming across Germany.

A few hours ago Hitler died by his own hand in his Berlin bunker, Eva Braun's body beside him. Two days ago the bodies of Mussolini and his mistress were strung up from the façade of a petrol station in Milan's Piazza Loretto. The war in Europe is almost at an end.

Lighting restrictions in Britain were lifted a week ago but the blackout lingers. Householders, conditioned by habit, still draw black-lined curtains. Street lighting is patchy but the face of Big Ben is lit once more and West End clubs, usually anxious to maintain their privacy, leave their huge windows defiantly uncurtained. Inside them elderly gentlemen can be seen reading newspapers or offering hospitality to young men and women in khaki and blue, for the nation is anxious to show its gratitude.

1

Celia, Joyce, Amy, Peggy
April 1945

From the depths of the worn leather chair Celia Blake surveyed the splendour of her godfather's club. Polished mahogany, here and there the gleam of silver, a dark, beamed ceiling that seemed to absorb the half-whispered conversations. It probably looked like this a century ago, Celia thought. She pulled her khaki skirt over her lisle-clad knees and tried to concentrate on what Uncle Philip was saying.

There was a sergeant's stripes on the arm of her ATS jacket, her dark hair was cut short and pinned back behind her ears and her expression was earnest, betraying the fact that she had spent her childhood among adults. She sipped what passed for wartime coffee as her godfather pontificated on the satisfactions of war and the dangers of the peace to come.

'It's a great pity FDR's gone. Lend-Lease will cease the moment there's an armistice, you'll see. And of course we're bankrupt – we'll have to cut back our imports. Food, petrol. What we make we must export if we're to survive, so there'll be shortages.'

'We can't do with less food.' Celia felt bound to protest. 'I don't know how manual workers exist on their meat ration.'

'Needs must, my dear. Would you like a brandy?' He was already nodding in the direction of a hovering waiter as Celia shook her head and she suppressed a smile. All this talk of shortages, but there was still the odd Armagnac around if you were in the right place. Sugar lumps, unheard-of luxury, were piled in a bowl on the tray in front of them. She thought of the huge bowls of sugar back at camp, tinged brown at the edges, an encrusted spoon standing to attention in the centre of the mound. She had used lump sugar all her life until Hitler intervened. Now she felt more at home with granulated.

'What will you do when it's over?' her godfather asked, leaning forward to take a sugar lump. As Celia watched he popped it into his mouth and let it dissolve, a look of satisfaction suffusing his face. She was fascinated for a moment and her answer was delayed.

'Well?' he asked impatiently when the sugar was gone. 'You should have taken a commission, you know. A girl with a good degree . . . I'm surprised they let you get away with it.'

Celia smiled. How could she explain to him that the

last five years had been the most fun she had ever known? She had been so afraid that first day, sipping the hot cocoa that was pressed upon them while an officer gave a speech of welcome. After that had come roll call and then a medical. As she had stood in line to strip off her clothes and place them, neatly folded, on a wooden form she had realised that life was going to be different. She could continue to tremble or she could enjoy it. It had been an easy decision to make.

Celia Blake had grown up in the home of two great-aunts, a place where windows were shrouded to prevent sun fading the furniture, and voices were never raised. There had been books galore and a tabby cat and much genteel kindness, but no sense of adventure and little companionship. As she had shuffled in line towards the medical room, clutching her newly issued underwear and her newly made resolution, she had felt first a surge of excitement and then a fellow feeling for the girls in front and behind her. Impossible now to explain that to Uncle Philip, however. He had more than once consoled her on being 'thrown in with all kinds of strange people'. Instead she smiled at him.

'I think they thought I was odd – mad, even – not to be jostling for place, so they left me alone. As for the future, I suppose I just want to do something useful.'

'Teaching?' He was eyeing the sugar again but to her relief he left the bowl alone. Instead he took a sip of his coffee, wincing as he did so. 'God, I'll be relieved to get a cup of decent coffee again.'

Celia had thought the coffee rather splendid but

perhaps years of sludgy army brew had ruined her palate. 'I'm not cut out for teaching, Uncle Philip. They did suggest AEC – the Education Corps – but I think not. I'd like to work in Europe for a while, perhaps with refugees or in the camps. There'll be a huge problem there.'

He shook his head. 'Not for much longer. They'll die, most of them. Too far gone and Europe hasn't the resources to save them. Half the continent has been displaced. Agriculture's done for. We'll be hard-pressed to feed our own this winter, never mind anyone else.'

Celia knew he was right, but the nonchalance with which he dismissed thousands of human beings was chilling. How could he see the pictures that had emerged from Europe and remain dispassionate? She made a conscious effort not to judge him. He was a dearly loved uncle and godfather – not a blood relative but someone who had brought her toys and sweets when her parents died and once even took her to Brighton for a week, to bathe in the sea. Tonight she could see signs of ageing. A looseness of skin at his neck and on the back of his hands, a yellowing of the whites of his eyes.

'You've had your hair cut,' he said suddenly. 'It suits you, but I still like a woman with a chignon.' He sounded so wistful that they both laughed aloud. 'Ah well,' he said. 'I'm showing my age when I hanker for bygone things. Let's order more coffee before you have to go.'

As they emerged from the club an hour later he

squeezed her arm. 'Good to see you, old thing. And keep in touch. I was fond of your father, your mother too. Still, isn't it splendid to see these steps at last? I've crept over this doorway, blind as a mole, for the past five years. It's a wonder none of the members have broken their necks.'

Once on the pavement he glanced skyward. 'We shan't see the stars so clearly now the blackout's over. Except in the countryside, of course. You must come to Gloucestershire soon.' He put out a hand and patted her cheek. 'You're a good girl. I hope life treats you kindly once you're out of uniform.' And then, aware that his voice was threatening to break, he glanced at the sky once more. 'None of those damn V things to cope with, thank God. Sky used to be thick with them once upon a time. I remember a meal at the Savoy – couldn't lift a fork to my mouth without one of the damn things cutting out above me. Ruined the entrée – such as it was.'

It is more than a month since the last V2 had landed near Orpington. 'Yes, it's good that it's over,' Celia said. 'They did enormous damage.'

She kissed him on the cheek before they parted, declining his offer to pay for a cab to take her to her destination.

'I'm meeting some of the other girls, Uncle Philip. There was a lorry coming up to town so we scrounged a lift. He's picking us up at ten for the trip back to camp.'

'I don't like the thought of you gallivanting around

in the dark, in a lorry of all things. Let me at least put you in a cab to this rendezvous.'

'I'd rather walk, Uncle Philip. London is so interesting.' But as she walked to meet the lorry that would take her back to camp Celia's thoughts were not of London.

She was thinking of the film she had seen in the news cinema that afternoon, made in Belsen and Buchenwald. The audience watched in shocked silence as the horror of the camps unfolded. Bodies piled mountain high. Gaunt, skeletal figures moving slowly as though through water, their faces impassive because liberation was too big a concept to grasp.

I must do something useful, she thought, as the meeting place came into view. In peacetime there had been a bustling department store on this corner. Now, a framework of ornamental masonry still stood but the huge windows were gone, along with floors that once were full of clothes and toys and household goods. Part of one storey hung drunkenly in a corner and tucked in a pile of rubble she saw the head and torso of a plaster mannequin, at a distance horrifyingly similar to the bodies in the film.

She had grown used to bomb sites in the last few years. Soon rosebay willow herb would assert itself and spread, turning the rubble into an impromptu garden. Once she had seen an area of dereliction bright with poppies, reminding her of Flanders so that her nose pricked and her eyes filled. Tonight, though, she was not in the mood for tears. She was full of the desire to mend, to heal, to create. It's going to be a wonderful peace, she thought.

In the back of a cab Peggy Bates and Amy Yeo sat side by side on their way to the lorry pick-up point. Peggy was small and sturdy and her dark hair framed her face in neat corrugated waves. She came from the pit village of Belgate in County Durham and was engaged to a miner there. She was almost as proud of the tiny diamond solitaire on her left ring finger as she was of her corporal's stripes, but tonight her principal emotion was disapproval of the extravagance of taking a cab when a bus would do. As usual, however, Amy's will had prevailed.

Amy – Alexandra Mary Yeo – was fair and blessed with what her father fondly called an English-rose complexion. It was Amy who insisted on the cab, firstly because she was afraid of arriving late at the rendezvous and secondly because she liked to be kind to Peggy.

Amy liked to be kind to everyone, just as life had always been kind to her. She was the favoured only daughter of George Henry Yeo, landlord of the George, a rambling riverside pub in Yorkshire, where he conducted a flourishing black market and wrung his hands that he had been unable to prevent the conscription of his only child.

'Such a lovely girl,' he told his regulars every night as they supped their after-hours drinks and plotted the progress of the war. 'Delicate,' he would say. 'Delicate.'

And he would glance towards the bar where his equally delicate wife, the true landlord of the George, was organising the best-kept pub in Yorkshire.

Amy was not at all delicate. The Army had declared her AI and she was a fully trained radar operative. Her blonde hair formed a fat roll around a chiffon scarf carefully concealed by the waves that framed her face. There was a small mole at the side of her mouth and dimples that came and went in her pale pink cheeks. Her hands were still the small soft hands of a pampered daughter but she could scrub a floor if she had to or incinerate rubbish with the best of them. She had enjoyed her war, seeing it not only as a means of escape from the fond but suffocating embrace of her parents but as the stroke of fortune that led her to Geoffrey Harlow, a full lieutenant in the Royal Corps of Signals and a qualified accountant to boot.

As the cab negotiated the city streets she thought of the prefabricated show house she and Peggy had visited that afternoon, situated in the shadow of the Tate Gallery. From the outside it looked remarkably like a mushroom growth, but inside it had been surprisingly spacious. Two bedrooms, a sitting room, kitchen, bathroom and separate lavatory, all painted in buff with green woodwork. The show house had been fully furnished and carpeted and Peggy had oohed and aahed in wonderment in every room. Amy had tried to look suitably impressed but all the while she had thought of the detached house Geoffrey had promised her, with French windows in all the downstairs rooms and parquet flooring in the hall.

While Amy thought of parquet flooring Peggy leaned her head against the upholstery of the cab and thought about marriage to Jim. If they could get a prefab she could turn it into a little palace. All those things built in! Bedding would be a problem with all her coupons going on the wedding but she would sleep on newspapers as long as she and Jim were together. Perhaps they'd get pillowcases for wedding presents. And her mam had plenty of sheets if she would part with some. Peggy thought of demob and the nice wad of coupons she'd get. She thought of Jim and what she would put in his snap tin before he set off for the pit. She thought of the years of separation and was glad they had not been wasted. She had a post-office savings book with three hundred and eighteen pounds eleven shillings and fivepence in it. If she'd still been living at home and working in the store she wouldn't have half of that. Not a quarter. And there'd be her gratuity and her post-war credits!

'It's exciting, isn't it?' Amy said as though reading her thoughts. For a moment envy overtook Peggy. Amy would have a wonderful wedding, her dad would see to that. Amy had everything money could buy. But it was not in Peggy's nature to be envious for long.

'Yes,' she said in the darkness. 'Not much longer now.'

'I bet you're thinking about that prefab.'

'No.' Fond though Peggy was of Amy, it was nice

to best her now and again. 'I was thinking that if I go back to the store I might pick up a few seconds – sheets and things. If I do go back. We might get married right away if we get a place, and Jim won't want me to work.'

'Sometimes,' Amy said, suddenly subdued. 'Sometimes I can hardly wait to get away. And other times . . .' There was a sudden silence between them.

'You can't imagine being a civvy?' In the darkness Amy nodded. 'I know,' Peg continued. 'It's the same for me. It's as though we've been together so long that splitting up seems terrible. And other times . . .' She chuckled. 'Other times I can hardly wait to see the back of all three of you.'

'We have been mates, though.' Amy was cheerful once more. 'Do you remember that first night? You had that bed by the stove and that awful Florrie said, "That bugger's mine . . ."'

'And then Celia said – quite quietly – I think, "Margaret got there first." And Florrie looked at her for a moment and then Joy said, "Seems fair to me," and Florrie backed off. It's funny that: Celia's never called me Margaret since. Still, like you said, we've been mates. And we've been lucky to stay together. If one of us had been posted . . .'

'We'd've had to go.' Amy was disconsolate once more. 'That's another thing. We've had years of being told what to do and although it gets on your nerves it's safe, isn't it? I mean you know what's expected so you don't worry.'

'Geoffrey'll keep you right,' Peggy comforted.

'He won't,' Amy said, complacent now. 'Oh, he'll take care of me and that sort of thing but he'd never tell me what to do. I'll just have to organise myself. And I will. I mean to be a perfect wife – well, as perfect as possible.'

'We're going to be happy.' Peg's voice was firm. 'That's the main thing, kidda. We're going to be happy.'

In a dimly lit room in the Hotel Ascot behind King's Cross, Joyce Latham, who preferred to be known as Joy, lay naked beneath a worn pink eiderdown. Beside her lay her fiancé, Andrew, the strain of eleven sorties over Germany etched on his sleeping face. From time to time she raised herself on her elbow to look down at him. She longed to kiss the closed eyelids but he needed his sleep. Tomorrow he would go back to flying duty and, as Joy subsided on to her pillow, she felt weak with relief that danger and separation were almost over. In the end she slid carefully from the bed and tiptoed to the washstand to begin preparations for her return to camp.

She was tall for a woman, five foot eight according to her paybook, her AB64, which also noted that she had green eyes, blonde hair, a fresh to sallow complexion, and weighed one hundred and eight pounds, which meant she was too thin for her height.

She usually wore her blonde hair drawn back into a knot on the nape of her neck but now it hung loose on her shoulders so that the face that stared back at her from the fly-blown mirror looked strangely abandoned.

She blinked to clear her bleary eyes and thought that you could always see when people had had sex. At least she could. As soon as girls came into barracks she could spot those who had and those who had not. And she and Andrew had never stopped, not until he had fallen asleep from exhaustion and she'd had to extricate herself from beneath his sleeping form. 'I love you,' she had whispered, and then again, 'I love you.' And he had gone on sleeping and she was glad.

When at last she was ready to leave she took a pen from her leather shoulder bag and wrote a note. 'Didn't want to wake you. Take care. I love you very much. Will write tonight.' In a year – six months if the war in Europe went well – they would be married and never need to part again.

'She's done it this time.' Amy shook her head at Joy's non-arrival.

'You know Joy. She always makes it at the last minute. Celia's always first, Joy's always last,' Peggy soothed.

'We've only got four minutes,' Celia said, checking her wristwatch.

'Charlie'll wait,' Amy said. 'He may be in charge of transport but he never sticks to rules, you know that.'

'He can't wait long.' Celia was remembering she was

an NCO. 'We're not supposed to get lifts. We could get him into trouble.'

'Never mind.' Amy was fumbling in her leather shoulder bag. 'I've got half a packet of Abdullahs in here somewhere. You know he never has enough smokes. He'll wait.' They settled their backs against a bit of wall that was still standing and fell silent until the covered lorry lumbered into view.

It was five minutes before Joy arrived, striding purposefully on her long legs, not running or panting. 'You've got to admit she's got nerve,' Peggy said admiringly and then, raising her voice, 'Get a move on, Joycey. You'll get us all shot.'

They didn't talk much on the journey home. Peggy wondered idly if they'd keep in touch after demob. Celia wondered what the others would do after the war and hoped they would all do well. Amy decided she would send Christmas cards to the others every year, signed 'Geoffrey and Alexandra' with their address embossed in the left-hand corner so no one would lose touch. And we'll all be happy, she thought, and smiled in the lorry's darkness. Joy didn't think of demob or keeping in touch or Christmas cards. Joy thought only of Andrew.

But as the lorry lumbered through the darkness all of them were sure that what lay ahead would be good.

2

July 1945 – Celia

Celia folded the last garment into her kitbag and drew it shut. The barracks was quiet and deserted, everyone elsewhere about their duties. On the narrow bed her biscuits were neatly piled. She put out a hand and touched the straw-filled mattresses, three of them for easy stacking. For five years they had supported her, sleeping and waking. Five years – a fifth of her life. Suddenly she was swept by nostalgia for the claustrophobic, regimented world she had inhabited and now was leaving. At times it had irked her but on the whole it had been the most exciting period of her life.

Until now! It was time to move on. She straightened up and took one last look around. There was a lorry leaving in five minutes, her lift to the nearest station. After that London and the first step into her new existence. She took the letter she had written to Joyce last night, and laid it on the adjoining bed. She had made her goodbyes at breakfast time as together they had rinsed their irons in the tub of cold, greasy water that passed for a washing-up facility, but there was more she must say and writing it was easier. It was two months since Andrew had died in the skies above Germany. For two days Joyce had been silent, her eyes empty and dark. And then, suddenly, she had been the old, insouciant Joy. Too suddenly. They had all been uneasy about it but none of them had had the courage to speak out.

'It's not right,' Peggy had said repeatedly. Amy had agreed. 'She's bottling it up. She must be. If it was Geoffrey . . .' They had both looked at Celia, expecting her to take charge, offer to counsel the bereaved, but she had looked away, painfully aware that she was not up to it.

Now, she hoisted her leather bag on to her right shoulder and seized her kitbag. She had said it all in the letter, or at least she had tried. She was due for interview at two o'clock. There was no more time to waste. She left the hut that had been her home for so long without a backward glance. There was no marching and wheeling on the square, no shouted orders, no one to take any notice as she made her last farewell to the camp. Truly, peace was upon them.

As the train rattled its way towards London she considered the last few weeks. First there had been the call to the CO's office. She had waited outside, racking her brains for misdemeanours that might only now have come to light. For the past few months they had not really been on active duty. Long before VE Day it had been obvious the war was as good as over and a mild euphoria had pervaded the camp. Had she been spotted idling? Had she left something undone?

She had spent most of her time assisting the Education Officer, who was trying to obey instructions to keep everyone's mind occupied with 'British Way and Purpose', the course that was meant to send everyone happily back to civilian life. Perhaps she had said something wrong in one of her lectures. Even something subversive. Some of the discussions had been lively, it was true, but surely not anarchic.

When she entered the office it was a relief to see that the CO's face was relaxed. There was another man with him, his uniform showing signs of wear but well pressed. There was a crown and two pips on his epaulettes and the hat on the table behind him sported a red band. A full colonel. Her heart lurched. Was this how they broke bad news? Who could have died? But even as she thought it she remembered her lowly rank. She would receive bad news from a warrant officer. This was something else.

'Sit down, Blake.' She subsided on to the seat facing them and folded her hands in her lap. The CO looked down at what she could see were her records and then looked up again. 'You have a first-class honours degree and yet you refused a commission?'

What was she supposed to say? Before she could form

a reply the other man smiled. 'Whatever your reasons, Sergeant, I'm sure they were good ones. I see from your records that you speak fluent French.'

'Hardly fluent, sir.' Fear impelled her to speak this time. 'I did Higher School Cert. I did get a distinction in oral French but that was luck.'

This time both men smiled but it was the CO who spoke. 'You spent time in France though?'

'Yes, sir. My godmother lived in Paris. Well, in Maison Lafitte. My parents were both dead so I was ferried around a lot between aunts and uncles. I went to France every summer once I was old enough to travel.'

The two men had looked at each other for a second or two and then the stranger spoke.

'We need people to go to Europe to join the Control Commission. Since April we've liberated one camp after the other. You must have seen the pictures. Uncomfortable, aren't they? The Allies are not prepared for the problem of feeding and caring for hundreds of thousands of civilians, many of them close to death. We've been giving ration packs to near-corpses and telling them to fend for themselves. Now we must do better. Since the war in Europe ended the Yanks have allocated the bulk of their transport to ferrying back ex-prisoners. We need people who can cope with this sort of thing – not pretty, I warn you. You seem to have some qualifications. I'm here to find as many people as I can. Are you interested?'

'It's entirely up to you, Blake.' The CO was holding her eye now. 'You can wait out your time for demob if you choose. You may have plans for your return to civilian life. Think carefully.'

Celia tried hard to keep the eagerness out of her voice. Here it was, the summons she had longed for, the arrow showing her the way to go. 'I think I'd like to volunteer, sir.'

'Good,' the stranger said and reached for the next folder.

Now she was on the train, her friends left behind her, the familiar, organised life where there had been a rule for everything no longer there to support her. She tried to tell herself that what she was going to was just another branch of service, but in her heart of hearts she knew it was not.

There had been a further interview in a dingy London office block. She had sat, knees neatly together, hands folded, trying desperately to give an impression of unflappability. What she learned there confirmed her worst fears – and her hopes too. Things were indeed desperate.

'We don't know where the hell we are,' the young major who interviewed her admitted. 'I'll never forget my first sight of it. It was at Gare d'Orsay. They were there in a huge space – hundreds of them, men completely naked. We were terrified of typhus so they had to be deloused. They were wailing skeletons, just eyes in foreheads. Bald, most of them, or covered in sores. They never looked you in the eye. They'd already been broken and here we were delousing them for all the world like the Gestapo. Still, it had to be done.

That lot are in the Hotel Lutetia now. It was Abwehr headquarters during the occupation, which is a nice irony. Things are better – just – but still chaotic. Everywhere swarming with people seeking family. Family they won't find. Eighty thousand Jews were taken out of France. I doubt if a tiny percentage will return. That's not to mention the Poles or the Czechs. Still . . .' He slapped the table with his hand and stood up to signify the interview was over. 'It's early days yet and we must do what we can.'

When Celia had come out into the busy London street her head had been racing with facts and figures. She would fly to Paris in a week's time, aboard an RAF plane, and report to someone in the Rue Saint-Beriot. It was all there, in her written orders. In the meantime she would stay at Warwickshire House, an ATS transit camp, where she would be fed and sheltered but left to her own devices. 'Try to forget about it for the next week,' the major had advised. 'It'll be all too real once you get there.' Now, as she mounted the step to the hostel, she reflected that forgetting about it would not be easy.

When she had checked into the hostel she had sought out a telephone book. 'Uncle Philip? It's Celia.' By the time she had put down the phone he had arranged where they would meet for dinner and expressed dismay that she would not spend the night at his London apartment. 'Is there a young man?' he asked hopefully and Celia felt her cheeks flush.

'No . . . it's not that. I don't want to put you to any

trouble. And I'm longing to see you and tell you what's happening. I'm going to Paris – seconded to the Control Commission.'

'Paris?' She could hear the dismay in his voice, a dismay that had not abated by the time she was seated opposite him at his club.

'Things are bad there, Celia. I had it from Lavinia Luscomb's son, the brigadier. He says the French are trying to suppress information but Eisenhower wants everything out in the open. I can't think what's come over the French. Of course the whole of Europe is one ghastly melting pot but by all accounts deportees are pouring into Paris, all the stations. Gare de l'Est, Gare de Lyon . . .'

Celia thought of what she had been told about the Gare d'Orsay, but somehow it seemed wrong to repeat something she had heard in the course of an official briefing.

'Things are getting better,' she said. 'They must be, now that there's an organisation.'

Philip shook his head. 'Not that easy, my dear. Not according to Ronny Luscomb. You can't take a starving man and give him food. You simply make him ill. Violently ill. They need simple food in the tiniest quantities. They need peace and quiet – and that's in short supply. Luscomb says they cower at an unexpected noise. They can't even sleep on a soft bed. Half of them wind up on the floor in the beginning. So used to planks they couldn't take a mattress. And he says the mood is sombre. No joy at being saved – too much guilt you see. We had that after the last war. Survivor guilt.' He went quiet, then and began to toy with his hors d'oeuvres.

Long after Celia was back in her narrow hostel bed she thought of the things she had been told. 'They have grey faces,' the major had told her. 'Grey-green with red eyes. And the eyes . . .' He had shuddered slightly and she had wondered if he was testing her. Deliberately exaggerating the horrors to see if there was the slightest withdrawing on her part. In the end, though, she had concluded that he was simply trying to cleanse his own thoughts of the horror of what he had seen so that he too could sleep. She turned on her side and tried to think of mundane things. Peggy and Amy and Joy would be asleep now. Well, perhaps not Joy, but the others would be asleep dreaming of wedded bliss.

She smiled in the darkness, a smile tinged not with envy but with resignation. She would never marry, she knew that. Had probably always known it. They had made jokes in camp about the girls who were mad to marry. 'On the hunt', Peggy had called it as girls had bobbed up and down in front of the barrack room's only mirror, desperate to get a look in to get lipstick right or smooth their brows with a newly licked finger before they went out in the hope of clicking with a serviceman.

All very well for Peggy to talk, with her tiny ring on a chain around her neck. Amy's ring had been pearls and opals, a huge cluster. 'Pearls for tears,' someone had said in an envious aside, but Amy would never know tears. She had been born to a charmed life. And Peggy would be happy too, as long as she had her Jim.

It's Joy I worry about, Celia thought. I must keep in touch with Joy. With all of them really, but especially Joy.

Scenes came into her mind then, happy times when they had lain on their beds and chatted or walked to the cookhouse or Naafi for breaks. There had been a war raging overhead but they had been strangely carefree.

In the latter stages they had brewed up in the barrack room, using a tin kettle and a plugged-in electric plate Amy had brought from home. They had boiled eggs in the kettle and toasted bread in front of the stove, taking turns to hold the fork when it grew too hot to handle.

I want it back, Celia thought. I was safe there. And then she remembered the Gare d'Orsay and the shambling figures walking around it, only half alive.

I will help them, she vowed, and counted herself to sleep by passing victims through an imaginary barrier to a better life on the other side.

3

July 1945 – Celia

Celia scarcely had time to adjust to the up-and-down motion of the small aircraft before the pilot was announcing sight of the French coast. It was her first flight and she was uncomfortably aware of the porage-and-toast breakfast she had dutifully eaten at 5 a.m. The crew were cheery young men, used now to hopping backwards and forwards between military airfields on either side of the Channel, but she sincerely hoped she wouldn't be airsick and need to turn to one of them for help.

'Where are you going?' one of them asked, crouching beside her seat as the journey commenced.

'Paris.'

He raised his brows. 'The city itself?'

'Yes. Well, at first. I'll go where I'm sent after that. Are things bad in Paris?'

He was smiling now, trying to reassure. 'It's hot in more senses than one. There's a heatwave and tempers are frayed. There are shortages and things are still a bit primitive. But it's the trial that has people really on edge.'

Celia had read accounts of the trial of Marshal Pétain, who had taken over the reins of government in 1940 and was now accused of treachery. He had been a hero of World War One, the defender of Verdun where his rallying cry had been 'They shall not pass'. But in the intervening years he had aged and his courage had diminished. He had handed France over to the Germans and now he was to be punished for it. 'He's ninety now,' Celia said. 'Too old to be put on trial surely?'

'Not according to the Parisians! The court's full to overflowing and the cafés around the Palais de Justice are packed with people howling for his blood.'

'Can it be a fair trial?' Celia asked, her stomach lurching as the plane suddenly lost height.

The airman shrugged and straightened up, and suddenly his face was the face of a boy. 'Search me! All I know is it's nearly over and soon I'll be out and I can get on with my life.'

As the plane descended they talked of interruption and recommencement, their every word optimistic. 'Good luck,' Celia said as he helped her on to the tarmac. Her legs trembled slightly but she marched briskly towards the cluster of prefabricated buildings at the edge of the landing strip. Someone there would tell her what to do next.

'Did you bring any coffee?' the sergeant who processed her papers asked as he handed them back to her.

'Coffee?'

'It's currency here. Cigs, nylons, coffee.' In spite of herself Celia's face must have registered disapproval. The sergeant smiled. 'You'll learn, kid. It's a den of thieves, this place – or a loony bin.'

As she was driven to the requisitioned hotel where she was to be billeted Celia looked out at the Paris streets with unabated curiosity. So much of it was as she remembered from visits before the war. Her godmother had brought her here in 1937 as a gift for her seventeenth birthday. The streets had been full of fashionably dressed Parisians, there had been the smell of good cigars in the air and always tinkling music coming from somewhere far off.

Now, the faces of the pedestrians were strained, their clothes shabby. As for the buildings, at first glance they were the same, but closer inspection revealed that here and there the brickwork was scarred by combat and everywhere paint was peeling and woodwork rotting. Poor shabby war-torn Paris, Celia thought, and then leaned forward to peer out as the driver gestured to a huge building.

'Hotel Meurice,' he said. 'Officers' mess for SHAEF. The Jerries had it before us. Eisenhower's lot are out at Versailles.' He cleared his throat before he went on. 'The Yanks aren't too popular with the Presshans.' Celia hid a smile at his attempt at a French accent. 'They think they can buy anything with a packet of

Luckys. There's girls – kids – hanging round their camps. Nancy's their rest area from the front. It's a scandal what's going on there, they say.'

There was a bitter note in his voice that Celia had heard before. Even the lowliest GI was rich in comparison with his British counterpart and there had been ugly scenes in British market towns when US and British servicemen competed for the available talent. She made soothing noises until they drew up outside the narrow, rather seedy hotel in a side street where she was to be billeted.

She was shown to a room up two flights of stairs. It was small and T fall but there was only one narrow bed in it, covered by a faded quilt, and she shivered with pleasure at the thought of having the place all to herself. She hadn't minded the barracks but a room to herself would be bliss! There was only time to deposit her bag and wash her face and hands with water from the jug on the marble washstand before she went down to continue her journey, meticulously following the instructions in her written orders.

She had been assigned to a house in the Boulevard Haussmann, where survivors who had been flown direct to Paris from the camps were being rehabilitated. She had been warned that their condition was bad but nothing had prepared her for what she now saw.

In the shabby entrance to the house a man was standing. At first she thought him elderly but closer inspection revealed that he was probably no more than twenty-three. The eyes looking out from dark hollows were the eyes of a centenarian and his skin was parched and papery. He had probably been handsome once. Now he was pathetic.

She moved past him, noticing the sweet sickly smell that came from a mouthful of rotting teeth. In the passageway that led to the back portion of the house a pegboard was studded with sheets of paper. One or two listless men were scanning it but there was a terrible resignation in the lines of their bodies, as though they did not expect good news.

'It's a Yiddish newsletter,' Glynn Chambers, the officer who greeted her, explained. 'It lists just who is looking for who. They look to see if anyone is looking for them or if anyone they're seeking is mentioned, but they know the odds are against them. Most of them are all that is left of a huge, extended family. Still, we're achieving something here. Every day they're a little more settled. Your languages will come in useful.'

Celia's heart sank. Had he been sold a false prospectus? Her French was schoolroom standard, her German basic. If all these men were Jewish surely Hebrew or Yiddish would be more use.

Glynn was pushing open a door. 'This is the quiet room. Some of them appreciate it. Most of them seem to want to cling together. We try to give them what they want and help them achieve their aims but the pressure's on to move them out. There are so many more to come through.'

'Move them out to where?' Celia asked. There was a young man seated in a corner of the room, his head bent over a book he was studying with the aid of a large magnifying glass. He had looked up briefly at the sound of their voices, now he went back to his reading.

'To hostels in Britain mostly,' her guide replied. He had not acknowledged the silent reader or appeared to notice his presence, but once they got back into the corridor he nodded towards the room they had just left. 'He's typical. A Polish Ashkenazi. His name is Aaron Gotz, liberated on a death march from Auschwitz. The Germans were hoping that if the front stabilised they would still have the makings of a workforce so their guards had a vested interest in keeping them alive. And if you were guarding slave labour you were regarded as being gainfully employed. If you lost your prisoners they sent you off to face the Russians. Aaron was on his way to Sachsenhausen when the Russians overtook them. He was given a ration pack and told to fend for himself. Eventually he was picked up, just wandering around half dead. It's more organised now. The initial rehab takes place near to where they're located and by the time we get them they at least look human, but I saw some ghastly sights here when we began.'

'How long has he been here?' Celia was looking back through the door to where the reader had suddenly buried his face in his hands.

'Since the end of January. He's a strange chap. Clever but morose. The Red Cross are trying to find out what's happened to his family but . . .' He shrugged his broad shoulders and then ran a hand through red hair that threatened to curl and she saw that he was genuinely moved by the boy's plight. He was in uniform but there was a scarf tucked in the neck of his shirt that looked suspiciously like a school scarf.

They were mounting the stairs now and peering into bedrooms. Beds were crammed close together, each with a makeshift locker beside it. 'They don't mind the cramped conditions. Compared with what they've been used to this is Utopia. But be very careful with their possessions. They don't have much so they tend to cling to what they have. Things you and I wouldn't hang on to are precious to them. A piece of blanket, half an old comb, stubs of pencils . . . they treat them as though they were by Fabergé. And books! Books in their native tongue are above rubies. Young Gotz is lucky. He has fluent English – not so much to speak but certainly to read.'

Looking through the bannister, Celia could see the door, see the boy slowly lift his head, letting his spread fingers trickle down his face. He left his chin supported on his hands, his eyes staring straight ahead, unseeing. Without asking her guide's permission she descended the stairs, stepped back into the room and moved quietly towards the boy.

'What are you reading?' He looked up, startled, and for a moment she thought he was not going to respond. Eventually he reached down and turned the book towards her so that she could see the title. It was a tattered copy of *British Birds – the ornithologist's guide* dated 1927. She looked up and their eyes met. 'Are you interested in birds?' For a second his eyes smiled but it was a scornful humour she saw there.

'No,' he said in lightly accented English. 'No, I am not particularly interested in birds.'

'I'll bring you other books tomorrow,' she said flatly and turned on her heel.

4

October 1945 – Joyce

'This is it then.' Peggy's voice was strangely morose as she looked around at the stripped beds, the straining kitbags. 'We're off.'

'Don't sound so cheerful, Peggy. Anyone would think we were going home.' Joy was outlining her mouth with lipstick as she spoke. As usual, Amy hurried to console.

'I know how you feel, Peg. If it had all been like the last few months I'd miss it too – but remember what it was like before. Drill, jankers, someone on at you every minute, roll call in the pitch dark with rain running down your neck, dunking your irons in greasy water after every meal. It's been cushy lately but cast your mind back.'

In the time since VE Day army life had changed beyond belief. As soon as demobs started parties had become the order of the day, some of them grand affairs with fancy dress and decorations, others impromptu get-togethers with fellow servicemen and -women going off in twos and threes.

Apart from compassionate reasons, age and length of service were the basic criteria for early demobilisation, but there was a fair amount of grumbling. Someone who had simply kept records in Aldershot could find himself in the same category as a war hero who had slogged through Burma, but no system was going to be perfect when there were millions of men and women to return to civilian life. And for women like Joy and Peggy and Amy, who had played an important part as radar operatives, much of the excitement was gone once the war was over.

'We're lucky to get out so soon,' Joy said, fitting her lipstick back into her case. 'I've had my fill of lolling about, thank you. I can't wait for Civvy Street.'

'Yesterday was lovely.' Peggy's voice was still nostalgic as she thought of the autumn sunshine with nothing to do but lie in the field and think about their futures. Her conscience pricked as she remembered that Joy had no future now that her Andrew was dead. 'Still, it'll be nice to get back home and start . . . well, start sorting things out.' She was choosing her words carefully, leaving out mention of reunions or weddings.

'No more British Way and Purpose,' Amy said brightly. 'I love the British way already and my purpose is to get back home and put my uniform on a bonfire. Roll on Guy Fawkes.'

'It's all very well for you.' Peggy's reproachful glance spoke volumes. 'I bet you won't have to exist on your coupons. I'm going to hang on to everything they've let me keep.'

'Not your passion-killers, Peg? Poor Jim!' There was laughter at the thought of the regulation army-issue bloomers. They had been allowed to keep their underwear along with some of their uniform, their kitbag and one pair of shoes.

'I wish I could've kept my tin hat,' Amy said mournfully. 'I wanted to put a plant in it just for remembrance sake.'

'We won't forget.' Joy said it lightly but they knew she meant it. 'Celia won't let us, anyway, not with her regular bulletins. We've had two already and she hasn't been gone five minutes.'

'Ceely will write a book eventually,' Amy said as she shouldered her kitbag.

'Called *The Saving of Aaron Gotz*?' Joy said, raising her eyebrows.

'She does talk about him a lot.' Peggy's eyes had widened. 'You don't think—'

'No, I don't. Not Celia. He'll just be some lame duck she's adopted.' Joy was pushing them towards the door of the barrack room. 'All the same, you know what they say about the quiet ones. Still, let's get going. We've got trains to catch.'

They had been through the process of demobilisation, medicals, dental examinations, handing in kit, receiving their paybooks with references concerning work and character included, the final payment of wages and travel warrants and, at last, transfer to a transit unit. Taking leave of the barracks they had occupied for two years had been hard – leaving this temporary accommodation was easier. What was more difficult was finally severing their links with the service that had both guarded and goaded them for five long years of war.

They didn't speak in the truck as it bounced along country roads to the railway station. 'Don't go mad with all that freedom,' the driver yelled as she reversed and began to move off.

'Freedom!' They stood and looked at one another for a moment and then hurried, laughing, towards the eastbound platform.

The journey to Euston took less than an hour. They had to sit on their kitbags in the corridor but for Amy and Peggy that was a small price to pay for the mounting excitement that was consuming them. Joy watched them, seeing their faces soften, their eyes glaze over, as they thought of home. There would be welcoming parties, no doubt, and a return to the rooms they had left in 1940. Clean sheets aired by doting mothers and sisters. Friends to help them settle down.

There'll be none of that for me, she thought, and then, as her throat constricted, she reached into her bag and drew out her cigarettes.

She had been nineteen when she was called up. Nineteen going on forty, her mother had called it on the odd occasion they met up. She had left home at fifteen, tired of the constant procession of 'friends' who shared her mother's home and, sometimes, her bed. She had been an assistant in a chemist's shop, her wages ten bob a week and for half a crown she had shared a bedroom in the home of one of the other shop girls.

She had never known her father, only glimpsed him once, standing in her mother's hallway. A tall man in a grey suit. She could remember his long legs in well-pressed trousers. She had peeped around her mother's skirts as the angry voices went on above her head. 'There now,' her mother said when the door clashed shut. 'That's your father for you!' She had gone into the room that served as living room and kitchen, folding some money into her purse as she went. And then she had turned and smiled. 'You're going to Auntie Maisie's tonight, our Joyce. Your mam's going out on the tiles.'

'Wake up, Joycey. We're here.' Peggy was standing up, trying to steady herself against the lurchings of the train as she settled her cap on her dark curls. 'Nearly home.'

They tumbled on to the platform amid a torrent of other servicemen and -women, harassed mothers holding children by the hand, elderly men looking anxiously for direction signs. The whole country's on the move, Joyce thought, and remembered Celia. If it was like this in Britain what must it be like in Europe?

'Have we got time for a drink?' There was a great consulting of watches and an exchange of glances between Amy and Peggy. They're humouring me, Joy thought, and felt her throat constrict once more.

'Time for a swift one,' Amy said, looking round for a bar.

'Tell you what – I'll come to King's Cross with you two,' Joyce offered. 'We can get a drink there and then I can see you both on to the train.' They stood shoulder to shoulder in the tube and emerged into the great, grey hall of King's Cross Station, awash with travellers now so that they were carried along on a tide of humanity until they found themselves in a corner of the buffet.

'We'll never get served.' Peggy was eyeing the ranks of men between them and the bar.

'Watch me,' Joy said and began to insinuate herself between khaki and blue until she could put a ten-shilling note on the bar and say, 'A port and lemon please, and two gin and orange.'

'It's funny, isn't it?' Amy said, when Joy returned. For once her face was without its habitual smile. 'I mean, we've been together for five years – and don't say four years, ten months and X days, Peg – or whatever it is. You know what I mean.'

'Yes,' Joy said. 'But it's not so much the time we've been together, it's what we've been through. That's the bond.'

'We've changed.' Peggy savoured her port for a moment before she went on. 'When I realised I was supposed to undress in front of other people I nearly died.'

'What about me? I was educated in a convent.'

Amy's eyes widened and rolled. 'We had things like white tents to dress inside. You put them on over your nightdress, took it off inside and passed your undies up underneath to put them on under cover.'

Joy smiled. It was impossible to look at Amy without smiling. Her blue eyes were like saucers, the lashes surrounding them thick and curling. She's like a Mabel Lucy Atwell kid, Joy thought and smiled again.

'Do you remember Florrie?' Peg asked between sips.

'Fast Flo? Who could forget her.' The other two were speaking in chorus.

'That first day when she just stripped off and stood there! I nearly died.'

'She had a lovely figure . . .'

'And she liked to show it off.'

Florrie had lasted a mere three months before the monthly FFP – Free From Pregnancy – test proved positive and she was sent packing.

'FFPs,' Peggy said wonderingly. 'As if we'd've dared get pregnant.'

'Lots of people did. Still, I'm glad we waited . . .' Suddenly Amy's voice faltered and Joy knew she was remembering Andrew. No joyous expectation of wedding and baby nine months later for the bereaved.

'No more FFPs and no more bath lists,' she said firmly. 'Now that I can have a bath whenever I like I shall probably live there, up to my neck in suds.' She didn't want her own bereftness to spoil their joyful anticipation of reunion.

They talked about shortages then. Would there be

the unlimited hot water and bubble bath of their dreams? How long would rationing last? And when would they meet again?

'Here's to Celia,' Joy said at last, raising the remains of her gin and orange. 'Let's hope we see her again when she's sorted out Europe.'

'She will, you know,' Peggy said. 'She's so well organised.' They drifted out on to the station concourse, a little misty eyed and somewhat lost for words.

I'll never see them again, Joy thought, and had to resist the urge to cling to them and beg them not to go away.

'We're platform four.' Peggy was returning from the destination board. 'And the train's in.' They clung briefly and called goodbye, leaning out of the doors to wave until the whistle blew and the train began to chug out of the station in a cloud of steam. Joy stood there for as long as she decently could, until the platform was deserted and there was no longer any excuse. 'I'm going to my cousin,' she had told the others. It was true. She was going to her cousin Edna, who had a flat in Bayswater. But the invitation in a scribbled letter had been vague.

> Don't be short of a bed when you come out. You can always bunk down here for a night or two till you get turned round. It's pot luck, mind you, and I'm never in, but you're welcome.

She spent a precious half-crown on a taxi, unwilling

to shoulder her way through the tube once more. As they moved away from King's Cross she closed her eyes. Hopefully Edna would go out tonight and she could simply sit in the quiet flat and recover her breath. So many things to think about. A job, a place to stay. Clothes to buy, which wouldn't be easy on little money and few coupons. Still, nice to start again. Nice to be out of uniform. No more bleaching khaki shirts to a more flattering eau-de-Nil, no more hitching up waistbands to raise the dowdy regulation hemline. No more rules!

But she could feel no exultation at the thought of freedom. In a way, it was frightening. How different it would have been if Andrew— She felt her eyes sting and squeezed her lids together. Mustn't, mustn't cry. 'Don't you dare cry, our Joycey. Tears don't cut any ice with me.' They had been her mother's words whenever tears had threatened. 'Can't stand cry babies, Joycey. Stop right now or I'll give you something to cry about.'

She quelled the tears but the pain remained. If only she had said goodbye that morning in that ropey hotel. Often he had woken before she left and they had kissed and planned their reunion. But not that day. That last important day. Alone in the back of the cab she kissed his sleeping face in her mind, her lips curling in pleasure at the familiar feel of stubble, the sweetness of his morning lips, the feeling of his body hard against hers.

It would kill her, the pain of losing him. For a second or two she lifted the lid and let out the black terror of her grief. Her ears sang with pain and panic rose up in her chest. Andrew, Andrew! If anything had hurt her he had smoothed it away. He had made her feel safe for the first time in her life.

He loved me! she thought. He would have gone on loving me for ever!

When his arms had come round her it had been like coming into heaven. And it had not been sex, good though that had been. It was love. I was loved, she thought, and let the sweetness of it roll around her mind.

But as the cab drew up at Edna's door she put memory away. If she was going to survive in the future there would be no room for the past. She paid off the cab and mounted the steps to ring the second bell from the bottom of the column.

As she waited for an answer she turned and looked at the street. There was a bomb site on the other side, rosebay willow herb peeping out from the hoardings which now surrounded it. An advert for Bile Beans was new and bright, a fresh-faced girl to show how well they worked.

She turned back as the door opened to see Edna in a white slip, clutching a cotton dressing gown around her thin body. Her hair was wound up in rag curlers and her face was bare of make-up.

'Our Joyce! I thought you'd got lost. Come in, the kettle's on. You're just in time. There's a party tonight.'

Joy's heart sank. 'I haven't got anything to wear, Edna. Besides—'

'I've got masses of things. We're on and off the same size. You'll love the boys – Yanks – and we're one girl short, anyway. Now put your bags down and get out of that uniform. God, I'm glad I was reserved – I couldn't've worn khaki and getting in the Wrens was like getting in Fort Knox.'

There were clothes strewn everywhere, on chair backs and tables and airing on a clothes horse in front of the gas fire. Edna snatched a pile from a chair and patted the cushion. 'Sit yourself down there and I'll make the tea. And then we'll get you something to wear . . .' She broke off and vanished into the bedroom, returning with an armful of dresses in the colours of the rainbow. 'There you are, take your pick. And perk up, our Joycey, the war's over. Now you're going to live.'

5

Amy

It was heaven to wake in her own bed. Amy lay back on the thick, soft pillows that smelled of lavender and let contentment ripple over her. No more biscuits and thin, tickly pillows. No more rising in darkness or washing in half-cold water trickling from reluctant taps. Last night she had lain in red-hot water with suds popping gently around her chin and promised herself that she would never again be subject to regulations.

She was still contemplating the wonders of the timbered ceiling of her room and rejoicing in the joy of living, when her father tapped at her door. 'Sit up, honey.' He was carrying a tray loaded with food and crockery. She struggled up on her pillows and let him plant it in her lap. 'Eggs,' he said, whipping off a plated cover to reveal a heaped plate. 'Bacon, sausage, fresh-picked mushrooms. Tea and milk over here. Your toast's in there to stay hot. Butter from down the road and home-made jam. And your mother says shout if you want something more.'

'Something more? I'll won't get through half of this. Still . . .' She struggled farther up on her pillows. 'It's lovely, Daddy. Thank you.'

He perched on the end of her bed as she began to eat. 'I can't tell you how good it is to have you back, Ally.' It was strange to hear the childhood version of her real name. She had been Amy ever since her first day in camp, when someone – had it been Joy? – had noticed her initials. AMY – Alexandra Mary Yeo. Amy! Eventually Lance Corporal Yeo, but all that was over. She was Alexandra Yeo once more. And soon she would be Mrs Geoffrey Harlow.

'It's good to be back, Daddy. Marvellous. And this . . .' She forked scrambled egg into her mouth. 'Scrumptious. Where on earth did you get it all?' But she knew, even without her father's knowing smile. There was a flourishing black market in North Yorkshire and the George was at its heart.

'Now, you stay there.' He was patting her bedclothes in the old, indulgent way of childhood.

'I wish I could, Dad. But I've heaps of things to do. They gave me piles of instructions yesterday but it was all so quick I didn't take everything in. I've got to get an identity card and a ration book. Where is the National Registration Office around here? And my clothing coupons – must get them.'

'Don't you worry about things like that. You'll need

your identity card, I suppose, but as for coupons, you tell your dad what you want, I'll see you get it.'

Amy smiled. 'I know you're a great fixer, Daddy. I won't call you a spiv. But we have a wedding to cater for, remember. And I'll need a trousseau, not to mention a wedding dress.' Her brow must have clouded here for her father winced.

'Hush. I won't have you worried on your first day home. Trousseaus and wedding stuff are your mother's department, but you won't go short. As for the reception, haven't I been preparing for that since the first time I saw Geoffrey in the bar? He'll wind up a major, I thought. I'll have him for my Ally. And so I have!'

When he had gone Amy thought over what he had said. Had it really been her father who had brought her and Geoffrey together? She had come down into the bar on the first night of her leave and he had been there, in uniform, leaning on the bar, smiling and chatting, and she had been glad she had on her red polka-dot tussore dress because it was short enough to show off her legs.

Remembering the red silk dress reminded her of clothes. She was taller and heavier than she had been in 1940. Since then there'd been the odd new piece of civvy clothing but the mahogany cupboards that lined one wall were mostly full of pre-war clothes which might not fit and would certainly be out of date. She finished her breakfast quickly, licking the knife so as not to waste the last traces of butter and honey, and then she leaped from the bed to explore her wardrobe.

She made a pile of discards, the careful clothes of adolescence, flashy things she had bought from her allowance before she went into the service, anything that wouldn't fit. Geoffrey liked her to be smart but anything garish made him frown. After all he was a professional man and came from a good family.

For a second the remembered chill of her infrequent visits to his home made her shiver. His mother was polite but distant, his father a shadow of a man who hardly seemed to be there. So unlike her own loving upbringing. Still, when they had a home of their own she would dictate the atmosphere and it would be warm and loving.

She picked out a grey linen dress with white collar and cuffs and a red patent leather belt and went off to run water for a second, wickedly unpatriotic bath. You were meant to save energy and bathe in five inches of water but her father had told her that was a nonsense as they had hot water going to waste.

In the bath she thought about life with Geoffrey. He had ruled out lovemaking before they were married, had even been slightly shocked when she had hinted that it might be possible. She had learned a thing or two in the last few years although she had not put the knowledge to use. At first she had been amazed at the way other girls had discussed sex. 'Can't get enough of it, he can't.' 'At it all night, I can hardly move now.' 'If I'm up the spout I've told him he's had his jollies.' And then her amazement had turned to interest and finally to boredom. Not much interest in other people's lovemaking when you were wanting your own.

She would have to be brave on their first night. According to some girls it was torture, others said it was nothing. 'Like a cork popping.' They all went into gory detail about the subsequent mess but that was what men expected so that was all right.

She closed her eyes, thinking of Geoffrey taking her virginity. Or rather of her giving it – the greatest gift a woman can give a man, according to her mother. She smiled, thinking of her mother's anguished face on the eve of her going away. Her father had hovered in the background, equally ill at ease and even tearful. Both of them were obviously imagining she was going off to a den of debauchery. If only they could have seen the army in action. 'A regulation for everything,' Joy had said once. 'Even sex.'

No, she would be all right with Geoffrey. He would be kind and gentle at first and then as demanding as anyone could wish. She began to feel a little uncomfortable, almost as though he was there with her, looming over her in the way he did. She loved the tall leanness of him in his smooth uniform. Officers' uniforms felt lovely. What would he look like in civvies? In pyjamas? She imagined him rumpled in the morning, the normally sleek hair tousled from a night of passion. Would he be wearing pyjamas? Would they ever be naked in bed together?

Her mother's flushed face at the bathroom door interrupted her shameless speculating. 'Geoffrey's on the phone. And do put some clothes on, pet lamb. The bar's full.'

She was breathless by the time she reached the phone in the lobby behind the bar. She turned her back so that no one would see her face as she listened to his loving voice. 'I'm going to Leeds, darling. Well, near Leeds. Wetherstone. An interview for deputy treasurer. I've got a twelve-hour pass. I can be at your place at five. Just for an hour, I'm afraid, but not much longer now and then we'll be together for good.'

'An interview?' She tried not to sound too eager. He might not get the job, except that anyone would see at once how wonderful he was. On her left ring finger her opals and pearls glinted. He would get the job and she would be the wife of a deputy treasurer. But only as long as it took them to see his worth and then he wouldn't be anyone's deputy. 'Come as soon as you can, darling. I can't wait to see you.'

While she waited for Geoffrey's arrival she walked on the river bank. However lovely her new home, she would miss the George. The long white building was set on the river bank, with an ancient bridge on one side and the river stretching away on the other. She had spent all her life in this place until war had taken her away. It had been the perfect place in which to grow up and she had hated leaving it, but without war she and Geoffrey would never have met. She would have come home from her convent school and married one of the local farmers and never known the joy of someone as wonderful as Geoffrey with his public-school background and professional qualifications.

She was smiling as she went back into the house to change into the grey dress she'd laid out. 'Wear this,' her mother had offered, holding out the garnet brooch that had been her grandmother's. When once more she walked on the grassy bank, trying not to get grass stains on her grey suede shoes, she knew she looked her best.

I am so lucky, she thought. The luckiest girl in the world. Life had always been kind to her, in childhood and girlhood. Even the army. She had made good friends and although their paths would seldom cross in peacetime she would always hold them in her heart. I've changed, she thought, remembering the child who had dreamed by the river. I've changed in the last few years. I've grown up.

She shivered suddenly, thinking of what being grown up meant. She couldn't run back to Dad any more. Not once she was married. She wouldn't have to salute anyone ever again but there would still be dues to be paid.

She would have to cultivate Geoffrey's colleagues and their wives, have them for meals and generally be a credit to him. He had been honest with her. 'I come from a good family, Alexandra, but there's no money. We wouldn't grub for it as others did so we're genteel poor. If there was money I'd go into practice. As it is, I must use the civic ladder. But I will get on, you can be sure of that.'

He had looked so serious then and she had not known quite what he expected her to say. So she had simply smiled and nodded and he had seemed satisfied.

She turned as she heard his voice. He was striding towards her over the grass, upright and handsome in his uniform, a smile on his face that told her the interview had gone well. When Geoffrey was displeased or disappointed it showed in a tightening of the lips, a coldness in the eye. She started to run, the narrow skirt of her dress hampering her steps, until she was in his arms, or rather he was in hers and she was lifting her face for his kiss.

'Steady on,' he said but he was smiling so it was all right. He kissed her on the temple and then again, glancingly, on the lips. 'It's good to see you out of that dreadful khaki.' She clung to him, wanting more affection, but he was already turning to go back to the hotel. 'Your mother has tea ready. Mustn't keep her waiting.'

If she had been Joy she would have said, 'Damn tea. And damn Mother too.' But she was Amy, who never made waves. She tucked her hand in the crook of his arm and walked with him towards the open door. And if she felt disappointment at the length or depth of his greeting she put it away. When they were married, when she was truly his wife, all would be well. Things always came right for her. Love would be no different.

They ate ham and tongue and salad and new bread thickly buttered and then they had home-made shortbread and curd-cheese tart. Her mother fussed over them and her father quizzed Geoffrey about the prospective job.

I want to take him to bed, Amy thought, remembering Flo, who had staggered back to camp, after every pass, eyes dark in a white face to declaim as she shed her clothes, 'Mah bugger never stops.' Would Geoffrey be a voracious lover? If not she would make him so. As they ate curd tart she imagined a trousseau lavish with lace and very décolleté. Never mind how many coupons it took – Daddy would see to it.

She cried when it was time for Geoffrey to leave. 'Sh,' he said reprovingly but he kissed the top of her head and shook her father and mother by the hand, and as he got into the cab that was to take him to the station he looked so handsome, so every inch the officer, that she felt her heart would burst.

'Everything all right?' her father said as the cab moved away.

'Everything's fine,' she said. 'Just fine.' There was a little sigh behind her and she turned to her mother. 'You look tired,' she said and linked her arm in her mother's to go back inside.

She came down into the bar that evening, something that had been denied to her before the war and allowed only as a treat when she was home on leave. Everyone was pleased to see her, exclaiming over her ring, wishing her well, making sly jokes about weddings and wedding nights until her mother clucked disapproval or her father said, 'Now then!'

This is a well-ordered hotel, she thought, and was suddenly proud of her parents for their total control of the atmosphere, a control that was imposed so congenially that no one even noticed their behaviour had been modified.

When she went back upstairs she continued to go through her clothes. They were all good fabrics with expensive buttons and buckles. On the ottoman by the window lay her discarded uniform. For two pins she'd make a bonfire of the lot, except that there were people who would be glad of such good-quality clothing. Other girls in the transit hut had talked of dyeing and altering. She would have no need of that.

She was struggling into a too-tight organza party dress when her mother appeared. 'I feel as if I haven't had a moment with you all day,' she said.

'You work too hard.' Amy put out her arms and drew her mother to her. She had always thought her mother pleasantly plump. Now she realised the frame within her arms was bony, almost fragile.

'You must let me help you now I'm home,' she said, conscience-stricken.

'Nonsense.' Her mother was pulling her away, smoothing her hair where it had straggled free of its pins. 'I'm going to go and make us both some Ovaltine. Get into bed and we'll have a little chat when I get back. But not for long – you need your sleep.'

Amy was in bed, her pillows raised behind her, when

her mother returned. They sipped their drinks for a moment, each of them wondering where to begin the conversation.

'Geoffrey looked well,' her mother said at last.

'Yes.' In spite of herself Amy felt her face crease into a Cheshire cat's grin.

'And you love him?'

'Oh yes.' She put out a hand and covered her mother's. There were large rings on her mother's fingers but the knuckles were rough and enlarged. 'I do love him, Mum. Don't worry. We're going to be very, very happy.'

Her mother's face was softening as she listened. She drained her cup and put it on the bedside table, then she put up her hands to her dark hair and began to pull out the pins.

'You haven't a grey hair,' Amy said proudly.

Her mother threw back her head and laughed. 'My pet lamb. Four years at war and still innocent. I'm grey as a badger, Ally. If it wasn't for my weekly visit to Darlington you'd soon see. Still, I'm no spring chicken. I shall be fifty-three next January. I'm a year older than Daddy, don't forget.'

Amy felt a sudden panic. 'You're all right, aren't you? Fifty-three's not old. You should retire, you and Daddy. Get more rest.'

But her mother was smiling and shaking her head. 'Take your father away from the George, pet? I couldn't do that. He wouldn't survive it.' She looked around the room with its white walls and apple-green paintwork, chintz curtains and cast-iron fireplace. 'And we've been happy here, haven't we?'

'The happiest in the world.' Amy was scrambling from the covers to take her mother in her arms. 'I have been the happiest girl in the world. Every day of my life, even when I was away, I always knew this was here, waiting.'

'And it always will be,' her mother said firmly. 'Now into bed, there's a good girl.'

'Do you remember when you used to sing me to sleep? "Loola, loola, loola, loola bye-bye . . ." That was what you sang.'

'Paul Robeson.' Her mother was smiling. 'Paul Robeson sang that in some film or other before the war.' She reached to smooth hair from her daughter's brow. 'Now go to sleep. Think of your Geoffrey and how happy you're going to be.'

And I am, Amy thought, when the light was out and her mother gone. As happy as happy can be.

6

Peggy

As the bus wound its way towards Belgate, Peggy tried to quell her excitement. She was going home. And this time for good! All through the war years she had gone backwards and forwards on this bus but the joy of going home had always been tempered by the knowledge that she would no sooner be home than it would be time to go back again. In the early months she had cried when it was time to leave but as time went on she had begun to look forward to seeing her mates again and that had made the parting from Jim less unbearable.

Remembering the camaraderie of the barracks made her think of the girls. Celia was still in Paris, unless she'd been moved on, which was quite possible given she was still in the service. Amy would be up to the ears in wedding preparations as soon as she got home.

Lucky Amy. And Joyce would soon be living it up in London. Except that the old Joyce who had loved life was gone, extinguished in that moment when the staff sergeant had come into the mess and for once her eyes had been kind and they had all known it was bad news for someone.

Joy would find someone else of course. Impossible to imagine her without a man in tow. Whereas, if anything happened to Jim, she would never remarry. Would never get over it. She settled down in her seat and closed her eyes. Three more stops to Belgate so she had time to think about Jim.

They would have to find somewhere to live and that wouldn't be easy. Jim had shown her a bit of a speech of Ernie Bevin's in which he had promised to build millions of homes as soon as the war was over. She had memorised the last line because it appealed to her. 'The one essential thing if you are going to stop moral disaster after the war is to enable these young folk to start off under reasonable conditions of home life as quickly as ever you can.'

'As quickly as ever you can.' If they had to live in for long there'd be trouble. She opened her eyes as the bus drew up in Houghton-le-Spring. There was a placard outside the newsagent's. 'Allies execute collaborator. Paris applauds as Pierre Laval dies.'

Paris! Celia was there and they were still killing people! Outside the bus window everything looked so normal, so peaceful. As the bus moved on into open countryside Peggy gave thanks that she was here, in

County Durham, when poor Celia was still caught up in death.

She had hoped someone would be waiting for her when she got off the bus. Not Jim, because he was on tub-loading and needed his sleep. But her dad was on night shift and could've been there. Or her mam or one of the kids. Five brothers and sisters. You'd think one could've made the effort. Disappointment was suddenly sour in her mouth. She'd gone to war for them, could've been killed if the Germans hadn't been so poor at hitting their targets.

She was fishing for a hanky when she heard her mother's panting voice. 'Our Peggy . . . I thought I'd be too late. Give us your bag, pet. By, I'm glad to get you back. Jim came round last night like a dog with two tails. He's coming round ours as soon as he's had his sleep out. I said you wouldn't want him to stop up. He's got news for you.' Her mother was beaming, so it was good news.

'A house?'

'No.' Her mother's disappointment was fleeting. 'No, not a house but as good as. They've made him a deputy.'

'That's good,' Peggy said, trying not to crow. A deputy meant promotion and promotion meant more money and the chance of a house. They walked home together, arm in arm, each of them carrying a bag.

'I wish I could've made you a better meal,' her mother said as she lifted stovies from the range. Peggy's mouth was already watering at the prospect of her mother's stovies, the appetising mix of potato and onion, seasoned to perfection, and with just enough liquid to make the pale confection melt on your tongue.

'It's OK,' she said. 'I love your stovies.'

'It's the dock strike.' Her mother was unmollified by the praise. 'Five weeks it's gone on. As if things weren't hard enough. How do they expect men like your dad – manual workers – to get by on veg? And bairns waiting for a few treats – oranges and bananas – I'd dock-strike them if I had my way.'

The lecturer in British Way and Purpose had spoken of a new purpose, a solidarity among the working class, but Peggy could see little sign of it here.

'They only want a better deal.' As soon as she'd said it Peggy regretted it. Her mother was waving the serving spoon to emphasise her point.

'We all want a better deal, our Peggy. They're not the only ones what's fed up. I've scrimped and scraped for five years, made meals out of thin air, washed pit togs without soap, made clothes out of stuff I'd've binned before the war. And all so things could be better. That was the carrot! Get the war over and then there'll be milk and honey. And things are worse! Worse! Less in the shops, rations cut. And what about bairns like you coming back home? What will you get? It'll be years before you and Jim can get wed. Years!'

A small knot of discomfort had formed in Peggy's throat. Her mother was speaking as though marriage to Jim was a hundred years away. She tried to enjoy the hot and tasty food but it had turned to ashes in her mouth and it was a relief when her mother switched on the radio. There was music playing, 'Cruising Down the River', the song that was on everyone's lips. Wherever you went someone was whistling or singing it. Peggy felt her eyes prick and blinked fiercely so as not to cry.

'What's the matter?' Her mother was eyeing the still-full plate.

'I've burned me mouth, that's all. It's so tasty – after army food.' She was trying to make jokes now to lighten the atmosphere. 'Army dumplings – Hitler's secret weapon, we used to call them. Heavy as lead.' Her mother had settled opposite her, arms folded on the table, scarred hands cupping the elbows of her shabby cardigan.

'Will you miss it, Peggy?'

'Some of it. The girls . . . I'll miss the girls. And you got into the routine. It'll be a change pleasing myself now.'

'Have the others gone home? What did they call your friends?'

'Amy was me best mate.' She had slipped back into the familiar sloppy speech. 'Me best mate'. In the last few years she had tried to talk more like other people, especially Celia, who had a lovely way of saying things. 'My friend', she would've said. Or 'My special friend'. 'Me best mate' was pure Belgate but she was home in Belgate now and had better get used to it. 'She's getting married soon. As soon as they can arrange it really.'

'Her dad's got money, though.' Her mother's tone was gloomy. 'And a pub. I've heard you on about it. It's scandalous what you can get if you're in the food trade. They should shoot black-marketeers and spivs. You wouldn't catch me lowering myself to grovel the way some of them do. I've made do for five years on what the government allowed. I'm not giving up now.'

Inside Peggy the last little spark of hope flickered and died. Without a bit of skulduggery there would be no hope of a wedding, not to mention a home. 'I think I might lie down for a bit,' she said. 'Before the kids get back from school and Dad gets up.' She had left most of the onion and potato. 'It was lovely, Mam, but I had a big butty on the train.' As she mounted the stairs to the bedroom she shared with her two sisters she could hear her mother scraping the uneaten food back into the dish from which it had come.

In the bedroom she drew the thin curtains across the window, although there was still black paint on the glass, so no one could see in. The obsolete blackout frames that had obscured the windows in wartime were stacked against the wall. Thin strips of wood to fit the windows, covered in blackout material. She fingered it, wondering if it could be made into garments. But who wanted to be dressed in black at twenty-four? That was for widows and grandmas.

She opened the door of the closet that filled one alcove. Her clothes were hung on the right. Two cotton dresses, two skirts, a green serge coat and her navy-blue mac. She looked down at her uniform. Would it dye? Could she shorten the skirt, change the buttons? In Yorkshire Amy would be planning her trousseau, standing arms raised so that her wedding dress could be fitted around her slender waist.

'Damn Amy.' She said it aloud and then was covered in shame. Amy was the kindest, sweetest girl in the world and instead of envying her she should be working out what to do for the best. She took off her uniform and crept between the sheets in her underwear. They were striped flannelette and welcoming and she felt her limbs relax.

I'll work it all out, she told herself as she closed her eyes against the soft flannelette pillowcase. I'll go back to work and we'll save up, both of us, and if a spiv offers me anything – anything – I'll have his hand off.

Soothed by this vow to resort to skullduggery if she had to, she drifted into sleep.

'Wake up, pet.' Her mother was standing at the bedside, a steaming cup in her hand. 'Here's some tea, and Jim's downstairs. He's that keen to see you. I said you'd be down directly.' As she sipped the tea and felt to see if her hair would be passable if it was combed, Peggy imagined what it would be like if her mother was like some mothers and would let Jim into the bedroom. She would move over so that he could have the warm patch and he would pull off his shirt . . .

She stopped, realising that she had never seen Jim naked. He was a collier so he'd have a body like her father, flecked with blue scars where coal dust had entered into the thousand minor wounds that were a pitman's lot. His chest was broad, that much she knew, and he had a tight bum.

They had talked endlessly about men's bums in the barracks at night, especially Ethel, who had described her boyfriend's buttocks in detail. But she had never really felt comfortable with such chat. The thought of her mother knowing she had been a party to such conversations brought a flush to her cheeks and she finished off her tea at speed.

She put on her best cotton frock to go downstairs, aware that the buttons were straining over her more mature bosom but determined that his first glimpse of her should be out of uniform. In the mirror her eyes were bright and she pinched her cheeks and bit her lips to make them glow. Not bad! But as she descended the narrow stairs she felt a lowering of spirits. They had talked about this so often, this moment when she would no longer belong to king and country but to him. And now it was all being spoiled by dock strikes and coupons and the fact that a place of their own was years away.

He was sitting on the fender but he stood up as she entered the room, his long legs untangling gracefully, his face lighting up at the sight of her. 'Peggy.' It was a formal acknowledgement rather than a greeting. He was conscious of her mother beaming in the background and so was she.

'Jim.' She was bowing her head as he had done, for all the world as though they were at court.

'Well, go on then, give the lass a kiss.' The maternal permission worked. He kissed her cheek and then, tentatively, her mouth.

'It's good to see you back.'

'It's good to be back.' She wanted to put her arms around him, thump him with love, kiss the hollow at his throat, which showed in his open shirt neck. I want to do it with him, she thought. Not wait for a hundred years. Aloud she said, 'Shall we go for a walk? I could do with some fresh air.'

Their conversation was stilted as they walked awkwardly up the back street, afraid to hold hands for fear of scoffing neighbours, each of them nervous to make the first move, although it was five weeks since they had last seen each other. But when they reached the hedged lane that ran towards the cricket field they turned to each other instinctively. 'Oh Peggy,' he said. 'Oh Peggy.'

He smelled of soap and new, sweet perspiration. She was sweating too. 'Let's go somewhere quiet,' she said. 'I want to be alone with you, pet. I want . . . I'm ready, Jim. I've thought about it. It'll be years before we get a place. I can't go on waiting, not now. We'll be careful . . . I know all about it. We got lectures . . . it'll be safe.'

She could feel him hardening against her. He wanted it too, as much as she did. More, even. She wound herself against him, rubbing her open mouth against his face, his neck, until he put her away from him. 'Wait, Peggy. It's not right. We don't want to start off on the wrong foot. Deputies get a house. We might have to wait a bit . . . still . . .'

She had never congratulated him on his promotion and suddenly she was conscience-stricken. 'I'm proud of you, Jim.' She felt herself go limp. He didn't want her, not as she wanted him.

'Never mind that.' He had sensed the change in her and was gripping her arms. 'I love you, Peggy Bates, and I don't want to get in bad with your mam and dad – or mine, come to that. We'll get somewhere. I'll ask me mam about the back room if I have to. It won't be for long. The important thing is to start off right because I want to be married to you for a hundred years.'

He was looking down into her face and his own was so earnest and troubled that her frustration melted in the desire to comfort him. 'I know,' she said. 'I know. It'll be all right. It's just that I love you so much.' They kissed once more, the slow kiss of people who know they have all the time in the world, and then, arms around each other, they walked on, planning their future.

7

Celia

'What are we going to do about Gotz?' From somewhere outside in the street Celia could hear music – the plaintive accordion music she always associated with Paris. 'J'attendrai', that was the tune. Somewhere a shutter rattled in the wind and she could see a brown leaf caught on a cobweb and shaking to break free.

'I don't know,' she said, turning towards Glynn Chambers. She had come to respect him now and trust his judgement. Again and again she had seen him cut through red tape to restore an individual's pride or self-confidence. Now they had a committee of residents in the house, who made decisions and implemented them themselves whenever possible. The system was working well but there would still be the odd scream in the night, the occasional outburst of temper. Aaron Gotz was different. No display of emotion, only a stoic silence.

'He doesn't want to make friends,' Glynn said. 'You've tried, I've tried.'

'I think he was disappointed not to have news of his grandparents.' Celia reached for the boy's dossier. 'They were taken to Theresien-stadt. He thought they'd survived. I don't know why. He accepted that his parents and his sister were dead. He just seems convinced the old couple will come back to their house.'

'We sent him to the house, didn't we?'

Celia nodded. 'Twice. Sergeant Mealy took him the first time and then Madame Mauriac. She told me he never spoke. Just went from room to room in silence. The house had been looted – it was a German billet. She said it was a shambles.'

'And now he sits all day staring into space and half the time returns his meals. He should be moving on, Celia.'

'He reads.' She felt defensive suddenly and agitated. She had grown used to the presence of the young Jew, enjoyed seeing the gaunt frame fill out a little and the eyes begin to come alive. She didn't want him to move on. But his rehabilitation had stalled – that couldn't be denied.

'Reads?' Glynn's eyes were kindly as he posed his question. 'Or hides behind a book?'

'He reads – he quotes bits back to me. Well, sometimes. I gave him my *Golden Staircase* and he enjoyed it.' In the street outside the music had ceased and the wind increased. Winter was coming.

'*The Golden Staircase*?' His eyes were kind but keen.

'It's a poetry book,' she said defensively. His expression softened but his words did not.

'I want him out of here, Celia. There's nothing for him here. Not now. He should move on. He's a clever lad. University's the place for him but he's lost education. If he's ever to catch up he needs help.'

He closed Aaron Gotz's file and rose to his feet. 'Take him back to the Rue Christine. It's probably been cleared up by now. They've locked up the empty apartments. Talk to Michael. He'll contact the Sûreté for you and make the arrangements.' He put up a hand and ruffled his red hair in what was a characteristic gesture.

'What will happen to the properties of people who've died?' Celia asked.

'Due legal process eventually, but I'm glad I don't have responsibility for it. According to the latest SHAEF figures a quarter of French Jews have perished. At least a quarter. The remainder are scattered to the four corners. Europe is in a state of flux, my dear. The only thing we can do now is let things settle. See who comes back to claim what's theirs. Then we can see what's left and talk about next of kin. In the mean time Gotz must be motivated. Take him there, let him see the place is safe, but make it clear it's not the place for him now.'

'He never asks about his own home,' Celia said, frowning.

'If you've been dragged from your bed aged fourteen, seen your sister molested and your father felled and spat upon you might be quite inclined to forget it,' Glynn said drily. 'Now, I was due at the Meurice half an hour ago. Get back to me when you've made the visit.'

She found Aaron Gotz in a small room with barred windows that looked on the rear courtyard. The light was fading but he had not switched on the light. When she did so she saw him blink and put up a hand to shield his eyes. She had learned in the last few months that it was best not to question why people sought sanctuary, so she crossed to the window and made a great show of drawing the curtains.

'Not long to tea,' she said as she turned back. There was a book on the arm of his chair and when she picked it up she saw it was the book of poems she had lent him.

'Are you still reading this? I must bring you something else.'

He reached out and took the book from her. 'If I can still keep this. I like it.'

'Which poem do you prefer?'

'The snow poem,' he said, without hesitation.

'By Robert Frost?'

Aaron nodded and began to quote.

'Whose woods these are I think I know . . .'

Celia finished for him: 'His house is in the village, though; He will not see me stopping here To watch his woods fill up with snow.'

Aaron smiled and Celia felt her own face relax at the sight of his pleasure. 'You are thinking of your English snow,' he said.

'Robert Frost is American – or was. I'm not sure if he's still alive but I love his work. I'll see if I have any more here with me. If I have you can borrow it.'

'Thank you.' He inclined his head as he spoke.

'Glynn wants me to take you to the Rule Christine tomorrow,' Celia said. 'Do you want to go?' He smiled suddenly but it was not a smile of pleasure, much less of amusement. It was a smile of scorn.

'Why not? If that's what you want, why not?'

'Glynn says the house has probably been put in order. He thinks the Sûreté will have the keys. And . . . and he thinks it's time you moved on. You want to resume your education, don't you?'

'I suppose so.'

She couldn't resist letting her frustration show. 'You don't give an inch, Aaron, do you?' Immediately she was contrite. He didn't give because he was bereft. He had nothing left to give, not even an answer. 'I'm sorry. I want to help you and you don't let me. If you'd say what you want . . .'

'Like the others?' He was bitter now. 'Yes sir, no sir, three bags full sir. Give me food, give me money. Set me up in my store, give me my business back. I don't want anything, Celia. I want nothing because there is nothing I want. Can you understand that?'

'Yes. I can understand it very well. But it's not an answer. You can't stay in this hostel for the rest of your life. Look at it. It's a shabby house full of requisitioned furniture. You get a clean bed and three meals a day. Is that all you want?'

'It's enough.' He had picked up the book and was making a play of finding his place.

'You're trying to shut me out, Aaron, but it won't work.'

'Of course not. You're responsible for me. Childish of me to forget that. You have a duty to me, don't you? And I have a duty to be grateful. And I am. Deeply, humbly grateful. Now can I read?'

Celia got to her feet. 'Read by all means. I'll go and arrange transport for tomorrow. Shall we say ten thirty?'

There was a soft rain falling as they left the following morning. Celia sat beside him in the back seat, trying to establish some intimacy. 'Did you come to Paris often before the war?' she said. She had expected a shrug or a muttered 'Sometimes.' Instead he seemed disposed to talk for once.

'We lived in Poland but we were moderately wealthy so we came once or twice each year. My mother was very attached to her parents.'

'The Meyers?'

'Yes.' He nodded and rubbed his hands together as though he was cold. Seeing her eyes on him he put his hands, palms down, on to his knees. They were still bony but they were a man's knees and a man's hands.

He has missed his boyhood, Celia thought. Or, rather, he has been robbed of it. Now he is a man and he can't cope.

'I loved the time we spent here because my mother

was always happy to be home,' he said suddenly. 'She loved my father but not Poland.'

'Will you go back?' They were on the Rue de Richelieu and he stared out at the Comédie Française for a moment before he answered.

'To Poland? I don't think so. We blame the Nazis for everything but it was Polish children who called me names long before the Germans came. "Dirty Jew". "Stinking Yid". They did not see us as fellow Poles.'

'Is that why your mother was unhappy?'

'Who said my mother was unhappy?' His tone was sharp and Celia back-pedalled furiously, terrified of stemming this sudden flow of conversation.

'I'm sorry. Of course you said she was happy in Paris – that doesn't mean she was unhappy elsewhere.'

'She was happy in the home.' He was mollified and Celia let out a small breath of relief. 'We celebrated all the Jewish holidays,' he continued. 'And on Friday nights all the family came. Papa and Mama Gotz and my aunts and uncles and the cousins. There were lots of cousins. My mother would light the candles. Our house was open house because it was bigger than the rest. My father was a doctor and one of my uncles also.'

Celia did not need to ask if any of them had escaped the camps. It was there on his file: 'No known family survivors'.

'My father went to synagogue for morning and evening prayers. That was the centre of his life. For my mother the home, for my father the synagogue.'

His voice was breaking and Celia put out a hand to cover his where it lay on his knee.

I'm not supposed to do this, she thought. This is not being objective. That was the shibboleth: 'Remain objective at all times'. But his hand did not flinch when he felt her hand upon it. His voice strengthened and he went on talking until they drew up at the door of 8 Rue Christine. It was an imposing house, or it had been once. Now, like every other building in the city, it was battle-scarred and shabby.

Once they stood on the pavement Celia handed over the bunch of keys with the Sûreté label attached. They were new keys and the lock they fitted stood out new and bright against the blistered paint of the big front door. In the lobby he paused and put out a hand to the jamb of the inner door. There were two holes where screws had been inserted. 'They have taken away the mezuzah,' he said and Celia nodded in sympathy, knowing that the tiny box containing extracts from the scriptures held enormous significance for Jews, who would touch it reverently as they passed through the doorway.

They moved from the hall into the large front room. Here and there were pieces of furniture, all of them broken or scarred by ill use. 'Everything good is gone. They took it, presumably.' Aaron's voice was matter-of-fact and she realised that he had come to terms on previous visits with the ransacking of the house. 'My grandmother was proud of her furniture.' He smiled at the recollection. 'She had a little maid but it was never polished enough unless she did it herself.'

They moved from room to room until they came to the small room at the back of the first floor. 'This was my room,' he said. 'I slept there, by the window. At night I would kneel to say my prayers. Outside the window there was a cherry tree. White blossom in spring. Such blossom . . .'

He was crying now, tears rolling unchecked.

'Cry,' Celia said. 'Cry as much as you want to – you have a lot to cry for.' And then she took him in her arms, realising they were almost the same height so that her lips were level with his chin, knowing she must remain objective and this was wrong and glorying in the feel of him in her arms in spite of that. Except for the terrible fragility of his thin frame. If it had not been for his sobbing she might have thought him lifeless.

She waited until his tears subsided and then she let him go and hitched up her leather shoulder bag. 'We're going for a meal and a drink,' she said. 'I'll tell the jeep to go back and we'll find a café.'

He was shaking his head. 'There's no need.'

'There's every need,' she said firmly. 'I need some food inside me – and so do you.'

They found a café in a side street and settled at a corner table. 'Coffee?' she asked. 'Or would you prefer something stronger?' The thin cheeks were suddenly flushed and she knew exactly what was going through his mind. 'It's not my money,' she said firmly. 'Glynn has funds for this sort of thing so have whatever you want.' She was lying but her conscience did not prick her at all. She had always accepted the concept of white lies and there could be no whiter lie than one that saved a young man's pride.

For a moment anger flared in his eyes and she wondered if he had felt himself patronised, but when he spoke his voice was almost apologetic. 'I don't know what else.' He gestured towards the row of wine and liqueurs behind the bar. 'We used to have raisin wine. My mother made it and my father would bless it on Friday nights, before the *kiddush.*'

'That's the prayer over the wine, isn't it?' Celia had learned a little about Jewish life from others who passed through the hostel and she knew she must encourage him to talk of his past. 'Friday nights are important, I know.' She saw that his eyes had grown bright and he was blinking to hold back tears. 'Tell me about Fridays in . . . Where was it you were born?' She knew full well that he had been born in Praszka, a small town near the German border. In 1924, so he was five years her junior.

'I was born in Praszka. My father was a rabbi, a teacher, and I began my studies when I was four. The Hebrew alphabet, reading and writing, the Torah. And my mother taught me to cook.'

'What did you cook?' The coffee she had ordered was brought to the table then, and they both sipped.

'It's good coffee,' he said appreciatively, and she didn't point out that it wouldn't have been dignified with the name 'coffee' before the war. After five years in a concentration camp even chicory would taste like nectar. He put his cup back in the saucer. 'We made *cholent* on Friday mornings. Meat – kosher meat – with potatoes and beans and onions. When I was old enough I took it to the baker to be cooked for Shabbes. Praszka was a small town. My parents knew everyone there. Our pot was blue so when I collected it I would get our pot back and not another family's poor meat.' He was smiling at the memory and Celia nodded to spur him on, liking the way the thin face moved with each new emotion.

'I loved *cheder,*' he said. '*Cheder* was Jewish school and I went there with my cousins and the neighbours' children. Sometimes I had money – five or ten groszy – to buy myself a paper poke of beans from Yentel Drora, who sat outside the school with a pot of them roasting over charcoal.'

He had paused and Celia said, 'It sounds like a happy life.' It was the wrong thing to say and she sensed his withdrawal.

'I can't remember,' he said. 'We should be going back now. The rain is getting heavier.'

I want to stay here, Celia said but only inside her head. This is foolish, she told herself as they walked through the autumn rain, past the shuttered Parisian houses and the narrow alleyways that gave glimpses of courtyards where people were living and loving and forgetting the war that had torn the world apart.

For some reason Amy's letter came into her mind. She had had it for three days now and must reply soon. She could go home for Christmas and attend Amy's wedding. She had more than enough leave to take. But she didn't want to leave Paris and her work.

You mean you don't want to leave Aaron Gotz, her conscience accused her. And it was true. She woke in the morning wondering how soon their paths would cross, if he would smile, show her some special attention. Be objective, she urged herself. Your job is to move him on. Back to his studies. Back to life. He's only a boy. But in her heart she knew he was a man and that she loved him.

She felt his hand on her arm then and looked where he was pointing. A dog sat just inside a doorway, gazing out mournfully at the rainsoaked pavement while a white cat solemnly licked its ear to clean it.

'Do you like animals?' she said, smiling at the dog and cat. 'My godfather sent me a new book this week. It's called *Animal Farm* by a writer called George Orwell. I won't have time to read it straight away. You can borrow it, if you like.' He would read and learn and move away from her and that was as it should be.

'Thank you, Celia.' It was the first time he had used her name and the pleasure of hearing him say it was unbelievable. 'I don't have to give back the poetry book yet, do I?'

'No,' she said. 'You can keep it for as long as you like.'

8

Joyce

There was a man with a hammer banging on Joy's left temple when she opened her eyes. She closed them again but the thudding persisted. She swung her legs over the edge of the bed, vowing to drink less in future, knowing as she made the vow that she would not keep it. The round green alarm clock on the bedside table said five to eight. If she didn't get a move on she'd be late again and Mr Henry Lavender would glower at her and sensitive Mr Neville Lavender would wince on her behalf. She levered herself to her feet and moved towards the door to the landing.

As she had feared, the WC was already occupied and she could hear singing from behind the bathroom door. 'Bugger,' she said aloud. Now she would inevitably be late and there was bugger all she could do about it. She filled the kettle to boil water and made tea in a cup, carefully scooping off the leaves that floated to the surface. Her mouth felt bad enough without having to pick tealeaves from between her teeth.

When she switched on the radio she half expected nothing but static. Instead she got the calm voice of a newsreader giving the latest details of de Gaulle's campaign to become President of France. As if there was any question of its being anyone else but the war hero! She fiddled around for a while, trying to find some music. When she succeeded it was a female voice singing the song everyone seemed to be singing. 'My Guy's Come Back'. Nowadays it was always that or 'We'll gather Lilacs'. Everyone, it seemed – or at least every woman – had a guy coming back with whom she would gather lilacs. Every woman except her. A tear escaped her eye and she wiped it away. No use thinking about Andrew any more. She reached in her bag, trying to remember if she had had any fags left last night. There was one in the packet and a half-smoked butt. What the hell! She lit the whole cigarette and dragged smoke into her lungs. That was better.

On the mantelpiece Amy's letter seemed to beam reproach. 'Please come, Joy. My wedding won't be the same if there are none of you there.' She had put it back in the envelope, acknowledging the truth that she wouldn't care if she never saw any of them again. Wouldn't care if she never met a single human being again or heard a human voice. And yet Amy and Peggy and Celia had been her friends. She reached for the letter again.

The wedding was on 29 December. The Christmas rush would be over and she could be spared from the shop for one day. She might take Chuck with her if he was still around! Let them see she could still get a fella! A door banged on the landing and she rushed to see who had vacated what. A few moments later she was locked in the bathroom, wishing she could use the lavatory, peering at the rings around her eyes that spoke of an excess of everything.

As she brushed her teeth she thought again of taking Chuck to the wedding. He was presentable, that was certain. Charles MacDonald Roche the third. She had met him on her first night in London when she had gone to the party with Edna. Unlike the other American servicemen there, he had been sober and well-mannered. He had taken her back to Edna's flat when she pleaded tiredness and as she had prepared to repel unwelcome advances he had tipped his cap and stood back until she was safe inside and the door closed behind her. She had stood in the hall then, half relieved, half sorry. He had looked so much like Andrew, except that his uniform was the strange pink of an American officer and everything about him spoke money.

'He's from one of America's top families,' Edna had said when she returned the following morning. 'You're on to a good thing there.' Joy had shrugged and muttered something about never seeing him again and then flowers had come and Edna had said, 'See. I told you you'd clicked.'

Someone was hammering on the bathroom door now.

Joy gathered her toilet things and quit the bathroom, seeing, to her delight, that the toilet door was open. Twenty minutes later she was hurrying into the tube, uncomfortably aware that she would be at least half an hour late for work.

She had got the job at Lavender et Cie through a friend of a friend of Edna. 'It's ever so old-fashioned. Mr Neville tries to make changes. Well, when he first came back he did. He's given up now.' Mr Neville had lost a leg at Alamein and had a medal, which Edna's friend swore was a Victoria Cross but was probably something much more mundane.

Lavender et Cie were makers of fine soaps and lotions. There was what purported to be a laboratory at the back of the shop, encased in glass and decorated with magnificent gold-embossed bottles, and that was certainly where the business had begun in 1743. Now, though, it had a large national turnover and all that went on behind the jewel-coloured bottles was commerce.

Mr Henry was lurking behind glass when Joy arrived, just as she had anticipated. And Mr Neville was lurking below, just as he did most mornings now. 'It's all right,' he said, seeing her agitated face. She needed this job, needed it badly if she was ever to get out of Saxton Street, the crumby bedsit Edna had found for her.

'I'm sorry.' She was shrugging out of her coat and reaching for the white overall with pink trim that all Lavender's female employees wore. 'It's difficult in my lodgings, you see. Sharing a bathroom, you can't just get away when you like.' Anyone else would've said, 'Get up earlier' but he just smiled that lop-sided, tolerant smile of the person who knows what difficulty is and limped off to the stairs that led to the offices.

Once behind her glass counter she began to relax, in spite of the hostile stares of the other girls, who were pretending to be busy with their own fixtures but had missed not a word of the exchange with Mr Neville. She checked her shelves, lining up the jars and featherweight boxes, featherweight because they were empty. Like everywhere else in Britain stocks were low at Lavender et Cie and each consignment that arrived from the factory in Stoke was already committed twice over, to women who seemed to have money to spare and nothing else to worry about but obtaining their favourite Fleur d'Amandier or Muguet de Bois.

When the shelves were dusted and to her liking she reached under the counter for the huge tub of sandalwood hand lotion that she was supposed to ladle into square, wooden-topped jars. She liked this task, enjoyed the heady perfume and the way the cream rippled and curled into the wide mouth of the jar.

She was lidding the last one when Mr Neville loomed up beside her. He had a large flat envelope in his hands. 'You mentioned you'd seen *Brief Encounter*,' he said, 'and liked the music. This is the Rachmaninoff theme you liked. You're welcome to borrow it for as long as you like.'

He was assuming she had a gramophone and all she had was a gas fire that took florins. She looked into his kind, rather careworn face and smiled. Easier to let him think he was doing a real favour. 'Thanks,' she said. 'I'll really enjoy that. I'll make sure you get it back.'

He turned away and then back. 'I was wondering,' he said, 'about . . . well, I wondered if you would have a meal with me sometime.' His eyes met hers and then fell away.

He's no flirt, Joy thought. And he is a war hero. But Chuck wouldn't like it. Besides, she couldn't really be bothered with that kind of thing. Not now. Not since Andrew. 'Sorry,' she said. 'I'd love to. Really, I would . . . but . . .'

'I understand,' he said. 'Of course, you've got someone. I only thought . . .'

'My fiancé was shot down over Germany,' Joy said, anxious to lessen his embarrassment. 'I should've told you about Chuck. He's an American.'

'Ah!' He had recovered his composure now. 'It's always an American.'

'Yes,' Joy said in mock regret. 'As they say, "over-sexed, over-paid and over here".'

He left her then, among the soaps and lotions, or rather the ornamental boxes that were supposed to contain them. She felt an odd sense of regret, odd because, although he was nice and every inch a gentleman, he wasn't really her type. And the exchange had made her think. About Chuck. About upsetting Chuck when, up till now, she had thought she didn't give a damn about him.

When it was time to go home she tucked the record under her arm and bobbed her head in Mr Neville's direction as she left the shop.

'Enjoy it,' he said, and smiled. When she reached the street and realised it was raining she put the cardboard-covered disc under her coat to protect it as she ran for her bus.

Chuck was waiting when she reached the flat, hunched under the overhang of the door to try to escape the rain. 'Let's get inside,' he said, taking her key from her. They were halfway up the stairs holding the shaky varnished handrail, avoiding the holes in the thin carpet and still shaking rain from their clothing, when the door to Mrs Mather's living room opened.

'Miss Latham, could I have a word?' Joy could see something was wrong. Mrs Mather's lips were pursed, her arms folded across her waist, fists turned inward.

'Go on up,' she said, anxious lest Chuck should hear anything unpleasant. There was a smell of boiling cabbage coming from the kitchen and somewhere a cat was miaowing. Bad enough that he had to come to a dump like this when he was used to better. Edna had said his family were out of the top drawer and everything about him spoke breeding. Now, though, he ignored her instruction to carry on up the stairs.

'I'll wait,' he said. 'I'm sure this good lady won't keep you long.' His young face was suddenly pugnacious, the freckles across the bridge of his nose standing out, the dark curling hair spangled with raindrops, which he shook free as he spoke. He was folding his cap neatly but there was no mistaking his determination. Here I am and here I stay, his expression said.

'I'm sure I don't want to delay anybody.' Mrs Mather had drawn herself up and was now clutching her waist, as though in pain. 'But it's not what I bargained for. I don't let to couples. I thought I made that clear.'

'I don't know what you mean.' Joy was bemused. 'You know I'm single.'

Mrs Mather's 'Hah' was a masterpiece not lost on Chuck.

'She means me,' he said affably. 'I'm here – here as much as I can be. Is that the problem?'

'I'm not casting aspersions, I'm sure. But single is single.' She softened a little, seeing Chuck's smile grow even wider.

'It's all right for an hour, this one time, and I'm not saying—'

What she was not saying, never emerged. Chuck leaned over the bannister to bring his face nearer hers. 'No, you sure as hell aren't saying, you sanctimonious old biddy. Haven't you heard? Jealousy gets you nowhere.'

'I won't stay here to be insulted. Not in my own house . . .'

'Ma'am . . .' His tones were silken now. 'You are welcome to your house, your mean, dusty, odorous little shack for which you charge exorbitant rents.' He gestured for Joy to pass him and proceed upstairs. 'Get your things, honey, and let me find you somewhere more . . . civilised.'

'Chuck!' She was pulling at his sleeve, knowing she

had walked her feet off to find a place she could afford and only got it in the end through Edna.

'Now, honey. Get your things now!' She looked at Mrs Mather's face. There would be no peace for her here, not after this. She sighed and eased past him towards the bedroom door. There was a further exchange and then Chuck was in the room, running his hands through his curling hair, biting his lower lip and breathing hard through distended nostrils.

'I should've got you out of here before, Joycey. Now don't you worry about a thing.' He moved towards her, sliding his hands under her coat and around her waist, moving them gradually until they cupped her breasts. 'I'm going to take care of you. Leave it to me. We'll get a place together. You'd like that, wouldn't you? Things are slack at base now. We can be together most days, I guess. We should've done this weeks ago. I love you, Joycey. Now, is that your only bag?'

9

Amy

Downstairs Amy could hear the comforting sounds of preparation. The chink of glass and crockery, the rattle of cutlery and bottles, the laughter of the George's entire staff and the extras drafted in to prepare for the best wedding reception austerity-bound Britain could obtain. She smiled to herself and wriggled farther down in the bed.

Tonight she would share a bed with Geoffrey. She had pictured it so many times, how he would take her face in his cupped hands and kiss her. So tenderly. So often before his hands moved to her shoulders, her arms, her breast. She shivered at the delicious thought.

Waiting had been worth it, just as her mother had always told her. Nothing to confess to Geoffrey tonight, nothing to hide. She thought of all the tales she had heard of girls faking virginity. She and Peggy were lucky in that they had no need to lie. Celia, too, except that it was impossible to imagine Celia doing it. She would in time, of course, but it would be different. More intellectual. For a moment Amy puzzled over how the act of love could be intellectual when it was such a very physical thing. But only for a moment. Today was her wedding day and there was a lot to be done.

As she went along the landing to the bathroom she could see the streamers decorating the hall below. A Christmas wedding. What could be better? And at least two of her wartime comrades to support her. Maybe three, because there had been no answer from Joy and she was so unpredictable. She might just turn up.

Her father had given her a dressing case last night. Green shagreen with silver fittings and a full compartment of toiletries inside. 'French,' he had said proudly, displaying the perfume and bath essence. 'Joy, by Patou of Paris, France.'

'Where did you get these?' she had asked, unable to believe her luck. Her father had tapped his nose and rolled his eyes, which meant 'Don't ask – black market' and she felt her eyes fill. However much she loved Geoffrey she would never, ever love anyone more than she loved her father. She shook a liberal sprinkling of bath salts into the gushing water and then, when the fragrance rose up to her nostrils, lowered herself into the scented water.

The George was filled with family. Aunts and cousins, some of whom she barely knew. It would be nice to have Celia and Peggy there, people who knew about her and Geoffrey, had been present at every stage of their love story. For it was a love story. She close her eyes and imagined it. 'I, Alexandra Mary, take you, Elliot Geoffrey. With my body I thee worship. To love and to cherish. Till death us do part.' No need to worry about the words. All she had to do was follow the vicar.

Geoffrey would look into her eyes and she would see herself reflected in his dark grey pupils, her face framed in mother-of-pearl, lily of the valley, her veil cascading around her like white smoke. She would lend the veil to Peggy if she wanted it. The dress, too, as long as it came back in perfect condition, to be folded in tissue and put away to be treasured until it was time for her eldest daughter to wear it to her own wedding.

There was a tap on the bathroom door and her mother's voice. 'Your friend Celia's here, Alexandra. Don't be too long.' As Amy reached for the soap she reflected how your thoughts could alter with time. She had longed to get away from the girls, if the truth were known, but all along it had only been the army she resented, because the thought of Celia's and Peggy's faces turning towards her as she walked down the aisle was suddenly comforting.

A tiny pang of guilt reared its head inside her. She wanted them to see that she was having her fairy-tale wedding but that wasn't the only reason, surely. She musn't turn into a show-off now that she had so much. She whisked through the rest of her bath and climbed out, resolving to be modest and grateful in the years ahead.

As she came down the wide stairs, her new underclothes covered by a housecoat, she could hear her father declaiming to the assembled guests. 'And of course Geoffrey being an accountant, they'll have to move around. Deputy treasurer now. After that, well, it'll be up and up.'

She halted for a moment, clutching the newel post. Be careful, Daddy, she wanted to say. Don't tempt fate. And then Peggy was visible through the glass door that led to the lounge bar and she was rushing forward to greet her friend and pull her into the warmth of the family gathering.

They had half an hour in her bedroom before it was time for her mother to shoo them away so that the anointing of the bride could begin. Celia perched in the window seat to watch and Peggy sat in the big, button-backed velvet chair. Both of them looked smart. Celia wore navy blue. She was noticeably thinner and looked somewhat older but there was a distinct air of chic about her, from the tiny pearls in her ears to her cream suede gloves with their elaborate stitching. It must be true what they said about Paris, that living there gave you an air.

Peggy, too, looked remarkably smart. Her blue tweed suit was a little too big and probably borrowed but she had nice tan suede shoes with a laced tab at the side and her hair had been cut and permed into two wings that went up from her temples and made her face less round. 'It's so good to have you here,' Amy said. 'Have you heard anything of Joycey?'

Celia frowned. 'I went to her old address as soon as I reached London. Apparently she left there weeks ago without leaving a forwarding address. At least, that's what her cousin said. I felt she was holding something back but . . . Well, I expect she'll surface eventually. You know Joyce.'

'Is this your dress?' Peggy was fingering the white watered silk that peeped from beneath its covering sheet, her eyes wide with appreciation.

'Yes,' Amy said proudly, whisking off the cover to reveal the wide skirt with its sweeping train and the lace-encrusted bodice.

'It must have cost a fortune,' Celia said faintly. 'As for coupons . . .'

'Don't ask,' Amy said, mimicking her father. 'I've had to forget about honour and sharing the post-war burden and just let Daddy have his head. But . . .' She paused for dramatic effect. 'It's yours if you want it, Peg. For your big day, that is. I must have it back because I want to keep it for ever and ever, but you can certainly borrow it.'

'I wouldn't dare,' Peggy said. 'What if anything happened to it?'

'Nothing will,' Amy said firmly. 'And you know it will fit. I'll pack it up as soon as I get back and you can keep it until your big day.'

'I couldn't,' Peggy said, but Celia laughed aloud. 'You're drooling, Peg. I'd say "yes please" if I were you. And what could happen to it on your wedding day?'

'Well, if you're sure.' Peggy took the edge of the skirt and held it up against her chest, turning towards the dressing-table mirror as she did so.

'See,' Amy said. 'It becomes you. You'll be a perfect bride and Jim will hardly get his vows out he'll be so bowled over.'

Peggy dropped the dress and flung her arms around Amy's neck. 'Ta, Amy. You're a brick. But I won't take it till we've set a date.' She looked around the bedroom. 'Our whole house would fit in this room. It's better off here till the time comes.'

As they took leave of Amy, Celia squeezed her friend's arm. 'That's put stars in your eyes, Peggy.'

'She hasn't changed.' Peggy's reply was fervent. 'I thought she might – once she got back to all this – but she's still the same old Amy.' She hesitated, as though plucking up courage. 'When you left, Ceely, did you ever wonder . . . well, think you didn't . . .'

'Didn't want to see anyone again? Anyone from the company? Sometimes I thought like that. We hadn't chosen one another, had we? We were just plopped down together, all quite different, most of us away from home for the first time. I used to think I was making the best of things, liking you all because there was no option. But when I got away I realised we clung together because we had something in common.'

'We weren't on the hunt?' Peggy was laughing. 'That was what set us apart. Amy and I were courting and

Joy never needed to hunt – they came running. And you, well . . . you never seemed . . .' She broke off and looked curiously at her friend. 'You've gone red, Celia. You haven't met someone, have you? Is he French?'

'No . . . I mean he isn't French. He isn't anything. There isn't anyone . . .' But Peggy was pulling down her lower eyelid with an index finger and pursing her lips in disbelief.

'There's no one. Really and truly, Peggy. I meet a lot of men, colleagues, some army types but mostly its DPs. Displaced persons. The people from the camps. You get attached to some of them but it's just on a friendship basis. Besides, I'm not supposed to get attached. It's frowned upon.'

'Fraternisation was frowned on but that didn't stop anyone,' Peggy said drily. 'There's GI brides flooding out and fräuleins flooding in if you believe all you hear.'

'Don't,' advised Celia. 'Rumour's a terrible thing. I've seen it in action in Paris. There were people there punished for collaboration when they'd actually been active in the Resistance.'

'Was it as bad as they say?' The question was never answered for Amy's mother appeared, list in hand, to shepherd them out to the waiting cars.

'I've just said goodbye to Alexandra,' she said a trifle tearfully. 'She looks a picture, I must say. Now you're going in the next taxi, Aunt Beth comes behind you with her brood and then it's me and the bridesmaids. They're Amy's cousins, you know. Little devils, I hope they behave.'

Upstairs, Amy contemplated her reflection in the mirror. God had been good. No last-minute spots, no falling out of hair, nothing to mar the picture. She leaned forward and pinched her cheeks until a satisfactory glow appeared.

'Can I come in?' Her father's face was anxious as it peered through the half-open door. 'You look lovely, Alexandra. I hope that Geoffrey's good enough for you.' He moved to stand directly behind her. 'You will still be Daddy's girl, won't you, when you're Mrs Harlow?'

She put up her hands to grasp his. 'You know I will. And Geoffrey will too – be a son to you, I mean.'

He was nodding. 'We had a nice talk last night. When I gave him your . . .' He chuckled. 'Your dowry, I suppose.'

'Dowry?' So Geoffrey and her father had talked behind her back. The idea both shocked and intrigued her.

'Two thousand pounds. Mother and I agreed you should have it towards a house.'

'Towards? Daddy, you could buy a mansion for two thousand pounds.' Her eyes had gone round with astonishment at the sum. Two hundred would have been nice. Two thousand was astronomical.

'There, there.' He was patting her hand. 'Never mind the money. It's not to late to back out. Are you sure you're sure?'

'I'm very sure, Daddy.' She knew he was serious and she tried to reassure him. Taken up with this wedding though he was, he would march into church and tell everyone it was over if she required it of him. 'I love Geoffrey and he loves me and we're going to be so happy. And we'll have dozens of children for you to spoil and you'll come to us and I'll come to you. Every week, you'll see.'

Suddenly his eyes were strangely sad. 'I know you mean it, pet. But you'll be a married woman: you'll have to do what's right.'

She rose to her feet, manoeuvring her heavy skirts. 'It's right I should go on loving you. Geoffrey knows that. Nothing will change, you'll see.'

But as she walked down an aisle bedecked with holly and white chrysanthemums, holding her father's arm, his words kept echoing in her head. 'You'll be a married woman . . .'

She felt her father trembling and then he was holding out her hand and Geoffrey was taking it, grasping it firmly, and she was looking into his eyes and saying the words she had so often practised. 'I, Alexandra Mary, take thee, Elliot Geoffrey . . .' And Alexandra Mary Yeo was no more.

They posed for photos, smiling interminably as the photographer popped in and out from behind his camera. 'One more,' Amy said when they were almost done. 'I want one with Celia and Peggy.' She sensed, rather than felt, a slight tensing in Geoffrey's arm but he moved obediently to stand between the two friends.

'My Jim would've come,' Peggy said when Amy had introduced them to her groom. 'But he's on piece work.'

Amy looked up at Geoffrey, expecting his reply to be reassuring. 'Ah well,' he said. 'We've got lots of people here, haven't we?' It was meant to be dismissive and it was. She saw the smile fade from Peggy's mouth, saw Celia's eyes first widen and then narrow.

'Why did you say that?' she asked when the girls had turned away. For a moment she thought he was going to ignore her question, but at last he looked down at her.

'Because it was true, Alexandra. We have other guests and your preoccupation with former comrades is a little tedious, to say the least.'

'They're my friends.'

'They were fellow servicewomen. Face the fact that you have nothing in common with either of them. We all have to face up to peacetime, tempting though it is to wallow in sentiment. Now, stop being silly, and come and meet my new boss.'

She followed obediently enough, but for the first time in her life a tiny sliver of ice had entered into her heart.

10

Celia

It was cold without any form of heating and Celia laid down her pen to flex frozen fingers. The windows were frosted, starry patterns that caught the late-afternoon sun. Outside, the Paris streets were relatively calm, a welcome relief after the bread riots that had erupted the previous day. She picked up her pen and began to write again.

> The riots were quite ugly and apparently there was trouble in Rouen too. It seems strange that people will riot over shortage of bread when they have so recently been liberated but I suppose their reserves of patience have run out. I hope things are better for you in England.

She smiled suddenly, remembering Peggy's tales of

breadmaking in County Durham and the famous stotty cakes. She began to write again.

Perhaps you should send me your recipe for those famous flat-cakes. I could make a killing on the black market and come back a millionaire. Seriously, though, I hope you feel better about your job. Settling down to Civvy Street can't be easy. In a way this has been a halfway house for me. I have a degree of freedom and I don't have to wear uniform but I still have the feeling of being protected.

Remember that no one can make you work where you're unhappy, Peg. See how things go and change jobs if you have to. It was so good to see you and Amy. I wish Joyce could have been there and it's a little worrying that she's answered none of my letters. However, no doubt she has such a dizzy social round that it leaves no room for letter writing.

What did you think of Geoffrey? I thought the wedding was superb. No expense . . . and no spivvery spared . . . which is fair enough when it's your only daughter. As for Amy, our girl looked a picture, didn't she? As you will when it's your turn. But I couldn't warm to the bridegroom. I'm sure he's a splendid chap but there's just something . . . of course he reached the lofty heights of major before demob and we all know what that extra pip can do, don't we?

Life here goes on much the same. We are resettling a few of the DPs but it's a slow . . .

There was a knock at the door and she laid down her pen and called, 'Come in.'

Glynn put his head around the door. 'Sorry to bother you, Celia, but there's trouble in the kitchen again and you're so much better than I am at calming it down.'

'The kitchen?' There had been trouble before over the kosher nature of the food they served in the hostel.

'Yes.' Glynn shook a rueful head. 'This lot are mostly Hassidic. The sooner we can ship them to London the better. Young Gotz is trying to restore the peace but I think he needs help.'

Celia capped her pen and pushed back her chair. 'I'll come.' Glynn stood back to allow her through the door.

'When you've placated the young lions how about an absinthe somewhere? I could do with getting out of this place.'

She didn't want to go out for a drink. She wanted to hurry to Aaron Gotz's side and support him.

Glynn saw her hesitation and misunderstood it. 'It's all right,' he said, putting a hand on her arm. There was a faint ginger stubble on his chin and the blue eyes were tired. 'I've clean gone off sex if that's what's worrying you.'

'Don't be silly. Of course I'd like a drink.' She pulled her cardigan around her. 'As long as it's somewhere warm. I've forgotten what it's like not to shiver.'

They walked down the stairs together, towards the kitchen, where raised voices could still be heard. 'It gets into your bones, doesn't it?' Glynn's smile was like his voice, full of longing for home, and Celia warmed to him.

'We'll find a bistro. The Café d'Or is usually warm, just up from Clichy. Let me see what I can do in here and I'll be with you.'

In the kitchen a handful of young men were clustered around the scrubbed-pine table. They were all too thin but in the last few weeks their eyes had lost the dead look of the camps. Most of them wore the traditional yarmulke on heads that were now free of the lice and sores that had been the product of the camps. 'Now,' Celia said. 'What's all the noise?'

It was Yasha Kisgerman who spoke first. 'I have done many things,' he said. 'When I was liberated I strangled a chicken, tore it apart and ate the liver. In Malhausen I stole bread from corpses but I swore, I swore, that when it was possible – when it was no longer survival – I would eat kosher.'

'So?' She was used to the heightened emotions of the DPs and kept her voice calm. 'What's the problem?'

He was gesturing towards the table, where a meal was set. 'Is this kosher? Where did it come from?'

'It's not easy at the moment, Yasha. Yesterday even Parisians were taking to the streets. Food is scarce. But what we give you is within the rules.'

'Be grateful!' Aaron Gotz was speaking now, the dark eyes alight in the too-thin face. Celia felt a surge of love for the boy. He was on her side. Always, she felt his support, his gratitude. 'Be grateful you no longer have to disembowel a chicken, my friend. And watch your tongue to Celia.'

Yasha was biting his lip. 'I'm sorry, I know it isn't easy. But . . .' Celia felt her eyes sting. She wanted to reach out to the boy and hug him, hug them all.

'The food is kosher, Yasha. It isn't good food, or appetising. But I swear to you it isn't forbidden.'

She knew Yasha Kisgerman and his story. He had seen his brother beaten to death by a Pole who recognised him as a Jew. He had waved his mother and sisters goodbye as a wagon bore him away to Skarzysko, the slave-labour camp. He never saw any of them again. Now he dreamed of going to Palestine and every day that he was detained in Paris was torture to him.

Celia put a hand to his arm. 'Eat up, Yasha. Soon you will be on your way. You need to be strong.' There was a moment of hesitation and then a boy – she thought it was Aaron but dared not look – pulled out a chair, scraping the legs on the stone floor. One by one they took their seats and the kitchen workers began to dole out the soup and bread that was their staple diet.

She let out her breath on a sigh and smiled around the room. 'I'm going out for a while but I'll be back later. Keep the peace till then.'

There was a wind whistling around corners as they left the hostel and their feet crisped on the icy pavement. 'Here,' Glynn said. 'Take my arm.' When she hesitated he reached for her hand and drew it firmly through the crack of his arm. 'Don't worry, Celia. As I told you earlier, I'm quite safe.' In the lamplight his face was weary, his eyes shadowed.

'You're not joking, are you?' Celia said. 'Is *it* getting you down?'

'A bit.' They had reached the corner of the Rue Malraux and they waited for a break in the traffic before they crossed the road. 'I'm tired of putting people off, breaking promises, seeing hope fade in eyes that had only just regained it. I want to go back to England, buy a sheep farm and never see a DP again. I have no money for the farm so it'll have to be my old trade, schoolmastering, but I still want to go.'

'But you won't.' They moved together towards the opposite pavement.

'No. I won't. I'm like you, Celia. A born martyr. When you went on leave, to your friend's wedding, I hoped you wouldn't come back.' He was pushing open the doors of the café. 'Not that I know how I'd manage without you. But for your sake I'd like to see you escape.'

They settled at a corner table in the half-deserted room.

'It'll sort itself out eventually,' Celia said soothingly.

Glynn shook his head. 'Didn't you dream of how it would be after the war? I did. I had this brilliant picture. The trumpet would sound the cease-fire and we'd all combine to tend the wounded, heal the sick, open up the camps and send them all home in ambulances. What a fool I was! This continent is so scrambled, Celia, that I doubt it will ever heal. We can't send them home because they have no homes. We can't reunite them with their families because their families don't exist any more. We can't even feed them, God knows, because there is no food.

'And it's going to get worse. Well, I could come to terms with all that. It's the people who disappoint me. There's no thankfulness for deliverance, no desire to repair. Only anger and hypocrisy. I was talking to a Frenchman yesterday. A barrister. He told me he felt uncomfortable about his time in the Maquis. Uncomfortable! He's obliged to wear his medals in court, which brings him into bad odour with the Pétainists. They feel ashamed of not being Gaullists, yet they can't forgive him for being one. The truth is that we have all learned nothing and forgotten everything.' He put his head in his hands in a gesture of despair.

'Well,' Celia said, unbuttoning the neck of her coat, 'what I prescribe for you is a drink.' A waiter was shambling towards them, ready to reel off what was available. Celia fixed him with a steely eye. 'I want a bottle of whisky. Scotch if possible. Bourbon will do. And don't shake your head. Anything is available if you have cash. I have cash. Lots of cash. Now, whisky please. *Vite! Vite!*'

There was a moment's hesitation and then the man turned on his heel and vanished into an alcove behind the bar. Celia felt her cheeks flush and put up a hand to smooth her hair. Beside her Glynn's face was still buried in his hands but his shoulders were shaking. She wondered what to do next, thinking he was overcome with grief, but when he straightened up she saw that tears of laughter were streaming down his cheeks. 'By

God, Celia,' he said, wiping his cheeks. 'I'm glad you're on my side.'

They talked of the future as they sipped the dubious spirit that had cost Celia almost the entire contents of her wallet. 'Things will be better for France now that de Gaulle is in power, surely?' It was two months since the leader of the Free French had been elected Interim President of the French Provisional Government by the unanimous vote of the 555 deputies.

Glynn shook a wary head. 'I wonder. Again I think he had the same dream as me. Everyone pulling together. He tried to include them all in his cabinet, even communists. He pardoned Pétain, who would certainly have executed him if he'd been captured. But he's bound to be disillusioned. I don't think he'll stay.'

'Well . . .' Celia spluttered a little as the spirit hit home. 'Things will be better when we get back home. And we're shipping off quite a few of the boys now.'

'Not to where they want to go. Palestine. You can almost see it lit up on their foreheads.'

'They'll get there eventually, if they want it enough.'

Glynn smiled. 'I can see why they like you, Celia. You give them hope.' He put out a hand and covered hers. 'Do you know what Aaron called you the other day? He said you were a Menschenkenner.' She wrinkled her nose to indicate incomprehension. 'Someone who understands people,' he said and smiled.

'Let's not talk about me,' Celia said. She felt uncomfortably warm now, out of the wind, drinking the unaccustomed alcohol. And uncertain whether or not to withdraw her hand from the large, warm one that now covered it. 'Tell me what you'll do when it's all over and you can go home.'

'I was a schoolmaster before the war. At Allingborough.'

'Ah, my cousin went there. A good school.'

'When was he there?'

'Twenty-nine, thirty. Sometime around then. I was staying with my aunt so it must have been early thirties.'

'Tell me about your family. All I know about you is that you were labelled bright and obedient but unambitious during your war service.'

'Was I?' She was laughing aloud at the thought of her service record. 'Did they say I enjoyed it? I did. Hugely! I had good friends and I was my own master for the first time in my life.'

'Really?' He took his hand away, much to her relief, and picked up his glass. 'You were at Durham for three years. Weren't you free then?'

'Not really. I was happy. Mary's was heaven and I loved my subject. I did history. But I felt I had to keep my nose to the grindstone. I had no parents, you see. They died when I was a child and my aunts and my godfather paid for my education so I had to do my best.'

'A double first. You certainly repaid them.' Suddenly he leaned across and put a finger to the side of her mouth. She felt her lips part involuntarily and wondered what to do next. But just as suddenly he was sitting back in his seat. 'Drink up, Celia,' he said. 'I think I'd better get you back before I forget what I said about being off sex. And don't wince at that word. It's what makes the world go round, after all.'

She didn't take his arm on the journey home but when they halted at kerbs or hit a bad patch of ice he gripped her elbow, releasing it as soon as danger was past.

They parted in the hall and she turned upstairs towards her room. There was a light in the tiny cubbyhole where they kept their meagre store of books and newspapers. When she peeped round the door she saw that Aaron Gotz was reading by the light of a small table lamp.

'Aaron, shouldn't you be in bed?'

He looked up and smiled at her and she felt her heart leap at the sight. 'You've been out,' he said. 'You have stars in your eyes.'

'Don't be silly,' she said, sitting down at the table. If there were stars in her eyes they were for him, and that he must never know. 'What are you reading?'

'Your book,' he said. 'It's you who makes me late.' The skull that had been covered by an uneven stubble when first she saw him was covered by tight black curls now and his eyes were ringed with black lashes. She looked at his long thin fingers with their bitten nails and saw that it was indeed the first book she had given him that he held.

'*The Golden Staircase*,' she said. 'My Uncle Philip gave it to me on my birthday.'

He nodded and turned to the flyleaf. 'For Celia, in the hope that she may climb the Golden Staircase of life' was written there in Philip's bold hand.

'I was sixteen,' she said. 'It's meant for children up to sixteen but I always loved the poems in it. I still do.' She began to quote from his favourite.

'Whose woods these are I think I know.' He joined in and they recited solemnly until it came to the last verse.

'The woods are lovely, dark and deep, But I have promises to keep, And miles to go before I sleep, And miles to go before I sleep.'

'It is beautiful,' she said when they were finished. 'And very true. We do have miles to go, especially you.'

'Hah!' He closed the book with a snap of irritation.

'You will go. Soon. I know it seems interminable but you will go.'

'Oh, I'll go all right. They will give me one of their little chits, the kind they give to people who have no homeland, and they will send me somewhere. Then somewhere else. And on. And on. But never to Palestine. You know what I think, dear Celia? I think we are the new Flying Dutchmen. They send us here and there, everywhere, until eventually they lose us.'

'Now you *are* being silly. You, of all people, should understand how difficult it is. There are thousands and thousands of people to resettle. It can't be done overnight.'

The urge to reach out and take him in her arms was

almost irresistible. She stood up abruptly. 'Go to bed and get up in a better mood in the morning.'

He was smiling again, good humour restored. 'It can't be done, Celia. I have miles to go before I sleep.' He was gesturing at the books around him on the table and she knew he meant he must catch up on his studies.

'I'll try and get you some better books,' she said. 'I'll write to my Uncle Philip and tell him what you need.'

'And then you will take back your *Staircase*?'

'No.' She turned in the door way. 'It belongs to you now. You can keep it for ever.' And in that gesture she was giving him more than a shabby volume of poetry.

11

Peggy

There was a hoar frost on kerbstones and walls as Peggy set off down the back street. There was ice in the gutters, too, and she offered up a swift prayer of thanks for her greatcoat, dyed a dark brown now and boasting mock-tortoiseshell buttons.

It was Monday. Amy would have been back from her honeymoon for two days and it was a safe bet that she would not be on her way to work wearing an ex-war-department greatcoat and shoes that had seen better days. Annoyed with herself, Peggy skirted a patch of ice and quickened her step. What was the point of envy? It didn't get you anywhere and why should she envy anyone who didn't have Jim? Geoffrey might be an accountant but compared with Jim he was less than a man.

Besides, what Celia had said in her letter was true.

She tried to remember the exact wording. What was it? Something about Geoffrey being a cold fish. As she rounded the corner and saw the Co-op store in front of her she regretted not bringing the letter with her. She could have read it with her eleven o'clock and seen if what she suspected was true, that Ceely had met someone. It would be in there, between the lines. Suddenly Peggy was filled with a desire to be back in barracks again, where there was always someone to confide in, someone you could trust. At work, here in Belgate, she felt alone and friendless. It's not how I thought demob would be, she thought, as she turned down the alley that led to the staff door, and schooled her face for the working day.

Mr Palmer was already behind the glass front that separated his cubbyhole from the store proper. He looked up as she came in, then looked to the huge wall clock and back to her. 'Good morning,' she said brightly and received a grunt in reply.

'Shall I go on softs again, Mr Palmer?' He paused and tipped back his chair as though considering a weighty problem. Since her return he had moved her from department to department as though she was a junior who needed experience. But she had served her time before the war, from the day she had left Markham Terrace Seniors until the day of her enlistment. She knew every department inside out and old Palmer knew it.

'Not softs, I think,' he said finally. 'There's not much call for softs with Christmas over and no one with coupons or brass. Not that we've got much if they were buying. And it's getting worse!' He blew down his nose rather like a horse and she saw the hairs on his nostrils quiver.

Disgusting pig, she thought, but he was also the store manager and she needed the job so she smiled sweetly. 'Where then?' she asked, trying not to sound impatient.

'Stockroom, I think. We need an up-to-date tally. Miss Robson and Miss Cairns can cope downstairs and Leslie's got upstairs well in hand. Now . . .' He glanced at the clock again. 'Isn't it about time you got down to some work?'

Peggy felt her cheeks flame, all the more so when she looked towards hosiery and saw Lily Robson's smirk. 'I went to war for this lot,' she said, but she said it under her breath.

She thought of Celia again as she counted tea towels and checked off thick woollen linings, the long underpants men wore to the pit. Celia had been so keen on their education for civilian life, the compulsory lectures that were supposed to fit them for a brave new world of peace. What had they discussed in those earnest sessions? 'The army obscures the individual.' That had been one and they had all agreed with the proposition. But the army couldn't hold a candle to Belgate Co-op when it came to crushing a person.

I've got to put up with it, she told herself, as she went up and down the wooden stepladder, balancing boxes of lisle stockings in unbecoming shades of brown. Just until we can get wed, until we have a place of our own. Then I'll tell him where to put his stocktaking.

Tonight she would write to Celia and tell her how lucky she was to still be a servicewoman. Even with all the problems Celia had told her of at Amy's wedding, anything had to be better than this!

She had promised to call on Jim's mother on her way home from work. Normally she dreaded these visits, but today she was so relieved to quit the store that she almost skipped up the wide back street that led to her future in-laws' home.

'You'd never think the war had been over for six months' was her greeting. Mrs Dobson was standing at the sink, up to her elbows in suds and pounding a thick workshirt in the foam. 'I have to wash this as it comes off his back. Can't get another for love or money. I've got the coupons but where does that get you. It's all under the counter nowadays. "See our Lily," Ethel Robson said yesterday. "She'll see you right." "Thanks," I said, "but I've got kin of me own in that store, or soon will have. If there's perks to be had she'll get them for me."'

No chance, Peggy thought, but she only smiled. So that was why no one was pleased to see her back. They had their own little deals going. She was an intruder.

They settled either side of the kitchen table when the shirt had been rinsed and wrung and pegged out to blow in the icy wind. It would freeze stiff as a board in no time and be brought inside like a dead body to hiss and steam under a red-hot iron. Truly, woman's work was never done, not in Belgate anyway.

'Jim was saying you were hoping to get a house.'

Peggy nodded cautiously, trying to work out whether Mrs Dobson was pleased or vexed at the prospect. 'As soon as one comes vacant. It might not be for a while yet. It'd be nice, though.'

'You'll have a better chance once the pits are nationalised.' Mrs Dobson lifted her mug of tea in both hands and sipped. 'We'll see our day when that comes off. They say Clem Atlee'll have it all through by the turn of the year. We'll have a knees-up then and no mistake.' She sipped again and then put up a hand coarsened by work and water to smooth her straggling hair.

'I don't know what's the matter with this village since the war was over. We put up flags, we had parties, but where's the jubilation? There's lads come back that don't even resemble the lads that went away. It's causing trouble, I can tell you. There's five divorces pending in Belgate. And I don't remember one afore the war.'

Suddenly she remembered that Peggy too was a returnee. 'It's different for you, being single. But remember Mary Letts, from the Irish back street? Big girl, married Alec Letsworth? Anyroad, she had a bairn first year of the war, just after Alec went off to Burma. And what does she do? She takes the bairn in bed with her for company. So Alec comes back thinking he's going to share a bed with his wife and get a bit of you know what for the first time in five years and there's a five-year-old lying there refusing to budge. Ethel Kennedy says you can hear the rows through the wall. There'll be trouble there before long, mark my words.'

There was a pause and Peggy sensed that something momentous was coming. 'You won't do anything silly, will you. You and our Jim, I mean. I know it's a temptation but a shotgun wedding never works. Besides, your mam would take it hard, her being WI and all that.'

'Don't worry,' Peggy said, carefully avoiding the other woman's eye. 'We don't want a bad start. Not when we've waited this long.'

'That's good then,' Mrs Dobson said complacently. 'I hope you don't mind my mentioning it, but it's better out than in, I always say.'

'No, of course not.' Peggy hoped she sounded convincing and that the red tide that seemed to be engulfing her neck would not spread to her face. Hurry up, Jim, she thought imploringly. Hurry up and get me out of here.

And then he was there, stooping through the doorway, his weary face creasing into a grin at the sight of her. He had washed at the pit but his blue eyes were rimmed with black coal dust. It was there at the base of his nostrils and in the shell-like contours of his ears. Coal dust was like that – she had seen it with her father. It clung tenaciously to every crevice and could be dislodged only with a soapy flannel and gallons of water.

'Aye aye,' he said. 'Fancy seeing you here.'

'Seeing as we arranged it last night, it's not all that strange.' They were both being flippant to cover their embarrassment. She had hoped he would kiss her but known there was not much chance of it with his mother watching.

She sat while he ate his way through a plate piled high with stodge: mashed potato and leek suet pudding and thick, glistening gravy. I'll feed him better when we're wed, she thought, and then felt guilty. Women were doing their best with what they had nowadays. Putting a meal on the table at all was a victory and not to be scoffed at by anyone.

When he was done he pushed back his chair and patted his belly. 'That was grand, Mam.' His mother passed him a plate of ginger pudding topped with custard and then handed round mugs of hot, sweet tea.

'I'd better be getting up home,' Peggy said, when her tea was done, knowing Jim would want to wash at the sink and might be embarrassed at her watching.

She just had time to wash face and hands and put on a clean blouse when he was there at the door, his eyes clean now, clutching his cap in both hands as he always did when confronted by her parents.

'You can't go walking on a night like this,' her mother said as Peggy reached for her coat.

'It's not cold,' Jim said eagerly, and then went red as her mother laughed aloud.

'God help us when it *is* cold then. Go on, get yourselves off, but don't stop out long. It's enough to freeze a brass monkey.'

They walked up the lane to their familiar place. 'Oh Peggy, Peggy.' His mouth was on her hair, his hands first on her waist then cupping her breasts. 'I love you, Peggy. Do you know that? I love you.'

She wanted him so much, wanted to feel him around her, in her, possessing her. She opened her mouth as their lips met, felt his instinctive withdrawal and would have withdrawn herself except that suddenly his tongue was in her mouth and because it was his tongue it was sweet. She felt her legs weaken and put her arms around his neck for support.

'Steady on, pet, you'll have us down.' And then they were lowering themselves to the frost-hard earth and suddenly they were out of the wind and she could see the stars, quite distinct and separate, and a ring round the moon as though it was an angora bonnet. 'Are you sure, Peggy?' His hand was on her bare thigh, above her stocking top, his fingers cold and trembling against her warm flesh.

'Yes,' she said. 'Yes.' If she fell for a baby they'd get extra points for a house. She lifted herself obligingly as he tugged at her underclothes and then he was against her, naked and warm, fusing with her and then seeking and pushing. She felt a sudden, terrible pain and then it was all sweetness and there was no point in worrying any more because it was done and there was no going back. 'Thank God,' she said aloud and sensed his momentary puzzlement before he was moving and moaning and riding them both to fulfilment.

12

Joyce

For a moment on waking Joy couldn't quite remember where she was. In her dreams she had imagined herself still in barracks, a dozen girls slumbering beside her, a day of safe routine ahead. But all that was behind her now. She was alone in the dingy bedsit that was all they had been able to find in a hurry and soon she must get up and go to a job that bored her, consoled only by the fact that tonight she would see Chuck. It was only when she was with him that the pain of losing Andrew would loosen its hold.

She turned on her elbow and looked at the alarm clock. Twenty-five past seven. She ought to get up now if she wanted to get to work on time but she didn't want to get out of bed. Not yet.

She snuggled down and thought about the last few weeks since she and Amy and Pegs had left the familiar barracks and gone to their dispersal centre. Her small buff-covered release book was still in her handbag. It had been stamped and had its perforated pages torn out and ten minutes later she had been a civilian, in receipt of an Unemployment Book, a Health Insurance Contribution card, fifty-six clothing coupons, a railway warrant and what had seemed like a satisfying amount of cash. She had also been given a leaflet which assured her that 'the ATS is still interested in your welfare and is anxious that your return to civilian life should be as smooth as possible'.

But they weren't interested. Not really. No one cared that life without Andrew was no life at all. She raised herself up in the bed, shivering a little in the unheated room, and tried not to think about him. It only made her eyes sore and she was tired of having sore eyes. Besides, Chuck didn't like to see her with puffy eyes and he might turn up at the shop at lunchtime. He'd done it before. And one of these days he'd have found her a decent place to live. He'd promised her that.

Thinking of Chuck and a new place to live cheered her a little but only momentarily before she was engulfed by another wave of nostalgia for wartime. It had been fun in the barracks. Why hadn't she realised how much she had liked the other girls, especially Celia. Good old Celia, who never put a foot wrong but had never been even faintly goody-goody. Would she ever see Celia again? Or Peg or Amy? Wild thoughts of getting on trains or cross-channel ferries came and went as soon as she acknowledged that she was down to her last ten bob and that was counting the two threepenny bits she used in her suspenders.

As she dragged herself out of bed she was remembering last night's Home Service broadcast. 'We've got to remember that civilians have been shifted about a bit as well . . . that the war's made a mess of some of their lives, too. First of all, about home. That's the place that every single member of the forces is looking forward to – home – but home isn't just a place: it's people, it's you and me, and you and I are not the same individuals we were two, three, four or more years ago . . .'

'You can say that again,' she said aloud and began to wash in the icy water.

What had she been like four years ago? She had been in the service for a year so she must have been over her initial uncertainty. In fact, she had been quite a competent servicewoman then and on good terms with the rest of the barracks. She had had a relationship of sorts with a sergeant called Alan Bryson and she had been quite keen on him until she discovered he had a wife and child in Leeds.

There had been good times, lots of them. Times when the war seemed far away and all that mattered was having fun. And then she had met Andrew and the war had suddenly become desperately important because Andrew was desperately important to her and when the war was over they could be together for good.

When she emerged from the tiny bathroom with its flyblown mirror she was dry-eyed but miserable and the letter on the mat was a welcome sight. She recognised the writing and Edna's scribbled re-addressing of the envelope. Good old Ceel. She never forgot.

She sat on the edge of her bed to read of Amy's wedding. Lucky Amy! No expense had been spared, which was predictable if irritating. But reading between the lines Celia seemed less than enthusiastic about the bridegroom, which, coming from someone who fell over backwards to see the good in people, was quite significant. She tucked the letter back in its envelope to reread later and hurried off to work.

The train was crowded with people who looked as weary and despondent as she felt. A woman stood up to alight but before Joy could slip into her seat a man beat her to it, unfolding his newspaper at the sports pages and holding it up in front of his face. She wanted to say 'What about chivalry?' but there was no point. At least Chuck had good manners.

For a moment, as she strap-hung, she thought of tonight. She liked Chuck, could love him in time if she let herself go. There was no future in living with a memory, not even the memory of Andrew.

Suddenly the headline on the newspaper caught her eye: 50,000 GI BRIDES EN ROUTE FOR THE USA. Her mouth formed a silent O of astonishment. Fifty thousand British girls marrying GIs! There had been plenty of romances but few of them had looked like ending in a wedding ring, however ardent they might have been. She leaned her head against her raised arm and let herself imagine going to the United States. She wouldn't miss post-war Britain with its shortages and its weather and the eternal moaning about everything. It's not what I expected, she thought, and then remembered that if Andrew had lived it would all have been so much better.

At Bond Street station the newspaper placards had a different banner: NATIONAL HEALTH SERVICE TO TARGET TB. She bought a newspaper and read the lead story. Aneurin Bevan, the Health Minister, had announced that illness and death rates had fallen but tuberculosis and venereal disease remained problem areas.

She grimaced slightly, remembering the grim service warnings about VD and the humiliating medical examinations. It was supposed to be rife and yet she had never met anyone who had it – or confessed to having it, which was probably different. Anyway, you couldn't visit a public lavatory without a warning notice staring you in the face, so they would probably get on top of it eventually, especially now that Atlee's government were setting up a service to provide free health care for every citizen from the cradle to the grave.

She folded the newspaper under her arm and turned towards Lavender's. But as she walked down Bond Street her steps grew slower and slower. She didn't want to go to work, was sick to death of ladling goo into pots and pandering to the whims of rich women with more money that sense. She paused at the window of a clothes shop and stared at the single model it contained.

The white plaster face was supercilious, the elbow

turned out, the foot pointed. Joy felt her own body move to correspond to the pose and then remembered she was in the public street and quickly corrected herself.

The suit the model was wearing was fabulous. Black bouclé with a small Persian-lamb collar and buttons made of curled cord. The jacket was short with a nipped-in waist, the skirt was knee-length. She felt her mouth moisten with longing as she looked at it. She still had most of her coupons but a week's wages would probably buy less than an inch of one sleeve.

She move on, into an arcade lined with the contents of a jeweller's shop. Rings and earrings, watches, bracelets, a tiger's-eye pendant on a chain . . . Who had money for such things?

She spent a pleasurable ten minutes choosing what she would buy if money was no object, all the while conscious that she would be late for work and there would be consequences.

They came within minutes of her entering Lavender's. 'Mr Henry wants you,' one of her fellow assistants said, scarcely able to conceal her triumph.

'I don't think your mind's quite on your job, Miss Latham,' he said when Joy stood before him in the inner sanctum. 'I'm sympathetic to the difficulties ex-servicemen and -women must have in settling in to civilian life but as I said when we took you on, we'd have to review matters after Christmas.'

She was out, a week's pay and a box of samples as a parting gift. As she left she felt a sudden sense of terror. How would she manage? What would become of her?

She had reached the street and was struggling to slow her breathing and calm down when she heard Mr Neville's voice behind her.

'Miss Latham . . . Joyce. Wait.' She turned to see him coming after her as fast as his artificial leg would permit. His face was twisted in pain at the impact of the limb on his stump and she stopped and waited for him to catch up. He was a war hero, after all.

'I'm so sorry. I'll talk to my uncle. Don't worry, I'll—'

She cut in before he could finish. 'Don't bother. It's kind of you but it would never have worked out.'

He looked so crestfallen she wanted to reach out and pat his arm but she resisted the impulse. Better not encourage him. 'How will you manage?' he said.

'I'll be fine!' She was back in control now and spoke with a certainty she did not feel. 'I've got something else lined up so don't you worry.'

He was fumbling in his inside pocket and for a moment she thought he was going to offer her money. To her relief, it was a card he brought out. 'Please take this. Ring me as soon as you're settled. I'd like to know you're all right.'

She promised to keep in touch and left him standing, bare-headed and anxious, among the crowds thronging the pavement. When she turned the first corner she took the card from the pocket where she had placed it and dropped it down a drain. It was better to move on in life and keep no ties.

*   *   *

She cried for an hour, then bathed her eyes and put on her make-up. When Chuck arrived he was carrying a holdall which he slung on to her sagging easy chair. 'There,' he said. 'That should keep you going for a bit.'

She unzipped it and looked inside. Tinned peaches, butter, candy bars, coffee, cigarettes! She squealed with delight at the sight of two packets of nylon stockings and a leather box with a mirrored lid which contained make-up. 'I can't take this,' she said. 'Not all this!'

Suddenly she was overcome. As she started to cry, forgetful of her newly applied mascara, he drew her to him. 'Hey! What's this? That's no way to treat a gift.'

She couldn't explain that she was crying at unaccustomed kindness, at the fact that kindness was coming from a man other than Andrew, that she had had enough of life and emotion and insecurity. Instead she said, 'I've lost my job. They didn't need me now that Christmas is over.'

'Is that all?' He was smiling and drawing her into his arms, kissing her nose and cheeks and complaining that they were salty. 'I'm glad. Now I can have you to myself.'

She wanted to shake her head and point out that she needed to work to live but his arms, the feel of his chest against her cheek was too much temptation. 'I love you,' she said. It was only when her mouth opened on his and she felt his tongue touch hers that she realised that what she had said was true. She did love him.

Not as she had loved Andrew, but enough. She put up her hands to wipe her cheeks and then began to unbutton his tunic. By mutual unspoken consent they began to move towards the bed, still locked together.

'Don't worry,' he said when at last they separated, he to pull his shirt over his head, she to reach behind her and undo her bra. 'I'll look after you.'

His body was young and strong and healthy. She had forgotten the pleasure such a body could give. They made love wildly at first, then gently, then again, neither of them willing to be the first to say enough.

'God,' he said at last. 'You're something.' A faint shiver of guilt overcame her. Andrew had not been her first lover but he had been the one from whom she had learned. No, he had not taught her: they had learned together.

'Are you cold, honey?' She shook her head.

'Someone walked over my grave, that's all. I'm all right now.' She put out a hand to touch his belly then, as her hand moved downwards, felt him come to life once more.

13

Peggy

For a while Peggy lay in the half-darkness, trying to convince herself that she felt the moistness between her legs that would signal her period. She mustn't – she couldn't – have fallen wrong. Not now. Not when they had plans and everything was going so well with both mams having come round to the idea of a wedding next year.

'Don't worry,' Jim had said last night, holding her close as they sheltered from the wind in Harrington's shop doorway.

'Don't worry?' She had wanted to hit him across the face for being so stupid.

'We'll manage,' he'd said then. 'You never know, we might get a prefab, if a colliery house doesn't come up.' And the urge to hit him had become almost unbearable because everyone knew the waiting list for a prefab was a mile long. Half of Britain was homeless and the other half living in. She turned her face into the pillow now and cried until she remembered that her mam could spot swollen eyes at fifty paces.

To take her mind off her troubles she thought about the prefab she and Amy had seen in London. It had been wonderful and they were even nicer now. Aneurin Bevan had called them 'rabbit hutches' but according to her father Nye Bevan was a troublemaker. The prefabs had built-in cupboards. One whole wall was cupboards, and roomy ones at that. There was a stove that heated your water and an electric immersion heater in case the stove didn't work. But it was the kitchens that really made them. You could get gas or electric and they all had a large clothes boiler. You needed a boiler for nappies.

Horrified at the intrusion of such a thought, she concentrated on the prefabs. One of the girls at work had said some of them had refrigerators but this couldn't be true. She'd only ever seen refrigerators in service kitchens, huge things you could get lost in. And in American films: they all had refrigerators in America. Still, even without a refrigerator, a prefab would be heaven. Two good bedrooms and a living room with plugs for a lamp and a wireless. A bathroom and a separate toilet so there'd be no one banging on the door in desperation when you wanted to wallow.

Through the wall she heard the springs of her mother and father's bed creak and then the sounds of her mother lumbering into action. Her dad was on back shift so it must be half-past seven. The thought of the house waking up aroused all her fears once more. If she was pregnant she'd have to run away. Maybe Amy would take her for a while or Joyce in London. You could get lost in London. And she'd need to get lost because if she didn't her mother would kill her – if her father didn't get her first.

'You're a woman now, Peggy,' Jim had said last night. 'If the worst comes to the worst – and I still don't think it will – I'll face your mam and dad. Leave it to me.' But there had been terror in his voice at the prospect.

She stayed in bed as long as she could, checking occasionally in the hope that the period that should've come a week ago had finally arrived, but at last the alarm clock showed her that she could put it off no longer. If she didn't appear dressed and ready for work her mother would appear in the bedroom demanding to know what was wrong. And once she knew there was something she wouldn't rest until she had ferreted it out.

She was drinking her second and final cup of tea, one eye on the clock, when nausea overcame her. She tried not to let it show in her face, fixing her eye on the mantel of the one room that served as both kitchen and living room. The blue Rington's tea jar, her mother's most prized possession, two opened letters, one brown and official, one white. The black clock that had been left to her father by his Aunt Ethel, a brass candlestick . . . Suddenly bile rose in her throat like lava and she made a dash for the sink.

When at last she straightened up she knew it was too late to dissemble. 'You've fallen wrong,' her mother said. It was a statement rather than a question. She had always been afraid of her mother, much as she loved her, much as she knew herself to be loved. Now the stocky little woman in the flowered crossover pinny, her hair skewered back from a face half raw from wind and soap, looked terrifying.

'I've eaten something,' she said feebly. 'It's nothing – just wind . . .'

'You silly little bitch.' Suddenly her mother sounded flat, less furious than regretful. 'After all the times I've warned you – after all the years you were away fending for yourself – you come back here and one sniff of a daft lad and you've a bun in the oven.' Her mother put a hand behind her and felt for a chair, wearily, as though her legs were failing her.

They both turned as her father appeared in the doorway, the toilet roll in his hand because it was too precious to leave in the outside lavatory nowadays, when anything could be lifted. 'What's up?' he asked, looking from face to face.

'She's having a baby.' Her mother had subsided into the chair and folded her bare arms across her lap.

'Whose?' His face had gone white except for a bluish line around his mouth. 'Whose?' he said more loudly, advancing towards her.

'Whose do you think?' She saw his arm come up but the blow, when it fell across her mouth and nose, was still a surprise. Her father had often threatened to hit her but had never done it until now.

'Dad . . . be careful.' Her mother was on her feet now, anxiety overcoming every other emotion. 'It's Jim's bairn – who else would it be? And that's no way to go on . . .' It had always been the same with her mother, quick to anger and as quick to simmer down.

'I'm going to work,' Peggy said and pushed past them both, wiping blood from her cut lip as she went.

She managed to put on a good face at work, blaming her cut lip on a night-time encounter with a door jamb, but as the day wore on it became harder and harder not to betray the terror that was engulfing her. How would she face people? What would they say? Where would she go if her father put her out of the house now? What would she do if she lost her job? They were looking for an excuse – now she'd given them one.

She compulsively tidied drawers, dusted displays, polished the glass jamb of the big cabinets behind the glass counters. At dinnertime she walked the streets, not caring that her stomach was empty and tying itself into knots. The afternoon dragged on, the hands of the big mahogany clock on the wall seeming to defy motion. 'Please God, let it be six o'clock,' she prayed and then remembered that meant going home and changed her plea.

But if the clock was contrary it was also remorseless. At five past six she was out on the January street, the last one to leave apart from Mr Palmer locking up behind her. She was turning off Front Street when she felt Jim's hand on her elbow, his breath on her ear.

'All right?' He drew her into the lee of the wind and stroked back the hair that was escaping from the hood of her raincoat.

'Yes,' she said and they both laughed at the forlorn sound of her voice. 'I don't know why we're laughing,' she said at last.

He drew her closer. 'I do. Guess what I got today.' He didn't wait for an answer. 'A house, that's what I got. It's only Morgan Street, mind, so it's no palace. But it's ours and we're getting wed pet, bairn or not.'

'We can't,' she said weakly. 'Can we?'

'Yes. And no argument. I'm going to be boss in my house and don't you forget it.' They kissed then, not passionately: this was the gentle kissing of two people who know they are in total accord. Eventually he stopped holding her close and linked her arm in his. 'Let's get home out of this wind. We've got plans to make.'

'Can we have a look at Morgan Street on the way?' She knew it well but she still wanted to see it.

They were passing a street lamp when Jim noticed her lip. 'I thought you were wincing just now. How did you get that?'

She couldn't tell him the truth. The last thing she wanted was him and her dad at loggerheads. 'I caught me mouth on a drawer in the shop. How will we pay for the wedding, Jim?' She had always wanted a big wedding, a great day. But if he said keep it small she would.

'We'll manage,' he said. 'One way or another we'll manage. And you'll be the bonniest bride in the six pits!'

I will be, Peggy thought, as they neared Morgan Street. I'll have Amy's dress and veil. Shoes as well possibly as we take the same size. As for a reception, it would be in the church hall and sparse. Rationing would see to that. Aloud she said, 'What will your mam say?'

'You leave mam to me. What about your folks?'

'They know,' she said. 'I couldn't help it. I was sick this morning and me mam guessed.' He halted and turned her to face him.

'Did she tell your dad?' Peggy nodded. 'So that's how you got the fat lip?' She felt his hands tense on her arms.

'No . . .'

'Don't lie, Peg. And don't worry, I'm not going in there hot-headed. But I tell you this, no one – no one – will ever lay a finger on you again.'

'Except you,' she said meekly.

'That's right, except me.' He bent to kiss her brow. 'And I'll never hurt you, lass. You know that.'

Over his shoulder she could see the moon coming over the roofs of the colliery houses, houses that ran in rows down to the railway track. 'Stables for workers', her father had called them once when he was calling the coal-owners. But the thought of one of those houses being hers and Jim's was so wonderful she felt as though she might burst with pleasure.

The houses in Morgan Street were small, two up, two down, the stairs leading up from the living room. 'Ours hasn't got a bathroom,' Jim said. 'But you can see the pit from the upstairs windows.'

'There's nowt like a good view,' Peggy said sarcastically and then squeezed his arm to show she understood he meant it would be handy to be close to his work.

'I like her nets,' Peggy said, as they stood regarding their new abode. 'Do you think she'll leave them?'

'I doubt it. But we can get new ones. We'll have everything just the way you want it.'

'It'll take time,' Peggy said. 'But it's a grand little house really – and nice big windows. I think we'll paper the walls. I've never liked distemper.'

'Me mam can paper,' Jim said.

'So can mine.'

'That's all right then. We can sit back and let them do a room each.'

'Daft ha'p'orth,' she said, nudging him. 'We'll do our own papering.'

They stood for a while in silent satisfaction, not needing to speak.

'Come on then,' Jim said at last. 'Let's go and face the music. And leave your dad to me. If he wants to clock anyone he can try it on a man.'

'You're half a head taller than him,' she said, trying

not to sound too proud. And then she chuckled, thinking how quickly life could turn around. This morning all had been tragedy, now there was nothing ahead but a lifetime of love.

14

Amy

When Geoffrey drove off and she could close the door, Amy put her head against it for a moment and tried to clear her thoughts. What she wanted to do was go back to bed, climb into the still-warm sheets, close her eyes, curl up and think about nothing. Absolutely nothing. But the last time she had done that Geoffrey had been scathing about the lack of progress in their home while he had been at work and the icy atmosphere had lasted for days.

She cast one regretful look at the staircase and padded through to the kitchen, her fluffy pink slippers flip-flopping on the parquet flooring as she went. The paper Geoffrey had leafed through during breakfast was still on the table. She topped up the lukewarm tea in the pot, smeared a slice of cold toast with marmalade and sat down to read.

The front-page headlines were bleak: WORLD FOOD SHORTAGE BRINGS RETURN TO WAR-TIME RATIONING. Bread would have less wheat and be almost black, all fats were to be cut and the government could hold out no hope for an increase in meat, bacon, poultry or eggs. And all because thirty million Germans were facing famine because of the collapse of their agriculture. To compound the agony there was a warning of a serious coal shortage. London, the paper said, had only a week's supply left.

She sighed and turned over to find, ironically, the story of a three-year-old from Yorkshire who had died from a surfeit of bananas given her by a doting mother who wanted her daughter to taste the luxury that had just returned to the British table.

A further search of the paper produced very little of cheer. The 1948 Olympic Games were to be held in London and there was an ecstatic report on New York from one of the first GI brides to arrive there. But the item that lifted Amy's heart a little was about the soon-to-be-formed British European Airways, which would transport passengers to Paris for a mere seven pounds ten shillings.

Paris! Amy sipped her tea and nibbled her toast and tried to imagine what life would be like for Celia in the gayest capital in the world. Not that it would be back to normal yet. Nowhere would be like that for another five years, according to Geoffrey. But the blossom would be out on the Champs-Élysées and there would be music and pavement cafés and smart women in the Bois de Boulogne. And, if it was only seven pounds ten, maybe she and Geoffrey could go.

She made her mind up to enrol at the library when she went shopping and get out a book on France. '*Parlez-vous Français?*' She had taken French at school. Geoffrey had clicked his tongue when she mentioned she couldn't remember a word of it. If she brushed up her French he would be pleased. Well, *might* be pleased. Nothing was certain with Geoffrey.

She felt her stomach lurch uncomfortably, as it often did nowadays when she let herself think. It was just because of the new job. He had so much responsibility, that was all. When he settled down – when the whole situation settled down – he would be more like his own self.

She cleared the dishes from the table to the draining board, thinking as she did so how lucky she was to have patterned china in these austere days when all you could get was white. Her father was a magician, no other word for it. Again her stomach muscles contracted. Mustn't cry. Must not cry. If she cried where would it end. She hurried upstairs and began to get dressed to face the day.

She had tidied and dusted the living room when the telephone rang. 'Daddy? I'm fine. How are you? And Mum? Yes, dying to see you. Well, Geoffrey's having to work so hard. Yes, I could . . . Of course I'd like to . . . Yes. It's just that I don't like to leave Geoffey when he's under so much pressure . . .' She put up a hand to catch the tears as they swelled on her eyelids and tumbled over. 'No. It's a bit of cold, I think. No, not flu – just a head cold.'

As she changed the receiver to the other hand the bruise on her arm showed beneath her cuff, yellowing now but still distinct. Geoffrey would never hurt her deliberately but sometimes he got exasperated. It was her fault. She shrugged until the bruise vanished beneath her sleeve and went on explaining why she could not go north to the George. Couldn't say because Geoffrey had forbidden it. He would change his mind soon. When things settled down. No point in upsetting Daddy for nothing.

She prattled on, looking around the room of the unfamiliar rented house in which her marriage had begun. Nothing was turning out as she had hoped. But it would be all right. When Geoffrey settled down and they could buy their own place. That's when it would all get back to normal. It must, it must! she thought, and then, because she had almost let out a sob: 'No, Daddy, honestly . . . I couldn't be happier.'

There was a plop from the hallway and when she had put down the phone she went through to collect the second post from the mat. Two letters for Geoffrey and two for her, one of them with a Paris postmark. She left her housework and sat at the kitchen table to enjoy her mail, vowing as she did so to write to the girls, all three of them, and bring them up to date on her affairs.

Celia's letter was full of descriptions of Paris and the poor young men for whom she was caring.

> They are so bereft, Amy, and perhaps I can understand better than most because of losing my own parents. But no one knows how they will turn out. Can they overcome all the horror of the past few years? Their education has been almost nil and this at the most formative time of their lives.
>
> However, they have the right spirit and intend to make something of themselves. At least, most of them do. Some of them seem lost in their misery and who can blame them? I don't have favourites but one boy – well, almost man – called Aaron Gotz is using some of my books to study. I have great hopes for him. He has such eyes!

Amy pulled a face. Celia using exclamation marks! That was something new. She searched the letter for a description of this remarkable man but it wasn't there. Instead, Celia turned to talk of Amy's life: 'Don't worry about answering my last letters. I write too much, I know, and you will be so busy with your new life.'

'My last letters.' There had been no last letters. Amy resolved to answer Celia without delay and explain that the letters had never reached her. First, though, she opened Peggy's letter. Shorter than Celia's, but just as full of news.

> So I'm holding you to your promise, if you still mean it. I would collect the dress somehow or, better still, you could bring it when you come to the wedding. I do hope you can make it although I'll understand if

> you can't. It's had to be planned so quickly. I don't want to go down the aisle unable to see my feet!

Peggy pregnant! Sensible, down-to-earth Peg who had been so adamant about starting off properly.

> Of course you can borrow the dress [Amy wrote five minutes later]. And all the etceteras. I'm sure we'll be able to make it, especially as it's a Saturday. Wouldn't it be lovely if we were all there, the Four Musketeers. I never thought of us like that before but of course we were. Who was D'Artagnan, I wonder? Celia or Joyce?

As she sealed the envelope she remembered that Peggy might never have heard of the Four Musketeers but it was too late to worry about that. She had to reply to Celia.

As soon as she posted the letters she hurried home. If she had everything in apple-pie order for Geoffrey he would be more amenable to the idea of a trip. They could go to the wedding and stay at the George overnight. She must go home soon because, although he was a fusspot over health, the way Daddy had talked about her mother was worrying. 'The weight's dropping off her, pet lamb. Dropping. She's pining for you, that's what it is. Do come soon.'

She had lamb chops for Geoffrey, their meat ration for a week, served with parsnips and roast potatoes and the rather scrawny cabbage that was all she could get by way of greens. She set the table with their best linen and cutlery, popping out all the while to check the vegetables. Geoffrey detested soggy vegetables.

He had not appeared by the time they were ready and she drained them and put them into a preheated tureen, turning the oven as low as she could. Please, please God, let them stay crisp. Her hands shook as she withdrew them and her forearm touched the over shelf. The burn seared her skin and she let out a yelp of pain. Mustn't cry. Mustn't make her eyes red.

She ran her arm under the cold tap and pulled down her sleeve. Thank goodness it was the same arm and easier to hide. She took up a position from which she could see the overgrown drive. It was a nice house, but neglected. 'We won't be there for long,' Geoffrey had said and she knew that meant better things were ahead.

When he had joined the New Towns Commission he had come home, eyes bright with ambition. 'We won't be going to Darley,' he said, barely able to conceal his triumph. He had been offered a post in a new organisation, set up to implement the government's pledge to build 300,000 new houses in two years.

'It's a mess,' Geoffrey said. 'Shortage of materials and skills and too many fingers in the pie.' According to Geoffrey the money would come from the Chancellor, the Minister of Works would issue building licences, the Minister of Labour provide the manpower, the Minister of Town and County Planning the sites and the Minister of Supply control the materials. In overall charge was Nye Bevan, the Minister of Health.

'But he's got his hands full with the doctors,' Geoffrey said. 'It'll be up to the local authorities to sort it out at grass-roots level.' So they had come to this suburb of London, to be part of the team that would plan towns that would mushroom from the bare earth all over the country.

And now, as they ate their lamb chops and vegetables, Geoffrey's enthusiasm remained undiminished. 'No one has any experience of an enterprise on this scale,' he said. 'But I not only have my qualification: I've got the administrative experience I derived from war service.' He didn't say it but she knew he meant he would have power. She knew, too, that he was probably right.

She waited until she was serving the pudding before she mentioned the letters. 'It's quite strange. Celia says she's written before. They've probably been lost in the post.' He didn't respond and she pressed on. 'Peggy's getting married. Quite soon – a week on Saturday. I thought we could call in on Mam and Dad as we go north.'

This time he looked up. 'I can't get away just now. You know that.'

'I could go on my own. Actually, it's quite important I go. I'm lending Peggy my dress and I don't want to trust it to the post.' As he put down his spoon she felt her stomach heave and put a hand to her mouth.

'All right,' he said. 'If you make me spell it out I suppose I must. Even if I could spare the time we wouldn't be going to that wedding. Peggy – I detest that name, it's a servant's name – is someone you were thrown up against by war. Without it you'd never have known she existed. The sooner you forget her, the better. As for letting her wear the dress you wore at our wedding, it amazes me that you could even contemplate it. We will visit your father and mother in due course but not until a sufficient time has elapsed for them to realise that you're not their little girl any longer. You're my wife, with all that entails. Now, if you have no objection to my relaxing a little after a hard day, I'd like to change the subject.'

She tried once more. 'You liked Peggy. When we were all together – you got on well. And with the others.'

'I neither liked nor disliked them – I did what needed to be done at that time. I was civil to people who – with the possible exception of Celia Blake – I didn't expect to meet again.'

Amy was unable to stop the tears now but they did her cause no good. 'And stop the little-girl antics, Alexandra. They may have served you well in the past. They don't work now.'

There was a tiny fleck of foam in the corner of his mouth and she felt an insane desire to giggle but the hands that were folding his napkin were strong, in spite of their leanness. She got to her feet and began to gather up the dishes. She did not betray emotion until she was safe in the kitchen and could tremble unseen.

15

Joy

From the window Joy could see a tree, bare now but already with the hint of buds. She had been in the new flat for two weeks and she still couldn't get over having a tree in her back yard. It was green when you looked out on it and in a wind twigs tapped at the window. She looked at it now, in the morning light, and was filled with gratitude to Chuck, who had found it for her.

'Are you awake?' she said softly.

Beside her, Chuck stirred. 'No,' he said.

'I love you.'

'It's the middle of the night.' But he turned towards her in spite of his words and reached for her breasts.

'There isn't time,' she said but his hand was already moving down over her belly and she parted her legs obediently. 'I'll be late.' His lips were on her mouth now, shutting out words as he entered her. 'There,' he said, when they had both collapsed, moaning. 'That didn't take long.'

'Idiot,' she said, hoisting herself on the pillows, but the way she said it made the word a caress. He loved her and love bred love. She knew that now. It was Chuck's money that had paid the key money on this flat, his friendship with people in the know that had got her her job at La Salle, his food that stocked her new fridge. 'You can't live without a refrigerator,' he'd said when it was manhandled into the flat and she had shaken her head at the gulf between their two ways of living.

They bathed together in the big white bath, she sitting facing away from him between his long brown legs. 'How did you get that tan?' she asked. 'I mean, how do you keep it?' He had been in Britain for a year and a half and still his body was Californian.

He put his arms around her then and tucked his chin into the side of her neck as he told her of his home amid orange groves. 'One day you'll be brown as a berry, Joycee.'

'Don't call me Joycee,' she said but there was no reproof in her tone, especially when he stroked her white limbs and called her his English lily.

'Are all Americans mad?' she asked as he would have made love to her again, there amid the towels and discarded nightwear.

'Just rich Americans,' he said, grinning to show he was only joking and didn't take his moneyed background seriously.

They ate either side of the pull-out bench in the kitchen – precious eggs he seemed able to produce at will, toast and butter and the English tea to which he had become addicted.

'I must get a move on,' she said, eyeing the clock. To work at La Salle was a privilege – her tips alone were a fortune – but not even Chuck's influence would save her if she turned up late and unkempt. He didn't answer for a second or two and she realised something pretty important was coming.

'Honey,' he said at last. 'It's not definite yet but it looks as though I'll be shipping out before too long.'

'Home?' As she said it she realised how silly was her question. Where else would he be going?

'Yeah, home. Or at least a transit camp back home. The formalities may take a while.' She was trying to smile but somehow it was difficult to get her breath. She might have known it was all too good to last. 'Hey.' He was reaching across to squeeze her wrist. 'It won't make any difference – not to you and me. For two pins I'd fix for us to get married before I went but that would upset the folks and I want them to like you. I want that very much.'

His hand on her arm was warm and comforting and when she looked into his eyes she saw that he meant what he said. 'How long before we can be together?' she said at last.

'A few weeks – three months at the most. I want to break it gently to Mom and Pop that I'm going to marry a foreigner!' He made the word sound sinister and she smiled obediently.

'They'll hate me,' she said.

'No they won't. They'll love you with your English ways. And the voice. Toe-mah-toes. Mom'll love that. Say it.'

'Toe-mah-toes,' she said and then again, because she loved to make him laugh. 'Toe-mah-toes.' And then she had to rush to apply her make-up and don the pale pink overall she wore at La Salle.

'Take care,' he said, helping her into her mac. 'I'll be round to take you to lunch. In the meantime, don't take any wooden nickels.'

There were three letters on the mat, one a bill, the others personal and forwarded from her last address. 'Celia and Peg,' she said, tucking them into her bag. She left him, hair rumpled, naked beneath his dressing gown – his robe – standing in the doorway of the flat, his tall, athletic frame almost filling it as she waved and waved until a bend in the stairs took him from her view.

She got a seat in the tube and opened Peggy's letter. 'I'm getting married a week on Saturday. You have to come.' Lucky Peggy, to have a lovely, uncomplicated wedding to the boy next door. They would have four children, two of each, and live happily ever after. Could she go? Did she want to go to see another girl walk up the aisle? As she folded the letter and tucked it back into its envelope she decided that she would go if Chuck was still here and he would go with her.

She leaned against the window then and wondered

what it would be like when he had gone back to America. Her life would be a wasteland, that was certain, and although he might talk about her going over soon she knew that in reality it would take time. His family were immersed in politics. He had a great-uncle who had been a senator and his cousin was in the House of Representatives.

She comforted herself with the thought that, while she waited to join him, she could borrow books from the library on American politics so that she would arrive there understanding his background. That should impress her in-laws-to-be.

As soon as she reached the salon she hung up her things and checked hair and make-up in the cloakroom mirror. She looked good, eyes glowing, pale hair contrasting with her dark brows and lashes. Love, she thought, as she pinched a little colour into her cheeks. It was true what they said about love being nature's cosmetic.

And then it was time to walk out into the pink and grey magnificence of La Salle and try to bring a sparkle to the eyes of women who might not have love but certainly had money unlimited.

She massaged limbs almost too feeble to walk, covered in wrinkled skin that smelled of Guerlain or Chanel. She anointed seamed faces with creams, working them in gently, kneading taut shoulders until the client purred with satisfaction. When it was all done and they had been tucked up in pink towels to rest after their ordeal, she would slip away to the rest room at the rear of the salon, to check that she was still immaculate to receive her next client.

As they left they would extend a bountiful hand and press a note into her carefully reluctant one. 'No need,' she would murmur, trying to tell from the size and texture whether it was a pound or ten shillings.

Today she was extra-attentive and extra-keen on being rewarded. She musn't arrive penniless in America, not if she wanted to impress the Roche family. In photographs his parents looked aristocratic, his sisters and brothers impossibly glamorous. The owner of La Salle, the lordly Monsieur Pierre, had raised his eyebrows one day and said, 'You've done all right for yourself there, my girl' and then, glimpsing an important client, he had reverted to his accented English and darted forward: '*Chère madame!*'

Chuck was there at twelve forty-five, the time for her break. They walked in Kensington Gardens, pausing to kiss by Peter Pan. 'Why can't you buy dogs in this neck of the woods,' he said and laughed when her eyes widened. 'Frankfurters, honey. Hot dogs, you know.' But the best they could do was hot chestnuts, bought from a funny little man with a creaking, iron stove on wheels. 'I'll take you up town tonight,' he said. 'Somewhere ritzy. You name it.'

All she wanted to do was stay in with him tonight, to cook for him and comfort him and take him to bed at an indecently early hour. She pretended to play the game, however, naming every establishment of which she had ever heard, the Café de Paris and the Mirabelle, the Savoy and even the Ritz itself.

'I'll be outside at six,' he said. 'Don't keep me waiting.' He smelled of soap and tobacco and that indefinable something that marked him out as a foreigner.

'We'll be happy, won't we?' she said, hating this new need for reassurance that had sprung up in her. I love him, she thought as he smiled and turned away. God help me, I really love him.

The thought that she could love again was both joyful and shocking. After Andrew she had thought never to love again and now she was doing it, head over heels.

'Now, now,' Mr Pierre reproved, eyes twinkling. 'Less of the starry eyes, Miss Latham, and a little more of the elbow grease.' He had given her a two-day training course when she started and emphasised the importance of pressure. 'They don't come here to be stroked, Joyce. They come to get their money's worth. Let them know you've been there, or, as we say in la belle France, make the buggers suffer.' He had had the great fortune to be born in Petticoat Lane to English parents both blessed with Gallic good looks. 'I decided that if Froggy was what they wanted, Froggy was what they would get,' he'd confided on the day she commenced work. 'But you're your typical English rose. Cool, that's your stock in trade. Never lose it.'

She should take his advice, she thought, as she relieved her first afternoon client of her sable coat. It was her distant air that had attracted Chuck in the first place. 'You didn't even see me that first night,' he had told her more than once. It would be a mistake to let him see how completely she now depended on him. Except that he loved her and when you were loved you didn't need to pretend. Andrew had taught her that.

She began to swaddle the inert figure on the couch in pink towels, all the while thinking how wonderful life in America with Chuck would be.

16

Celia

'That's it, then,' Celia said, pulling tight the strap that bound Aaron Gotz's shabby suitcase.

'This is yours,' Aaron said. He was holding out *The Golden Staircase*, the book of poetry she had lent him.

'You must keep it,' Celia said. 'To remember me by.' His eyes were on her, eyes sad and questioning.

'Will you be here when I go?'

Celia nodded. 'It's my day off but I couldn't miss you going. I'll be back.' She felt as though her heart would break but she was glad for him just the same. Sometimes it seemed as though the cruelty of the Nazis had been replaced by the indifference of the Allies. Boys – men – like Aaron were homeless, stateless and, even worse, becoming more hopeless. It was time he moved on.

President Truman had asked the British government

to allow a hundred thousand Jews into Palestine but as yet it had not happened. A trickle was entering legally under the immigration quota and there were rumours of illegal immigration arranged by Aliyah Beth, an underground organisation.

Ostensibly, Aaron was travelling to England to resume his studies, but Glynn believed he was probably going to seek illegal entry into his beloved Eretz Israel, the Land of Israel. Privately, Celia hoped he was going to take up his education, in Britain or elsewhere.

'I'm too old,' he had said, when first it was put to him. 'I can't learn. I can only read.' She had admitted the difficulties of becoming a scholar again when you were a man of twenty-one. 'But you can do it, Aaron. I know you can – and you must. You owe it to your parents, to their hopes.' Now, she smiled at him to show she wished him well.

He was glancing at the clock on the wall. 'I have four hours, Celia. Four hours. Will you share them with me?'

'Aah.' In spite of herself a little moan escaped her lips, but she managed to turn it into an exclamation of pleasure. 'Of course. Four hours? Time to see Paris, I think.' They ran from the building like children, he anxious for one last fling before he moved on, she afraid that Glynn might see and disapprove. Not because he was a killjoy but because he knew or half suspected how she felt about Aaron and would be fearful for her.

There was no time to go far afield. They took a cab to the Faubourg-St-Honoré and wandered open-mouthed past the shop windows being redressed for peace. At last they found themselves in a side street near Palais Royal. Someone, somewhere, was playing an accordion, the sound that symbolised Paris for Celia. They moved on towards Rue de Valois, wandering almost blindly because they were together and still had three hours at least ahead of them. They turned a corner and suddenly she saw that Aaron was sniffing the air and looking towards a café which boasted the name of Toutes les Mondes.

'Do you want to eat?' He nodded and took her arm.

'Yes,' he said. 'But I must pay.' She was about to remonstrate when she realised that she must give way. He would have been given travelling money, French and English, enough to see him over the next few days. If he wanted to play the man for the first time in his life she musn't spoil it.

They ate a thin soup, mopped up with rounds of delicious bread, and then a passable tarte tatin. They lingered over coffee, laughing and talking until they could occupy the table no longer. 'That was delicious,' Celia said, wiping her lips. 'Now, we have two and a half hours. What shall we do?'

They wandered the streets for a while, glorying in the architecture, the sights, sounds and smells of a city that was licking its wounds and slowly returning to normality. They wound up in the Tuileries Gardens, the vast rectangular park laid out in the formal French style and decorated with statues.

The harsh afternoon sun was fading and it was

growing colder. Celia looked at Aaron's face and saw that it was shadowed. 'What are you thinking about?'

'That I can't believe it. Believe that I'm going. That I'm on the first leg of my journey to Israel.'

'Well, you are.' She wanted to say something warm and comforting but she was afraid of showing too much emotion. In an hour or little more he would be gone for ever. She mustn't disgrace herself now. 'And it's not the first leg of your journey – that began when you left the camp.'

He nodded. 'That seems a long time ago.'

There was a look in his eyes now, a look she had seen in him and in others, the light of memory. 'Often we used to think about rising up. They would kill us, but could it be worse to be dead than alive like this? And then someone, one of the wise, would say, "Wait for the day." And I used to think: Which day? Why wait? It will never come. When it did come, the liberation, I thought: Now it's over. Now I'm free. For that first day I thought it was as simple as that.'

He had put his hands on the stone balustrade in front of him. They were too thin, so that the fingers looked unnaturally long, and the nails were bitten, but she wanted to take them, one by one, and hold them against her mouth. Instead she said, 'What happened then?'

'On the second day, as we were lining up for the daily soup, I felt my senses going from me. When I came to I was in a hospital tent. They told me I was bleeding from my lungs. They gave me salt and calcium and then, as I grew stronger on the extra food, they got me to walk, each day a little longer. "Pretend you're walking to Israel," one of the nurses said when I would have given up. And she quoted from scripture: "I am the Lord that brought thee out of Ur of the Chaldees, to give thee this land to inherit it . . . unto thy seed have I given this land." And so I started walking.'

She moved towards him now, not caring whether she betrayed herself or not. 'You were brave.'

'No.' The word came out with venom. 'No! That first day people were dancing – those who had strength were dancing – and I just wanted to curl up somewhere, somewhere in the dark, and sleep. Someone had killed a German. "Come, help me rifle his pockets," they said but I did not dare. So many years of propaganda . . . I had been told I was "vermin" and "a parasite" until I myself believed it.'

'And now you're going to Israel.' She put up a hand and turned his face to hers. 'You're going to live the Frost poem – you have miles to go.'

'And promises,' he said. 'I have promises to keep.' He bent to kiss her then, on the lips, but even as they kissed she knew it was a kiss of friendship, of gratitude, nothing more.

He took her hand as they walked on. He went on holding it in the cab that carried them back to the hostel. But when they entered the hallway she saw him put back his shoulders as though preparing to take leave of the past. His bags were already there, Glynn beside them.

'At last,' he said. 'I was beginning to worry.' He was

looking at Celia as he spoke, his freckled face creased with worry, and she smiled to reassure him.

'Nothing to worry about,' she said. 'Aaron has been saying farewell to Paris, that's all.'

The car came for him then and she was glad. She stood in the doorway and watched him climb aboard, keeping the smile on her face, wanting to wail like a child who sees all of life slipping through its fingers.

And then Glynn's arm was around her. 'Brace up,' he said in her ear and she lifted a hand to wave. She went on waving till the car turned the corner and Aaron was gone.

'You need a drink,' Glynn said. She shook her head.

'Thank you. You're kind and I appreciate it. But I think I'll go up and lie down for a while.'

He pursed his lips in disapproval. 'If that's what you want.'

She did not sleep. Instead she searched until she found a book containing the Frost poem. Not that she needed to read it, for it was written in her head. 'The woods are lovely, dark and deep, But I have promises to keep, And miles to go before I sleep, And miles to go before I sleep.'

'God speed, Aaron,' she said aloud and turned her face to the wall.

17

Peggy

Her sisters had risen and departed early, tiptoeing from the room in an almost reverent way. They're leaving me to myself, Peggy thought. So this was what it was like to be a bride – important! She lay on her back, contemplating a room illuminated by the weak sun that flooded through the flimsy curtains. It was a nice day. That was good!

On the wardrobe the dress hung. The lumpy, yellowing travesty of a bridal gown that was inches too long and would surely have her flat on her back before she made it to the altar. She groaned and turned on her face, trying to forget the pain of Amy's second letter with its cold little refusal. 'I'm afraid it is not possible for me to forward the dress just now.'

'But you promised,' Peggy had said aloud as she read and then she had cried as the last possibility of a decent wedding slithered away. She had trusted Amy, believed her to be the kindest person in the world. Of course your wedding dress was important, not something you would share lightly, but Amy had offered – it wasn't as though she, Peggy, had asked for it. It had been offered and now it was being refused.

There had been neither the time nor the money to go shopping then, even if they had had spare coupons or the shops any choice. 'Don't worry,' her mother had said, and a day later she had a dress, Louie Ramsay's pre-war dress that had done for half the brides in the neighbourhood all through the war, and looked it.

The first time she had tried it on she had half gasped in disbelief at the picture that confronted her from the mirror. And then she had seen her mother's face reflected over her shoulder, filled with a terrible anguish, the shame of knowing she was not doing right by her daughter.

'It's lovely, Mam,' Peggy had said then, adjusting the neck that hung on her like a horse collar, fingering the crumpled lace as though it were pristine Brussels worked by nuns, smoothing the skirt that billowed over her now gently rounding stomach in the worst possible way.

She was resolving to keep a smile on her face throughout the ceremony when there was a tap on the bedroom door. No one had ever tapped on that door before. They had come and gone, naked or covered, through all the years of her growing up. She felt tears prick her eyes at the realisation that when she left this room as a bride she would never return to it as a girl again.

'Come in.' Joan was first, carrying toast and tea on a tin tray. Marge was behind with a bunch of cards and her mother brought up the rear bearing a tissue-wrapped bundle.

'There now.' Sister number one plumped the tray in her lap and exited. Sister number two laid down the cards and followed her. Her mother sat down on the edge of the bed and said, 'Get your tea.'

As she spoke she unfolded the tissue. 'I'm sorry about the dress. I know you were disappointed and I'll never forgive that Amy. It's a good job she's not coming, I'll tell you that. I did me best but . . . well, I hope this'll make up for it a bit.'

'This' was a set of shell-pink camiknickers in artificial silk. Bought from the Co-op, where Peggy had often handled their like, but special because there, on the bottom right-hand hem, were her initials, beautifully embroidered in satin stitch in a deeper shade of pink: 'MD'.

She put out a finger and touched the monogram. 'Mam . . . it's lovely. They're lovely. I've never had anything so nice.'

'Your new name,' her mother said, her voice suddenly gruff. She put out a hand, the pads of the fingers work-roughened but for once strangely tender, and patted her daughter's cheek. 'New name but still my bairn.' And then, afraid she had gone too far, she stood up and cleared her throat. 'Get a move on now. You can't be late today. Your dad's like a cat on a stove top.'

When she was alone Peggy sipped her tea and opened the first of the cards, recognising Celia's familiar handwriting on the envelope.

How I wish I could be with you today but, as I explained, so many of the boys are leaving here now, that it's impossible for me to get away. I will be thinking of you, Peg, and wishing you and Jim all the joy in the world. I know you will be happy because I have seen how strong your love for Jim has been through all the years I've known you. I'm sure Joyce and Amy will be with you if it's at all possible.

I haven't heard from either of them lately so I'm a bit out of touch. If you do know how they are or have new addresses for them let me know, but not until you come back from your honeymoon.

I hope you're going somewhere lovely and private. Weddings can be so hectic; it's good to get away. Give Jim a hug for me and know I am thinking of you.

Celia.

The second envelope contained a card. 'Best wishes on your wedding day,' it said in silver script. Inside the silver 'Best Wishes' was followed by 'From Amy and Geoffrey'. And then, in brackets, 'Sorry. I'll explain when I see you. I hope everything goes well. I'll think of you. Much love, Amy.' It was a very Amy-like message, unlike the cold formality of the letter of refusal. Peggy shook a puzzled head and turned to the next letter.

Well, kiddo, you've done it now. Or, if this arrives in time, you've almost done it. Don't say I didn't warn you often enough. Still, Jim is a good bloke – the best – so I suppose he'll put up with you. Tell him he has my sympathy.

I've got a flat now in quite a nice part of London. Yours whenever you can get down here, don't forget. Also a new boyfriend. Well, not new but special. I've mentioned him before, I think, I'm such a lousy letter-writer I can never remember what I've said or not said. Unlike our lovely Ceel, who is the nearest thing to the Recording Angel we're likely to meet. I bet she's got those poor DPs organised to their fingertips. Incidentally, has she mentioned Aaron? He crops up quite often when she writes. You don't think there's something going on, do you? They always say the quiet ones are the worst but I can't imagine Celia carrying on in the line of duty, can you?

Anyway, enough of the rest of us. Incidentally, how is Amy? I haven't heard for yonks.

But to the wedding, I hope the others are there with you and holding you down when you try to run away. Give them my love. We'll get together soon and catch up on all the news.

Much love to you and the lucky bridegroom. I'll raise a glass to you on the day.

They're all imagining the others will be here, Peggy thought. But none of them are. She might have cried then but the door opened and her sisters peered round.

'Are you getting ready? Me dad's getting himself in a right state.'

She got up then, washing herself in the basin on the wash stand, with water from her mother's pride and joy, the matching jug, specially placed there for the occasion and filled with water warmed on the range below. When at last she was clean she put on the camiknickers, feeling the silken material unaccustomed to her flesh, fingering once more the painstaking embroidery, fidgeting for what seemed for ever with the two buttons between her legs.

She made up her face then, cream and powder, pale pink lipstick as befitted a bride, spit to uplift her lashes and smooth her brows and finally, a dash of rouge from the little blue Bourgeois box because her eyes looked huge and dark in a too-pale face.

Marge was ready with the tongs then, heated in the fire so that they crisped and crackled the paper placed between them and her hair. It took two more trips downstairs to warm them before her head was ready to receive the wilting wax orange-blossom that was her headdress. But first the dress!

'It doesn't look bad,' Joan said, hitching up the hem of her own borrowed bridesmaid dress as she spoke. And indeed it did not, for when Peggy looked in the mirror the dress seemed to have taken on a new lease of life.

Her mother came into the bedroom for the final

anointing, lifting the waxen wreath and lowering it on to her daughter's head as though it was a crown. There were oohs and aahs of approval and then her mother was blowing her nose and reaching for a final hug. 'I would've had it different, I can't deny, but that's water under the bridge now.'

They embraced and then she stood back for a final look into her daughter's face. 'I hope everything turns out all right. It's a pity they won't let you stay on at the store but that's the rule – no married women. Still, a deputy's wage is something.' She sounded almost wistful, thinking of her own man, never more than a datal hand, the lowest form of pit life. 'I'd better get down. Watch your hem on those stairs.'

A few moments later Peggy came down to an empty house, save for her father standing at the bottom of the stairs. 'By, lass,' he said, suddenly full. 'Thou's a bonny bride and no mistake.' He put his hand in his pocket and jingled coins. 'I'm all ready if you are.' But first there were amends to be made. 'I'm sorry I hit you, pet. I shouldn't've done that. I was wrong.'

'It's all right,' Peggy said. 'You had good reason to be mad.'

'That's right then.' His face brightened, then clouded again. 'Are you sure . . . I mean, now's the time if you want to change your mind.'

She almost laughed aloud at his tortured expression. 'No, Dad. I'm quite sure.' His face cleared.

'That's all right then.' He held up his arm in a gallant gesture and she laid her hand on it, the right hand now ornamented by the tiny diamond solitaire Jim had bought and which she usually wore on the left. She looked at the clock. In twenty-five minutes that left ring finger would wear a plain gold band and nothing would ever be the same again.

Outside the neighbourhood children were gathered, eyes bright at the prospect of the traditional throwing of coins. Her father threw up the handful of copper and they scrambled for it, whooping with glee, for it was a large handful. Peggy felt her throat constrict. Money was so hard come by in her home but they were doing her proud on her wedding day.

On the way to the church he made an obvious attempt to take her mind off the forthcoming ordeal and she encouraged him, knowing he was far more nervous than she. 'Nye Bevan's got a battle on his hands with the doctors.'

'Get away,' she said. 'How's that?'

'It's the BMA – the doctors' union. They're going to fight the Health Scheme – tooth and nail.'

'Will they win?'

'Not a chance.' He was both triumphant and scornful. 'Win against the Welshman? They haven't a hope in hell.' And then they were at their destination and she was patting his arm on the way up the aisle to soothe a trembling that threatened to bring them both down.

Afterwards she couldn't remember much of the service, just Jim's anxious face as he looked down the aisle towards her and his smile as he saw that she was there and all was well. They sang 'Love Divine' and 'The King of Love My Shepherd Is' and someone poked her in the back when she was slow with her responses.

The walk down the aisle was a blur but the re-entry into the open air a relief, that and the moment when Jim, having stumbled through his speech at the reception, sank down with a fervent 'Thank God'.

People were tucking stray crumbs of austerity wedding cake from their mouths when news came of a disaster at the Bolton Wanders ground. 'Dozens dead,' someone said morosely although no one had a reliable figure. It was an FA cup tie with Stoke and the crowd had broken down barriers in their enthusiasm. 'Chuter Ede'll find out who's to blame,' her father said, displaying once more his complete faith in the entire Labour administration.

'That's put a damper on things,' the best man said darkly, but Jim just took her hand and whispered, 'Not long now,' for they were catching the five-thirty bus.

'Take care,' her mother said on the steps of the church hall. 'Was the spread all right?'

'Marvellous,' Peggy said, though the meal had resembled no more than the Naafi on a bad day.

'Watch yersel',' her father said gruffly, and then, under his breath, 'You can always come home if he doesn't come up to scratch.' She smiled and kissed him twice, to show old wounds were healed, and then they were off in a flurry of goodbyes and confetti painstakingly cut from the rare coloured pages of magazines.

'By, I'm glad to be out of that,' Jim said when they were safe on the bus. And then, seeing her put-out expression, 'not that it wasn't a lovely wedding, mind. Your mam and dad did us proud.'

He loosened his tie and undid the laces of his new and squeaky shoes. Peggy sat bolt upright as Belgate fell away and they were in open country. They changed buses twice, once in Darlington and then in Barnard Castle. Jim insisted on carrying her case as well as his own cloth bag and when they were on the final leg of the journey she saw that he was sweating.

'You're not coming down with something, are you?' she asked anxiously.

He shook his head. 'No. Never felt better. I've supped a bit too much, mebbe . . . last night and today. I'll feel better when we get to this place and see what's what.'

They were going to a rented cottage in Romaldkirk, a village in Teesdale. It belonged to the tallyman, who hauled goods around Belgate, and two nights there would cost them four shillings 'with everything in'.

A fear came over Peggy. She had never given the cottage a thought because the ceremony had been such a huge hill to climb. What if it was a dump, a place crawling with cockroaches or damp? Even haunted?

When they had trudged the remaining two miles from Cotherstone to Romaldkirk and the cottage came into view she let out a sigh of relief. It was straight out of *Snow White*, low and whitewashed with latticed windows and a garden which, even in the dark, seemed to glow with daffodils.

'Right,' Jim said, putting down the bags and opening the door with the key provided. 'Let's have you.' He swooshed her up in his arms, pretending to stagger at her weight, in reality lifting her as easily as though she were made of feathers. When at last he set her down inside a hall smelling of lavender he cupped her face between his large hands. 'I mean to do right by you, Peggy Dobson.'

'I know,' she said. 'I know.' And she began to draw him up the stairs to bed. As he took her in his arms, the scented linen enfolding them, she closed her eyes and felt for his mouth with her own. So this was what perfect happiness was like, peace in every part of you and the knowledge that it would go on for ever.

Afterwards, when Jim slept, she lay wide-eyed in the soft feather bed, thinking about war. It had been worth it, going away to fight for right. Some people had died for freedom: she and Jim were two of the lucky ones who had been spared to enjoy the peace. She thought of Celia, rebuilding Europe. Of Amy, making Geoffrey happy and going up in the world. Even Joy had found love again, after all her sadness. It was there in her letter, however she might play it down.

'It's going to be wonderful,' she said aloud. 'For all of us.' And then, before she snuggled down beside Jim, she put her hands together and gave thanks for all the joy that was to come.

Wait For The Day

Book Two

1953

18

Celia – 1953

The Home Service was full of details of Stalin's death and the power struggle in the Kremlin that was sure to follow. At least it makes a change from the coronation, Celia thought, but she switched it off just the same. She was not in the mood for doom and gloom after a long day at work. She walked to the window of her flat and stared down at Kingsway, semi-deserted now on this March evening.

She had been in this flat, high above one of London's main thoroughfares, since she came back from Paris. Six years! Six years and still she hadn't got over the pleasure of having a home of her own. Her flat was on the fourth storey of a corner building. The ground floor housed the premises of Quiller & Sons, high-class furniture makers. Above them were the offices of Stock & Co, Chartered Accountants, then the third floor, divided into two flats, Mr Tripper and Mrs Lewinski.

Her own flat was an eyrie high above the bustle of London. The whole building was a masterpiece of Victorian architecture, ornate and turreted with round windows like towers to every storey except the first. Here, in her own round window, she could look down towards Waterloo and up towards Holborn. It felt like being at the hub of the universe.

There was a soft purr at her feet and then the sensation of a small furry body weaving between and around her legs. She bent to pick up the cat, sleek and grey and, for once, affectionate. 'Hello, Sam,' she said, letting him climb to her shoulder, his claws sinking into her woollen cardigan as he went. I am a typical old maid, she thought, with my lonely flat and my pussy cat.

She bent to kiss the cat's sleek head, suddenly remembering Paris and Aaron Gotz. She had never seen or heard of him since that day when he had climbed into the car and been driven off to fulfil his dream. And yet hardly a day passed by without his coming, unbidden, into her mind.

She had thrown herself into her work then in an effort to forget the boy who had so stirred her. She had wandered the streets and gardens of Paris, remembering that last, sweet day with Aaron. It was a wonderful city in those first heady months of peace. As Simone de Beauvoir had written, 'All roads opened up. Journalists, writers, budding film-makers, discussed, planned, made decisions with passion, as if their futures depended only on themselves . . .'

There was no more hated curfew so the young tended to stay out all night hanging around the jazz clubs in Saint-Germain-des-Prés, sleeping in doorways to walk home at dawn. The economy of France was in a desperate state and, after de Gaulle's shock resignation, Celia feared for his nation, but gradually life, certainly in Paris, assumed a semblance of normality. Food became more plentiful, the flood of DPs coming to be rehabilitated slowed to a trickle, and it was Celia's turn to go home.

She was sad to leave Glynn but suddenly hungry to take up civilian life.

On the night of the day her posting back to Britain came through he took her to a small café on the Left Bank, becoming noted for its black-market food and drink and the quality of the jazz that was played there. There had been an odd intimacy between them that night, as though they were marooned in the pool of light that came from the table's flickering candle.

Around them the air was filled with cigarette smoke and here and there the aroma of a rare cigar. Across the table Glynn's eyes were wise and kind, twinkling now and then when they remembered the few times there had been cause for laughter. 'It will do you good to get home,' he said at last, and she knew that he sensed she was thinking of Aaron.

He put out his hand and covered hers, to stop her toying with the salt cellar – but when her hand was still he didn't take his hand away. She was the one who withdrew her hand to wipe eyes suddenly grown misty. And then he was calling for the bill and they were out in the dimly lit street, a glittering sky above them as they headed for home.

'I'll miss you,' he said when she left and she promised to keep in touch, but somehow the promise was never kept. She did not even send him her new address and so she never knew whether he had returned to England or continued his work in Europe. She came back to England to begin the peace and now she was a principal, the first step in the top echelon of the Civil Service.

'Being groomed for the top,' Philip had called it when she took advantage of the reconstruction competitions arranged and publicised at the end of the war by the Civil Service Commission. As a graduate she had had the option of competing for entry as a cadet or to the assistant principal grade. As a cadet she would be assessed to determine whether she was administrative grade material. If she went for a post as assistant principal promotion would be assured.

'That's what you should go for,' Philip had urged. 'Your experience in the Control Commission will be invaluable. You could go to the Home Office or the Ministry of Labour – they're immersed in the employment aspects of the Commonwealth immigration policies. You'd do well there.'

Celia had opted for the Ministry of Labour and National Service and was appointed to the regional office in Red Lion Square, there to specialise in the

Rehabilitation and Resettlement of Disabled Persons. Philip had found her a flat, this flat, somewhere that felt like a home, and she worked hard enough to quell any uncomfortable thoughts of loss.

She had been a principal for seven months and three weeks now, on a salary of eight hundred and eighty pounds per annum, and her annual leave stood at thirty-six days annually plus public holidays.

I'm lucky, she told herself, pressing her face into the cat's fur. I am lucky, lucky, lucky. And then the voice in her head that would not be stilled: I am lonely, lonely, lonely. She thought again of Aaron on that last day, setting off towards his dream. Had he reached Israel? She hoped so. The poem came into her mind then, or rather the last verse:

> The woods are lovely, dark and deep,
> But I have promises to keep,
> And miles to go before I sleep,
> And miles to go before I sleep.

'Not for us, Sam,' she said, sighing. 'We live here.' And then, knowing where this mood would take her, she put the cat down and seated herself at her desk to reread and reply to Peggy's latest letter.

Dear Celia,

Hope things are OK with you, as they are with us. Jim is fine and in line for Deputy Manager so cross your fingers. You can't believe it's eight years since that night we all went to London and they lit up Big Ben, can you?

I'm so happy, Celia. Sometimes I ask myself what I've done to deserve such happiness and I always hope it's the same for you and the others. Well, if not the same then just as good. Margaret starts school in September and the baby is dry now. A big relief as nappies and the wretched Milton bucket are the one thing I hate about motherhood.

Still, enough of me rabbiting on. Have you heard from Joyce or Amy lately? All I had was a Christmas card from Amy and Geoff but nothing from our Joy. I expect she's married a millionaire by now and is sunning herself in the Canaries. She always was a one, wasn't she, but losing Andrew hit her hard. The war caused so much sorrow but we were lucky, you and I.

I expect you're as sick of talk of the Coronation as I am. I wish it was over but the children will love it, I expect. All the children in Belgate are to get a mug and we're having street parties. You'll be right there, in London, and probably in the Abbey, you being a Senior Civil Servant. What did you say in your last letter . . . a Principal? It sounds very grand. Do you have a secretary?

Celia reached for her pen and began to write.

Dear Peg,

You ask if I have a secretary. Oh, that I did

then I'd answer my mail more promptly. I've had your letter for two weeks but can only excuse myself by saying that I've read it over and over again and rejoice at how happy you sound. It must be wonderful to be married to the right man and have a family. I've given up all thought of meeting Mr Right. Civil Servants are rather pompous, I fear, and male ones always married, and I seem to do nothing else but work.

I haven't heard anything from Joyce for ages and then a postcard arrived out of the blue. It had followed me from Paris, believe it or not, which would be the last address she had. And with typical service efficiency it took two years to track me down. And it makes you wonder if there were other letters. Still, no point in wondering about that. Apparently she's working on a cruise ship as a beautician, or she was then, about two years ago. There wasn't room for much detail but she said she'd done it because she needed to get to America. She says she'll be in touch when she's next in England so perhaps we'll have a reunion one day. It was her old breezy style so hopefully she's happy.

As for Amy, I rang her ages ago. Geoffrey answered and I asked if I could speak to Amy. He said 'There is no Amy here,' which quite flummoxed me for a second and then I said, 'Well, Alexandra,' and the next moment she came on the telephone. But it wasn't the old Amy. Quite stilted and I felt she wanted rid of me so I shan't ring again unless Joyce turns up and you can get down here, in which case I'll attempt to get us all together. My flat is small but if you're all prepared to bunk up we could manage and it would at least be more comfortable than barracks.

I don't know, though. Sometimes, I look back on those days in camp and they seem to be nothing but laughter. Was it that good or have I got a severe case of rose-coloured spectacles?

She ended with best wishes to Jim and the children, folded the two pages into an envelope and licked down the flap. When she looked at the clock it was seven thirty. Time for supper. She stood the letter on the mantelpiece and went into the kitchen to prepare a coddled egg on toast and two pieces of shortbread to have with her cup of Horlicks. I really am an old maid, she thought. Thirty-four or not, I am set in my ways.

She turned on the wireless again as she ate and drank. Someone was giving details of preparations for Queen Elizabeth's coronation, which was still three months away. If she had to listen to this for twelve more weeks it would surely drive her mad.

She had hoped for a play or an interesting talk. Even light music would have lifted her spirits but when the programme changed it was some esoteric science subject and she switched off in disgust.

She had intended to post Peg's letter on her way in to work in the morning but on an impulse she put on her tweed coat and tied a silk head-square under her chin. A walk in the cold March night air would settle her down. When she got back she would pop a bottle in the bed and have an early night. She pulled on her fur-lined gloves, picked up the letter and let herself out of the flat.

Mrs Lewinski was on the first landing, peering from the door of her flat. 'I thought I heard you, Miss Blake.' Inwardly, Celia groaned. Outwardly she smiled encouragingly. Mrs Lewinski was old and lonely and hungry for the sight of a friendly face. A chill came over Celia as she looked at the old lady. Was this how she would wind up, lurking on landings in the hope of a friendly word?

She talked for ten minutes, or rather listened to a catalogue of complaints about the building, the district, the state of the country and life in general. At last she freed herself with a promise to come down to tea on Sunday and then she was out in the crisp night air and hurrying towards the post box on the corner.

But when the letter was posted she was still not ready to turn for home. Instead, she walked on and turned towards Waterloo Bridge. It was almost deserted of pedestrians and she paused halfway to look down towards St Paul's and up to the Palace of Westminster, romantic now in moonlight.

She was almost home when she saw the man in front of her, his figure and gait so familiar that her heart lurched within her. She quickened her step, trying to breathe easily, tearing the scarf from her head and running a hand through her hair to improve her appearance. 'Aaron.' He didn't hear and she called again. But when the man turned she saw that he was not Aaron Gotz. He did not even resemble him.

19

Amy

As she made for the door to Selfridge's Amy had to pass a newspaper vendor. OLD QUEEN DIES IN SLEEP, his board said. She fished in her bag for coins and bought a paper. QUEEN MARY PASSES AWAY PEACEFULLY, said the headline. There was a picture of the Queen Mother, stiff and regal, dressed as she had been dressed throughout Amy's life, in an ankle-length coat and a matching toque. Amy folded the newspaper and put it in her shopping bag. It would be something to read over lunch.

As she moved around the jewellery department she thought about the royal family. Did they grieve as ordinary people grieved? When her mother died she had cried for two weeks. Cried until the lining of her eyelids burned as though on fire and she could only peer at the world through slits. Her mother had been dead for six years now. Ever since Princess Elizabeth's wedding in 1947. And now that young bride was a queen and soon to be anointed before the crowned heads of Europe.

Geoffrey had grumbled about the influx of visitors the coronation would bring. She closed her eyes momentarily, hearing his voice in her head. 'We don't need gawping crowds. They throw things into confusion.' When she opened them she saw the bracelet, silver filigree set with blue stones. Pretty. So pretty. The assistant was at the other end of the counter. She did not see as Amy unhooked it from the stand and dropped it into her open bag.

Her heart took a while to settle back to its regular beat and she dawdled between counters until it did. If she got flustered her neck grew red and it was an unpleasant feeling. Whenever she thought of her father, alone at the George – a George that seemed strangely echoing and silent now without her mother – her neck felt strange. She had not seen him since the week before Christmas. 'He must learn to stand on his own two feet,' Geoffrey had said when she had begged to be allowed to stay with her father for Christmas, or at least to bring him home with her.

'No,' Geoffrey had said and she had known there was no point in argument. Besides, Adam had begun to shiver as he always did when there was tension between his parents. 'Ssh,' she had said then. 'Everything's all right.' And Geoffrey had pulled her son from her.

'You mollycoddle him, Alexandra. Why don't you ever learn?'

She was in the children's department now. Sweet little dresses with matching knickers. Age 6–7, 5–6, 4–5. Alice was six. She ruffled through the racks with one hand, taking down a size six with the other and placing it in her bag. A glow of satisfaction went through her. I am winning, she told herself. In this at least, she was winning.

She smiled left and right as she mounted the marble steps. She was still smiling when she sat down in the restaurant and ordered a handsome lunch. She could afford to pay for it. Whatever else he was, Geoffrey was a good provider.

She made her way to lingerie when she had finished her lunch. She loved to finger the slips and nightdresses, satin lavished with lace, fine cotton trimmed with broderie anglaise, ruched bodices with tiny roses pinning them here and there. She waited until the assistants were huddled together at the till before she slipped a pale lemon petticoat from its hanger and twirled it around her hand to put it into her bag.

It was then that she saw the woman watching her from the other side of the display. Her eyes were wide, as though with shock. She knows, Amy thought, and felt a sudden wetness between her legs. The next moment she had thrust the petticoat into her bag and turned away. Would the woman cry out? Her heart pounded in her ears like bells until she was out of lingerie, through swimwear and on her way downstairs. And then, as her palpitation subsided, she was suffused with triumph!

At home she took out her booty. She was pleased with them but not as pleased as she had been in the shop. When they were yours they were never the same. The thrill was in wanting them, in obtaining them. Having them was nothing. She hid them at the back of the linen cupboard, along with the product of so many shopping expeditions. Soon she would have to find another hiding place, but not yet. She would worry about it tomorrow.

Amy walked to school to meet her children, thinking, as Adam and Alice walked towards her, how beautiful they were. Beautiful but subdued. They did not shout or run as the others did but they were pleased to see her, pressing against her, each taking her hand for the walk home.

She had given them milk and biscuits and was settling at the table to hear their news from school when the phone rang.

'Jenny?' It was the cook from the George. Strange for her to ring. She listened, only half comprehending at first, then letting out a howl of anguish as the truth hit home.

'So he's in the Cottage Hospital, Mrs Harlow. He was conscious when they took him away but he couldn't speak. Well, not to me, that is. I think you'd best come as quick as you can. And then there's this place. Not that we're busy, and I expect me and Joe can manage . . .'

Geoffrey sighed when she telephoned him. 'I'm

coming home,' he said. 'Don't do anything foolish. I'll see to it all when I get there.'

While she waited for him she prayed. 'Please let him let me go. Please don't let him stop me.' But she knew that he would. That he would do anything to make her suffer. That although he would never lift a hand to either her or his children, except to grip her arm to emphasise a point, he was crucifying them just the same.

But Geoffrey did not refuse her permission to go. 'I've arranged for the children to go to the Hargreaves,' he said. 'I'll drive you to Yorkshire. If I don't you'll do something idiotic.'

She kissed her children as they were led away by her neighbour and then she climbed into the front seat of Geoffrey's dark blue Morris. She was afraid to speak, terrified that she might say the wrong thing, that he would change his mind and prevent her from going to her father. There was silence in the car and she hardly breathed until they were past Stamford and heading for Doncaster and she knew they had reached the point of no return.

She wanted to go to the hospital but he pooh-poohed the idea. 'We'll go to the George and get our room settled. If there's time we'll go to the hospital then.'

Mustn't argue, mustn't demur. Keep him sweet. Daddy, Daddy, she thought. Just hold on until I get there.

The faces of the cook and the potman and the barmaids were strained. 'We thought you'd go straight there,'

Jenny said. Geoffrey did not dignify them with an explanation. 'Take these bags,' he said, 'and we'll have tea in the lounge.'

She sipped tea and nibbled biscuits, hearing minutes tick away on the big grandfather clock, wanting to scream, to run all the way to her father's bedside. It was nine o'clock when Geoffrey glanced at the clock. 'No point in going tonight,' he said. 'They wouldn't let us on the ward.'

He did agree to ring the hospital. 'He's stable,' he said. 'Now, let's get some sleep.' And then, as they mounted the stairs, 'Have you noticed how run-down this place has become? He's certainly let things go. I'm surprised the brewery lets him stay.'

As she lay beside him in the dark, hearing the dear familiar George creak around her as it settled for the night, she wondered how it would feel to kill someone. To take a pillow and hold it over narrow, unsmiling lips until every breath of life had been eliminated from the body beneath. And then, fearful of God's punishment, she prayed that her father would last the night until she could be there to hold him in her arms.

20

Joyce

Joy had only a forty-five-minute break in the middle of the day. She was too tired to eat so she went straight to her cabin, kicking off her white shoes as soon as she entered and flopping down on her bunk. I hate this life, she thought, and then sighed at the futility of her own action. She was sick of crossing and recrossing the Atlantic but she did nothing about it and probably never would. She lay, hands behind her head, staring up at the polished wood above her, and reviewed the last seven years.

Andrew had been dead six months by the time she was demobbed. She remembered those first aching weeks without him, when her limbs had felt so heavy that it seemed she was walking underwater. It had been worse after Celia went. However hard Peg and Amy had tried, and they had tried, their joy in their own relationships had spilled out, a living reminder to her that she was alone.

She had gone to work at Lavender's and there had been parties every night, parties full of her cousin's friends, young men and women drunk with the euphoria of peace.

And then she had met Chuck. She closed her eyes so that she could see him, lithe and brown and insatiable. 'Is that good, honey? Is that good?' He liked to bring her to climax again and again, sometimes with his mouth, his hands, sometimes by entering her, always thinking of her pleasure as much as his own.

She thought of his breath warm on her neck as he entered her from behind; she thought of his body slippery with soap as they loved in the shower; she thought of the security of knowing he would always give her fulfilment. Which perhaps explained why she had been willing to traipse back and forth across oceans for so long, just for a snatched few days together.

She had hoped to meet his parents when she went to America that first time but the promised meeting had never materialised. 'You have to give them time, honey,' he had pleaded, his eyes moist with anguish. So she had given them time and still Mr and Mrs Roche refused to acknowledge that their son had a woman in his life. Or, rather, they refused to acknowledge that he had any other than an *American* woman in his life.

'You have to understand, honey. They have this dream, this ambition for me. They intend me to follow the family tradition and go to the Senate. These are crucial days. If I want to make a mark I've got to become a delegate.'

She had wrinkled her nose in incomprehension and he had explained. 'Each state holds a party convention to select delegates to the national convention. When they get there they'll pledge the votes of their state to a particular nominee for the Presidency. This is the time to catch the eye of the party bosses. After that . . .'

He had paused then, pursing his lips and rolling his eyes to indicate that the sky was the limit. 'And I would be a liability?' Joy asked.

Chuck shook his head. 'No, honey. It's not that. It's just that staying single – looking free – at this stage . . . well, every party boss has a daughter. You smile at them all and that way you get Daddy's vote. Once I'm out there, though, once I get a nomination . . .'

He had explained to her that to be a senator he must be at least thirty years old. 'One more year, honey, and then I'm eligible. I live in the state and my family counts. I'm young, that's both for and against me. But once I'm there, I'll have you there, on my arm. You could be the first English First Lady.' He had made it seem so easy, so certain of fulfilment.

Now she lay on her bunk, blowing smoke rings against the polished wood ceiling. She ought to walk away but that was easier said than done. I'm lonely, she thought, and was suddenly filled with nostalgia for wartime, when she had been surrounded by friends and

Andrew had been alive and loving and full of plans for their future.

She had understood the difficulties Chuck faced in acquiring an English wife too soon. There was resentment in some parts of America against the influx of English war brides, many of them seen as having snatched GIs who had left loving sweethearts back home. Not that the English wives had had an easy time of it. One departing group were greeted by an officer with, 'You may not like conditions here, but remember, no one asked you to come.' Other women were made to stand naked on a stage in front of US officers while a doctor shone a flashlight between their legs to check for evidence of VD.

So she accepted the need for patience, never imagining it would last as long. Now she closed her eyes for a few moments, longing to sleep but aware that there was not time. At last she swung her legs to the floor and got ready to return to duty.

By 5 p.m. her back was aching intolerably but Joy kept smiling as she massaged rounded limbs too lazy to lift themselves from the bed. At first she had envied the pampered women who occupied the couch. Now she almost pitied them, having listened to them moan and bitch about their lot.

This last one was different, however. Almost purring with contentment, which was not surprising as the three-stone diamond ring that flanked her platinum wedding ring would be worth a cool two thousand! She had perfect, if slightly supercilious, features and her dark hair was cut short in gamin style. She said very little as the head-to-toe massage continued, except to murmur 'Hmm, nice,' from time to time.

She had booked an hour and Joy kept one eye on the clock as she kneaded and stroked alternately. With a bit of luck she could squeeze a five-minute break before her next client and put her feet up while she had a fag.

'Do you enjoy your job?' The question was unexpected and Joy stumbled over her answer.

'Yes . . . well, sometimes. It's like any other job, I suppose.'

'Like the curate's egg,' the woman said.

'Sorry?' Joy was still nonplussed.

'Like the curate's egg – good in parts. Oh, never mind – it's an old joke. How long have you been on cruise ships?'

This was easier. 'Four years. I started on the *Pandora* – her first voyage after refit. She was a troop ship in the war. Can you turn over, please. That's lovely.'

'It must be a wonderful life. Exotic places, wonderful food . . .' The woman gave a low chuckle. 'Handsome matelots . . . what more could you want!'

For a moment Joy was tempted to tell what it was really like. A poky cabin that was stuffy and claustrophobic. Meals that were cold by the time you got them but it didn't matter because you were too tired to eat. Crew who were always trying to get into your bra and passengers, male and female, who thought you were one of the creature comforts provided on voyage.

Before she could answer the woman gestured towards

her bag. 'There's lotion in there. Could you use it for the final massage – I'm rather fond of it.'

'Of course.' The bottle was heavy, opaque glass in the shape of an urn, and when Joy unscrewed the top the smell was glorious.

'Hmm, it smells wonderful.' Joy looked at the label. Lavender et Cie, it said. Londres.

'Lavender's.' She couldn't hold back her amazement. 'I used to work there once. After the war. Only briefly but I've never forgotten it.'

'It's my husband's firm. Their products really are good. I'm not just saying that. I use them myself and they work!'

The woman's smooth body was testament that something worked, Joy thought. She moved round the bed, trying to catch sight of the appointment book. She had simply looked down the treatment column before the woman's arrival. Now she looked for the name. 'Lavender. Mrs C. Lavender.' But it couldn't be *her* Mr Lavender. She had seen the woman about the ship often enough, wrapped around a young man with dark curls and a dreamy expression.

'I knew a Mr Lavender in those days, Mr Neville Lavender.'

'That's my husband. He went back to the firm during the war. He lost a leg at Alamein, poor thing. It's frightfully limiting for him.'

'Well,' Joy said. 'It's a small world.' She kept her voice smooth but her mind was racing. So Mr Neville had got himself a wife! Got her but couldn't keep her, if her behaviour with the other man was anything to go by.

'I must tell my husband. He's meeting me at Southampton. What's your name?' She was looking at Joy without a trace of embarrassment that her affair with the boy might have been noticed.

'Latham. Joyce Latham. I went to Lavender's in 1945, straight after demob. Your husband was very kind – I do remember that.'

'He would be.' She did not sound proud of her husband's noble nature: rather she seemed a little contemptuous.

'Right,' Joy said, to suppress her irritation. 'Can we have you on your tummy now, please?' The woman's back was smooth and rounded, not a spare ounce of flesh nor a too-prominent scapula, and her skin was warm peach. She's beautiful but she's a bitch, Joy thought, and began to apply the lotion.

She had two more clients, each of them wanting full body massages, so it was seven forty-five before she could take off her pink and white overall and make her way back to her cabin. She brewed coffee with the kettle she kept there and nibbled on a biscuit, too tired to go in search of a proper meal. When she lay down on her bunk her legs throbbed and her head ached. She settled back on her pillow, closed her eyes and remembered Lavender's and 1945.

And then she had met Chuck and life had begun again. She sighed and snuggled farther down on her pillow. They had been in New York for three days but he had not been able to come over from Washington. 'I want to, darling,' he had said on the phone. 'You know I want to – God, I want to. I want you. But things are crucial here. I'll fly over if you don't get back here soon. We'll be together, I promise you.'

Joy had wanted to remind him that things were always crucial where he was concerned but he would only have smiled and teased her out of it. Seven years. She had listened to his promises for seven years. Listened and believed. But believing was becoming harder and harder. Soon there must be an ultimatum and she was not sure of his reaction. How would she manage without Chuck in her life if he walked out of it? Could she manage? Discomforted, she turned on her side and tried to sleep. If she slept for an hour or two she would get a shower and go on deck for a while before bedtime.

But sleep would not come. Instead she thought about Mr Neville. She could see him in her mind's eye, with his anxious face and his limping gait. He had given a limb for his country and now his wife was making a fool of him on a transatlantic liner.

The injustice of it drove her up and out of the cabin in search of fresh air but it was cold on deck and she shivered inside her thin jacket as she watched the ship's wake cream into the dark sea. She was on her way back down when she encountered the man, a beefy individual who was given to making suggestive remarks about masseurs whenever she was within earshot.

Now he put out a hand to impede her progress.

'Well,' he said. 'Here's a turn-up.' His southern accent was slurred now and she realised he had been drinking.

'Good evening, sir.' She kept her voice deliberately civil. 'I hope you had a good dinner. And now, if you'll excuse me, I have work to do.'

'At nine o'clock? What kind of work can you do at this hour? You don't call that work, do you? That's fun, or should be. I could make it fun for you.' His breath smelled sweet and alcoholic as he leaned over her and she felt herself flinch.

'I'm sure you could but I'd like to pass.' He didn't move. 'Please, sir. I don't want trouble . . .' She put a hand behind her and felt the smooth panelled wood of the corridor wall.

His hand was on her waist now and moving up to cup her breast.

'Get off,' she said, raising an arm.

'Come on.' He was trying to ingratiate himself. 'Where's the harm? We can go to my cabin – I've got vodka, Bourbon, you name it . . .'

'I'll name it all right. If you don't get out of my way I'll cripple you. And if you doubt I mean it . . .' She poked a stiff index finger into his paunch, just below his bottom rib. She meant to hurt him and his grunt of pain showed she had succeeded.

He stood back but as she moved past him he recovered himself and gripped her upper arm, intensifying the pressure until it was her turn to moan. 'Bitch', he said. 'Whore! Call it what you like, wear your pretty overall . . . but it's still whoring.'

'No,' Joy said cheerfully. 'I may administer to whores but I don't join them. Your wife is one of my clients, isn't she?' She smiled sweetly. 'Goodnight!'

There was a brief moment of triumph as she walked away but once she was safe inside her cabin she wept. She had never wanted to work on cruise ships. She had been happy at La Salle. This, though, was the only way to see Chuck.

But thinking like that was dangerous. She blew her nose and washed face and hands in the tiny wash-basin. She would sleep and get up early tomorrow and swim before work. She shook two sleeping pills into her hand and washed them down with gin and Italian. It was a kind of Russian roulette she played almost every night but tonight, as usual, the pills and alcohol blurred the edges of her pain and she could sleep.

In the five days it took to reach England she watched Circe Lavender. Circe! It was a strange Christian name and the purser who told it her had explained just who Circe had been, a siren, a sorceress who exploited men. But Circe Lavender was not exploiting the dark young man. Rather the opposite. She appeared to pay everything for him, lavished gifts upon him and twined herself around him whenever the occasion offered. Poor Mr Neville, Joy thought, but, conscious of the corridor Lothario's baleful eye upon her, she spent as little time as possible out of her cabin or the beauty rooms.

Instead she wrote a long letter to her cousin, Edna, asking her if she could find out the whereabouts of Celia

Blake, her old service comrade. 'She had an Uncle Philip who took her to the Central Club,' she wrote. 'Perhaps they might know something. It's worth a try if you have time. Failing that, she's something important in the Civil Service. See what you can do.'

She went on deck when the ship docked at Southampton. It was interesting to stand and look down on her disembarking clients as they fussed over their matching luggage and looked at the dockside to see if they were being met.

She saw Circe Lavender take leave of the slender youth, standing in the lee of a companionway to kiss him as though she would never get over parting from him. And then Mr Neville was fighting his way up the gangplank, removing the black Homburg he wore and gazing anxiously right and left in search of his wife. Joy had forgotten that he was handsome – or else he had become so in the intervening years.

He was almost at the deck when something made him look up. Their eyes met and she saw recognition there. He raised a hand; she raised hers in reply. She saw him glance down at his leg and knew he was contemplating climbing up to her level. She shook her head and mouthed, 'I'll come down.'

Below and to the far left she could see Circe, still entwined. Better divert him for a moment or two or he might see more than he should.

He was waiting at the bottom of the stairway. 'Miss Latham? What are you doing here?' He reached out and took her hand in his.

'I'm a crew member,' Joy said. 'A beautician. Your wife has been a client of mine on voyage.'

'Ah.' He nodded but did not pursue the matter of his wife's treatments. 'I've often thought about you – wondered if you were OK. I was sorry that my uncle let you go.'

'Sacked me,' Joy said ruefully. 'I was sacked.'

'I know. I'm sorry. I would have liked you to stay.'

'Yes,' she said. 'Yes, you were very kind.'

'Will you stay with the ship – when it turns around, I mean?'

'Yes. I'll go back one more time, I think. After that, who knows?'

He fished in an inside pocket and brought out a slim leather cardcase. 'Take this. If ever you need a job – that's my private line.'

Joy watched as he limped away, turning once to bow in her direction. And then his wife was kissing him on the cheek, a trifle unenthusiastically but kissing him nevertheless, and they were moving towards the gangway that led to the dockside and home.

21

Peggy

Peggy raised herself gingerly in the bed and reached over to still the alarm. She was wide awake now. No point in letting the alarm jar Jim out of a sound sleep. As if he had sensed her thoughtfulness he stirred and fumbled for her hand, pulling it towards him until her arm was around him. 'What time is it?' he said.

'Close your eyes for five minutes. I'll see you don't sleep in.' He purred and curled tighter into sleep but only for a moment before turning to reach for her.

'There isn't time,' she said but she said it half-heartedly. She loved him, loved his need of her and the fact that hardly a morning or evening passed without his expressing that need. This time they made love in the leisurely way of two who know they have the rest of their lives before them.

'If we're not careful . . .' he said, when it was done

and they lay snugly like spoons. 'If we don't watch out you'll be in the family way again.'

'Well,' Peggy said, philosophically, 'there's worse things happen at sea.'

'Two's enough,' he said, but this time it was his turn to be half-hearted.

'Our Peter's five,' she said. 'You don't want too big a gap. If we had another, mind, I'd like it to be another girl.'

'I'm happy enough with two,' he said. 'I wouldn't swap our two. But another one might be nice. Mebbe after the coronation.'

Peggy began to disentangle herself, thinking of the day ahead. 'We're having a meeting tonight to plan the street party. You can come if you're back in time.'

He put up a hand to touch her naked back as she pulled her nightdress over her head. 'Parties is women's work.'

She turned, smiling in the half-darkness of the curtained bedroom, seeing his face dark against the white pillow slip, wanting to get back into the bed and love him till she had squeezed all the maleness out of him. 'What *isn't* women's work, Jim? That's what I'm always wondering.'

But when she had served him his bacon and sausages, his fried bread and sliced tomatoes, all set in a cake of egg, she stood at the door to wave him off, glorying in being his woman and serving his whim. 'Hurry back.'

'Don't I always?' As he moved down the backstreet towards the dark outline of the pit she thought how handsome he looked seven years into their marriage. If she had an itch it was to have more of him, not to spread her wings. He turned on the corner and waved.

'Watch yourself,' he said and was gone.

It was time to wake seven-year-old Margaret then and five-year-old Peter. She sat with them as they ate out the centre of their buttered toast and dipped the crusts into their boiled eggs. 'We're having a meeting tonight,' she said. 'To plan the coronation.'

Peter was ever practical. 'The Queen plans that.'

'I know,' Peg said, secretly proud of his grasp of national affairs. 'I mean here, in Belgate. We're having a street party and games on the field and you'll all get a mug with the date on.'

'Will there be shuggy-boats?' Peter asked. There was a moustache of milk on his upper lip and she put out an indulgent finger to wipe it away.

'Mebbe,' she said. 'If we can raise the cash we might have shuggy-boats.' There were two bills on the mat as she let the children out of the door. Two bills and a letter from Celia, whose familiar writing was instantly recognisable.

'Watch the road,' she called as they walked away, experiencing the usual terror that any harm might befall them. She watched until they were across the road and then went back into the house to brew her own pot of tea and settle down with her letter.

Nothing much had changed in Celia's life since the last letter. She still had her flat and her cat and, although she played it down, obviously she was important now and must earn a good wage.

When she had finished rereading it she folded it and put it back in its envelope. Amy and Joy were almost out of the picture now. Only she and Celia to keep up the friendship. She resolved to write back that very day and tell Celia her flat sounded lovely. It was nice to think that someone as important as a principal, whatever that might be, wanted to keep in touch and it would be a pity to let the old bond fizzle out. After all, they'd fought a war together.

She washed her face and neck at the kitchen sink when she had done the breakfast dishes, squinting at herself in the mirror as she dried herself, seeing the lines that had not been there at demob. We're all getting older, she thought. If she and Jim were going to have a baby they'd better get a move on, never mind waiting for a coronation that was still weeks away.

She bought the makings of soup in the corner shop, a nice ham shank and a pack of veg: turnip and leeks, carrots and tatties. Jim loved a pot of broth and she would drop in dumplings as soon as she heard him at the door. She bought a writing pad and a packet of envelopes too, the best ones in the shop, vellum and thick. You couldn't write to a senior civil servant on any old paper.

She was so taken up with her purchase that as soon as she had put on the ham shank, bringing it to the boil and then changing the water, she sat down at the kitchen table to pen her reply.

'Dear Celia,' she began and then licked her pen. Celia's letters always flowed, line after effortless line. This was Chinese torture. 'It was nice to get your letter.'

She had completed one tortuous paragraph when the knock came at the door. The moment she opened it she knew there was something wrong. Every wife in Belgate knew what a visit from the under-manager meant.

She put a hand to her mouth, hearing such a whistling in her ears that she could hardly make out what the man was saying. The colliery nurse was behind him, a navy mac over her uniform, her face whiter than a sheet.

'He's in the hospital – or he will be by now.' So Jim was alive! There was hope after all.

'I'll get my coat,' she said and put a hand to the door to steady herself.

They drove in silence, the traffic mercifully light at this time of day and seeming to part miraculously to let them through. As they drove Peggy made her plans. She would bring Jim home as soon as they would let him out. She could bring a bed downstairs and he could lie in the living room and talk to her as she got on with things. Her mam had a commode and you could borrow a bottle from the district nurse. The bairns could go to her mam if he needed quiet at first and then, when he was up and about, she'd get Edie's Matty to take them out for the day. By the time they reached the hospital she was almost enthusiastic about the opportunities opening up to show him how much she loved him.

She wanted to rush on to the ward but a sister barred her way. 'In here, Mrs Dobson. Doctor won't be long.' Peggy looked at the woman's face and knew, by the sliding away of the eyes, that it was bad.

He came at last, no more than a lad, his tie tucked into his shirt, his white coat hanging from his bony shoulders. She wanted to say, 'Fetch a real doctor, you're only a bairn,' but she held her tongue.

'Your husband was caught in a fall of stone, Mrs Dobson. Apparently coal-cutting was held up, he went to sort it out and the roof collapsed. We have two other men in here with multiple injuries.'

'The price of coal,' she thought, and realised from his startled face that she had spoken aloud.

'Your husband has crush injuries to his chest and some internal damage. We think it's a ruptured spleen. The surgeon's with him now.' He pulled a rueful face. 'I'm just a house surgeon but we wanted to keep you informed.'

'Will he live?' Peg asked simply, and knew from his downturned head that he had no comfort to give her.

22

Celia

Celia awoke at six fifteen. She had slept well but she felt no urge to get up. Instead she lay and listened to the sounds of London going about its morning business. Sometimes, when she told people that she lived high above Kingsway, they would widen their eyes and murmur 'traffic' as though it must be intolerable to live on a main thoroughfare. But I love it, she thought now, turning on to her side and snuggling down. Mornings were still faintly chilly but spring was definitely here and summer would follow.

As she washed and dressed and fed the cat she thought about June. London would be a bull-bait at the time of the coronation. Already there were plans for coping with the people sleeping out on the route to be sure of a sight of the golden coach. It might be a good idea to take leave and go away. Alternatively she could stock the flat with provisions and hibernate until it was all over. Actually, that might be fun. Being there but not being there! She could be in her stronghold, quiet and serene, while below London went mad with celebration.

I am turning into an old maid, she thought, but it was not an entirely unpleasant feeling.

She walked to work, loving the feeling of being part of the bustling pavements. People were responding to spring, casting off the dark colours of winter and lifting their faces to the sun. By the time Celia sat down at her desk she felt at peace with the world. There was a hard day's work in front of her but tonight there was a Rachmaninoff concert on the Third Programme and she had a trout for supper. Bliss!

She worked steadily until her break, reading through one document after another, initialling some, putting others aside for further checking. She was putting one such paper, a list of names, into an out-tray when a warning bell rang in her head. Something had jogged her memory, making her think of Paris – she retrieved the paper and ran her eye carefully down the column. It was there: 'GOTZ, Aaron David, 7b Letchworth Road, London, WI.'

For some reason she lifted another paper and hastily covered the first one. It was a full moment before she put it aside and looked at the name once more. 'GOTZ, Aaron David.' Could it be? How common a name was Gotz? She had not encountered another, in Paris or anywhere else, but that didn't mean it was rare.

She sat for a while, chin on hands, thinking the easiest and probably the best thing to do was to carry on with her work and forget she had seen the entry. What if her Aaron Gotz was in London? He probably had a wife and child in tow. Children, even. There had been time.

On the other hand he might be ill. Or in need. She took out her diary and copied the address carefully on to the last page. It was only then, heart beating a little uncomfortably, that she could carry on with her work.

But, however hard she tried, the image of the boy she had known seven years ago intruded into her every thought. At four o'clock she pleaded a headache and took herself off. But she did not go to Kingsway. Instead she summoned a cab and gave the WI address.

As she had suspected, it was a recognisably Jewish neighbourhood. Hassidic Jews were going about their business, the men sombrely dressed and wearing Homburgs, the women with their hair covered by scarves, holding their children by the hand and talking animatedly to them or to other women, similarly clad and burdened with children. And there were Ashkenazis too, probably Polish like Aaron.

Her heart beat faster as she gave the driver the number of the house – 'I don't want you to stop there: just drive past.' She felt her face flush as she said it, knowing he would think she was up to no good. Chasing an errant husband, probably. She didn't look the type to be – what was it they called it in gangster movies? – 'casing the joint'.

But as they neared the house she was suddenly seized with terror. What would she do if she saw him? If he saw her and called out? What would they have to say to each other after seven years? He might even turn his back. If only she had not put on her old and serviceable navy suit this morning, her sensible lace-up shoes.

'I've changed my mind – drive on!' she said imperiously and then, as the taxi speeded up and away, a huge feeling of relief overcame her. Thank God I didn't see him, she thought. I must have been mad.

What was he doing, here in England? The lines from Frost came into her mind then: 'And miles to go before I sleep, And miles to go . . .' Had he reached Israel? If so, why had he returned?

She felt much calmer when the cab deposited her at her corner. The fare was astronomical but it had been worth it. As she put her change into her purse and fished for her key she thought of Rachmaninoff and her trout. She would grill it and sprinkle it with almonds.

Mouth watering, she scurried up the stairs but as her eyes came level with her own landing they encountered a neat pair of ankles above extremely high heels. Her heart sank at the prospect of a visitor until, as her eyes travelled upwards, she saw who was standing there. 'Joyce,' she said. 'Of all people! What are you doing here?' And then they were in each other's arms and hugging until they both gasped for breath.

They settled in the kitchen, almost inarticulate at first as news spilled out of them. 'How did you find me?' Celia asked as she put the trout under the grill and opened a bottle of wine.

'Sancerre!' Joyce said, sipping appreciatively. 'We have come up in the world. I asked my cousin Edna – she can find anything. Actually, she knows someone in the Home Office. When I said you were a high-up civil servant she went to him. He got your address.'

'I hope she didn't say I was high up. I'm enormously low-down . . .'

'Oh, Ceel, take that horrified look off your face. I found you – that's what counts. I've been away for most of the last few years. I sent you a postcard occasionally – Peggy and Amy too – but I was never sure they would reach you.' She grinned ruefully. 'I haven't kept in touch as much as I should have done. Sorry! Did any of my cards get through?'

'One did,' Celia said. 'Now, this is just about ready.'

'Tell me about the others,' Joy said when they were seated either side of the kitchen table, ready to eat.

'About Amy I'm not sure. You know I've always had my doubts about Geoffrey?'

Joy nodded. 'This fish is gorgeous. I never knew you could cook?'

'I couldn't – until I had to. Now I quite enjoy it.'

'To get back to Amy's Geoff – I thought he was cold on the odd occasion we met during the war. Very charming around the mouth, very flat around the eyes. Anyway, what about him?'

'Well, nothing really – except that Amy seems to have gone into seclusion. You get the odd flash of the old Amy – you know, warm and friendly, a card at Christmas, my birthday – but that's all. It's as though she doesn't want to keep in touch. I've suggested once or twice that we get together but she either ignores it or fobs me off with some weak excuse. So I'm forced to conclude she doesn't want to see me – see any of us.'

'Or isn't allowed to,' Joy said thoughtfully. 'You know Amy, always a daddy's girl. I expect she depends on Geoffrey now and would do anything not to displease him.'

'And she must be all right for cash because her father would make sure she was. Her mother died, you know. Way back, 1946 I think it was. I couldn't go but I wrote to her.'

'You're a wonder, Ceel, the way you've kept in touch and tried to link us to one another. I know I haven't responded always but I have appreciated it.'

'I know. Now, before I make the coffee, what about you? And then I'll tell you about Peg. She is unbelievably happy.'

'Still with her Jim?'

'Oh yes, that's for life. They have two children, a boy and girl, and he's done well. I'm not quite sure what he is but it's something for the National Coal Board in a supervisory capacity.'

'Good,' Joy said. 'He always sounded nice. I can't boast any children but I'm happy. I suppose I am. I'm still with Chuck, the American. He's been back in the

States since forty-six. We see one another as often as we can. He comes over here once or twice a year. I see him whenever we dock in New York. Well, almost every time. He's in Washington and he can't always make it to New York.'

'What does he do?'

'Well . . . he's in politics, actually. Or hopes to be. His family are very involved. They're Republicans. Their money comes from canning, Californian peaches, that sort of thing. Chuck's only on the very bottom rung of the ladder. He hopes to get into Congress eventually but of course it's a long haul.'

Suddenly her enthusiasm bubbled over. 'He's very good-looking, Celia. You have to be if you want to get on in the States. But he is so . . . well, he has dark hair and blue eyes and freckles across his nose like Van Johnson and when I dock in New York and he can't get across to me it drives me crazy!'

'So it's love?' Celia said.

'I think so – but it's difficult when we're on other sides of the world.'

'America's a huge country,' Celia said, pushing back her chair and gathering up the plates. 'I mean to travel one day. I'd like to see New York.' She smiled suddenly. 'I might have known you'd be the one who travelled. We're all turning out as predicted, aren't we? I'm the old maid, you're the globetrotter, Peggy and Amy . . . well, we don't know about Amy but Peg's got exactly what she wanted. Lucky girl. And Amy's probably all right.'

They carried their coffee into the living room and subsided into the velveteen chairs. 'This is fabulous,' Joy said, reaching to stroke the cat, which was perched above her. She looked around the room with its timbered ceiling, leaded windows and plaster walls. 'It's like a lovely cottage high up a mountainside. Still, enough of that. What about you? It is good to see you again, Ceely. I've thought of you often. Tell me what's been happening to you.'

'There's nothing to tell. I work hard, I've achieved promotion, I'm happy in this place in spite of the rent – well, *because* of the rent actually, because it's amazingly reasonable. And that's about it.'

'No private life?'

Joy's tone was teasing and Celia felt her neck flush. If she told of that foolish taxi ride what would Joyce make of it? 'Not really. I go to Warwickshire sometimes, to see my Uncle Philip. He's retired now.'

'No boyfriend?'

'No boyfriend!' Celia said firmly. 'Now, drink your coffee and stop being intrusive.' She chuckled suddenly, the years slipping from her face as she did so. 'You haven't changed, Joycee. You're still a monkey. I bet you run that ship, captain or no captain.'

They were deep in discussion of life aboard an ocean liner when the phone rang. Celia looked at the clock. 'No one ever rings at this time.'

'It's only nine o'clock,' Joy said.

Celia was already moving to the phone, her face anxious. 'Hello, yes.' As Joy watched she saw Celia's anxiety turn to something akin to horror. She tried to look away and not to eavesdrop but it was impossible. 'Of course, yes. I'll take leave. Give her my love, please . . . and if there's anything I can do . . .' She put down the phone and stood, motionless.

'It's not your uncle, is it?' Joy asked. Celia lifted her chin, as though seeking strength.

'No, it's not Philip. It's Peggy. That was her sister on the phone. There's been an accident in the pit. Jim's injured and it doesn't sound good.'

'Oh God,' Joy said. 'If he dies how will Peg live without him?'

23

Peggy

Sometimes it seemed as though she had been here for ever, sitting in the quiet room, hearing footfalls in the corridor outside or the rattle of trolleys. Only the silent figure in the bed for companionship. And sometimes it seemed only an hour ago that she had been planning Jim's meal. A nice pan of broth and then the meat from the ham bone with mashed potato and sago to follow.

There was saline dripping from a bottle high above the bed, dripping into Jim's vein. She watched the plastic tube, fascinated by the passage of the fluid, the little vacant spaces between the drops, the obscene fatness of the sagging plastic bag. There was another tube too, one that snaked unobtrusively from under the bedclothes. It was connected to a plastic bag but no fluid dripped along it because Jim's kidneys had failed and urine did not flow. Sometimes she fixed the tube with her eye and willed it to be filled with yellow liquid until the bag overflowed and cascaded on to the polished floor. But nothing came.

If only he had been conscious when she got to the hospital. If she could have spoken to him she could have drawn him back, willed him to live. She touched his hand now, finding it clammy and cold where once it had been warm and dry. And loving. He had always had loving hands.

In desperation she turned her mind back to their courtship. She had still been at school when they had met. She could remember dodging down the backstreet so that he, a jaunty seventeen-year-old on his way home from the pit, would not see her in tunic and ankle socks. And now he was lying, white and silent, in a hospital bed and all she could do was listen to his troubled breathing, willing it to continue.

They had known almost from the beginning that they would stay together. Even when her call-up came neither of them had wavered. 'It should be me going away, not you,' Jim had said, irked by his reserved occupation. He had bought her the tiny diamond ring that bit into her finger now.

She looked down at her hands, surprised at how her fingers had thickened and coarsened. I'm not a girl any longer, she thought, and was shocked by the revelation.

A nurse came in then, to check the vital life signs and monitor tubes and equipment. 'Any change?' Peg asked but all she got in return was a sympathetic smile.

Peg closed her eyes then, thinking of her children. Were they safe in school? Missing her? Wanting their dad? When Jim was better they'd all go off on a holiday and damn the expense. They were doing all right now, anyway. It had been hard at times but they had won through. 'Get better, Jim,' she prayed. 'Don't spoil it now.'

But thoughts of death and funerals came unbidden into her mind. She would have to wear black and see her children broken-hearted. To banish the black fear that threatened to overwhelm her she thought about the girls. Celia had sent flowers the very next day and was coming as soon as she could get time off work. Nothing from Amy so far but there had been a three-page letter from Joy. Just out of the blue after all these years!

She smiled to herself, thinking of that day on the station and how she had wanted to get away from them, to get back to Jim. Jim! As if had heard her he moaned suddenly. She was at his side in an instant. His mouth had opened and she could hear a rattle in his throat, as though it was obstructed by phlegm. For a second her hands hovered but what could she do? Nothing, except run to the door and call in anguished tones for a doctor or a nurse.

They barred her from the room while they fought for his life. She paced the corridor, shaking off hands that tried to restrain her, all the while repeating a litany in her head: Don't die, Jim. Don't leave me. Don't die, Jim. Don't leave me alone.

'I'm sorry, Mrs Dobson,' the doctor said when he emerged from the room. 'We did all we could.'

'You don't mean he's dead. Not Jim.' The sister was reaching for her hand but she threw her off. 'You can't be sure. I've heard of cases before . . .' And then someone was wailing, not her, but everyone was looking at her with eyes that said they wished they were somewhere else.

They brought her a cup of tea then, yellow and sweet in a thick white cup. She sipped it obediently, feeling unreal, seeing them mutter and plan, talking about her as though she wasn't there. 'I want to see him,' she said at last. And then, in case they argued, 'I've *got* to see him.'

He lay in the narrow bed in a side ward. There was mucus around his mouth and nose and his hair was ruffled. 'We'd've cleaned him up if you'd waited,' the sister said, her professional pride ruffled. Peggy put out a hand and smoothed the hair from his brow. 'What've you got yourself into now?' she said, as though to a child.

'He told me to watch myself,' she said to no one in particular. 'That last day he said, "Watch yourself, Peggy." And then he goes and does a thing like this.'

He would never hold her again or say 'That was grand' when he finished his tea. 'I love you,' she said and then, more fiercely, 'I love you.'

'He knows,' the sister said and led her gently away.

24

Amy

Amy kept her eye on the pan, willing the egg not to crack and allow the white to escape. Geoffrey was back in the bedroom now so he would be down soon expecting his egg on the table. If it burst, something he would not tolerate, there wouldn't be time to boil another. She glanced up at the clock. Thirty seconds to go, so almost safe. She reached for a spoon and, as the pointer came round, moved the pan off the flame with one hand and scooped out the egg with the other. As she did so her wrist passed over the flame and she let out a yelp of anguish, jerking her burned hand towards her and almost dropping the egg in the process.

When she realised it was still safe on the spoon relief flowed over her. She lowered it into the eggcup and then, not hearing Geoffrey on the stairs, was suddenly seized with fear that it might cool down too quickly.

She cupped her hand around the shell, the heat of it burning her fingers but not deterring her. She felt tears brim over her eyelids but they were tears of weariness rather than tears of pain. The next moment she heard the stairs creak and, sniffing madly to clear her eyes, transferred egg and eggcup to the breakfast table.

Geoffrey sat down without speaking and reached for his orange juice. So far, so good. If there had been anything wrong with the table settings he would have spoken. She pressed down the toaster and took the lid off the butter dish.

He had cut the top off his egg and found it cooked to his liking before he spoke. Amy was longing to go to the lavatory. She should have gone before this. She couldn't leave the kitchen now. She would have to wait until he was gone.

'What are you doing today?' he asked her.

Amy licked her lips. 'Just some shopping.' He nodded and the fact that he made no demur made her bolder. 'I was wondering whether we might go up to see Daddy – or I could go on my own. I know how busy you are.'

'I'll have to see. There's not a great deal of point in going up. You can't do anything for him.'

Useless to say her father's eyes lit up at the sight of her. He couldn't speak now, not with his voice, but his eyes spoke volumes. Instead she tried a different tack. 'And then there's the sale. I want to take some things – personal things, things of Mummy's – before they do the inventory.'

'That's not a good idea. By rights everything should

go to your father's creditors. He owes a small fortune. Everything's in the hands of the Receiver now. You can't interfere.'

'I don't mean valuable things, Geoffrey. I'm just thinking about little things – things that wouldn't make money. Mum's workbox and her embroidery frames, little things like that.' She was pleading even though that always made him worse.

'Do you embroider?'

'No. No, but I—'

'Do you intend to learn to embroider? I hope not because that attempt would undoubtedly be as unsuccessful as everything else you try.'

'I'm not going to use them. It's just—' He didn't wait for her to finish.

'What is the point, then, of cluttering up the house with things of no value for which you have no earthly use?'

'They've sentimental value, Geoffrey. They were my mother's.'

'*Were*, Alexandra. "Were" is the operative word. They *were* your mother's, your *dead* mother's. Now they belong to your father's creditors. I have given you a beautiful home, a home that would content most women. You, it seems, want to fill it up with tat. I'm sorry, but I won't indulge you in this.'

She sought for something to say that would change his mind. 'I just thought—'

But he was rising to his feet. 'If you're determined to ruin my breakfast at the start of what will be a very strenuous day, I suppose I'll just have to leave it.' He had finished the egg and almost all of the toast, so why did she feel guilty? 'Shouldn't you be seeing to the children now? Or do you want them to be late for school and fall behind?'

She stood dutifully at the door until his car had vanished from the drive and then she went upstairs to wake her children. They were both awake, lying on their backs in their single beds, their faces impassive. But she knew they had heard every word of the altercation down below, knew it from the very absence of any kind of emotion in their speech or actions. They are little automatons, she thought, and could hardly contain her pain until they had left the house.

She went upstairs then, to the bathroom, where she turned on the hot tap, letting it run until it gushed steam and she could hold guilty hands under the scalding flow.

When at last she withdrew her hands, red and throbbing, the fingernails feeling as though they would burst asunder from her fingers, she went to her bedroom, but instead of shedding her nightdress and dressing gown she retrieved her photograph album from the wardrobe drawer and carried it over to the unmade bed.

As she sat down her own body odour wafted up to her, strong and unpleasant. She hadn't bathed for days now and the uncomfortable folds of her body told her so. What is happening? she thought. Where has Amy gone?

She was there in the book. Grinning from a flower-filled meadow next to the George, aloft her father's shoulder on the riverbank, wearing her first high-heeled shoes and looking self-consciously grown up. The summer of '36. She had been sixteen and there had been a wind-up gramophone playing 'The Way You Look Tonight', and she had thought then that the life that lay before her would be filled with joy.

There had been a boy called Archie staying at the George and he had given her her first kiss, tickling her lips with his soft, unshaven fuzz.

'Darling, never, never change, keep that breathless charm . . .' The words of the song played on in her head as she turned another page.

The year before the war, the dress made of poppy-print Liberty cotton. It had had a mother-of-pearl buckle to the stitched belt and her mother had bought her tiny red flower earrings. The hit of the year had been 'Somewhere Over the Rainbow' and by Christmas they were all at war.

The war years went through her mind in a jumble then. Induction and training, making friendships, Joy and Peggy and Celia. Midnight rides in rocking lorries, dancing cheek to cheek with men in khaki and blue who might not live to the end of the week. When she had met Geoffrey, in the smoky blur of the George, she had thought him the finest man she had ever met. But it had been the uniform, only the uniform.

She had known it really, if she was honest, on the day of her wedding, when he had dismissed her friends as though they did not exist. And then that night, in bed and afraid, but proud too that she was bringing him something of worth, her virginity.

'Oh God,' he had said when she squirmed with pain at the first penetration. 'Lie still and let's get this over.' She had not let out as much as a whimper until she was sure he slept, and then she had cried for her father, her mother, the George, for lost illusion and childhood hopes. But if, in her heart of hearts, she had hoped her swollen eyes would bring consolation when morning came, she was disappointed. 'Hurry up,' he had said, when he returned from the bathroom to find her still in bed. 'We don't want to waste the day.'

She had found she was pregnant within six weeks of the wedding. She had longed for that moment all through adolescence, the moment when she would tell a man she was going to give him a child. There had been a gleam of satisfaction in his eyes at the news, but she knew it was pride in his own achievement, not in hers. He had been assiduous in his attention to the detail of her pregnancy, making her take the government vitamins and drink her extra milk, but he had never held her in his arms and told her she was clever. In fact he decamped as soon as he could to the spare room, leaving her to lie dry-eyed contemplating a sterile future.

And then Adam was in her arms, warm and alive, dependent but giving her so much that for a little while she was happy. Until she realised what she had done to her son by bringing him into a world dominated by Geoffrey. Her father had clucked over the baby and she had smiled and told him all was well. Out of pride, because it was difficult to admit a mistake, and then out of compassion, because her mother was dying and her father had enough to bear.

Geoffrey had returned to her bed when Adam was eight months old. 'It's time to stop all that,' he decreed when she wanted to continue breast-feeding. Adam was banished to the newly painted boxroom and within three months she was pregnant again and her mother was dead.

She cried then, closing the album and laying her head on the pillow. She was still crying when the phone rang in the hall. She let it ring until she remembered that it might be the school ringing to say one of the children was ill or had had an accident.

She ran down the stairs then, ricocheting from wall to bannister, desperate to reach the phone before it stopped ringing.

'Yes?' For a moment she didn't recognise the voice. When she did the relief was almost overwhelming, so that she had to question and cross-question Celia to get the facts straight. And the facts were terrible. 'So he's dead. Poor Peg. Poor Peg.' But all the time she expressed sympathy she was thinking how she would feel if Geoffrey were dead. Happy, happy, happy!

'I can't come, Celia,' she said at last. 'You know I would if I could. I was so fond of Peg. Give her my love but there's no way I could get to Durham. I can't get to Yorkshire to see my father. He's dying, Celia. Slowly dying and I can't see him . . .'

She slid to the floor then, tears and mucus mixing around her mouth and chin, flowing on to the receiver so that it became slippery in her hand. 'I am trying . . . I'm sorry . . . I'll stop in a moment. Just don't ring off, Celia. They're going to sell my mother's things. Everything – her thimbles and her Crown Derby. I can't . . . I have no money of my own . . . No, he pays the bills now – he says I'm not to be trusted. Tell Peg – please tell Peg – I'd come if I could. I am trying – honestly . . .'

She could hear Celia's voice at the end of the line, exhorting her to be calm. She ought to be calm and think of Peg but all she could think of was that Peggy was free.

She wiped her nose and mouth with the sleeve of her dressing gown. 'I'm sorry. This is very wrong of me. I *am* trying to think, Celia. The sale is on the nineteenth. At the George. Why do you want to know? What are you doing about Peg? If I could only think of a way . . . Joy? Joy's with you? Yes, put her on. Joy? How lovely to hear from you. I was just thinking about you all . . . the good, old days. Yes, it would be lovely to see you sometime. Weren't you on a ship? Peggy said something about a ship . . .'

She knew they were trying to calm her, bring her comfort. She tried to give them what they wanted, tried to keep her voice steady so it would seem as though she had got on top of her misery. She did not cry again until she had put down the phone and could go in search of a drink.

25

Celia

They set out as soon as it was daylight, driving a dark-green Wolseley borrowed from someone Cousin Edna knew.

'It's huge,' Celia said when Joyce stepped from behind the wheel.

'Drives like a piece of silk,' Joy replied with a confidence she was far from feeling.

'I've never driven anything as big as this.' Celia was still doubtful.

'Look,' Joy said, picking up Celia's suitcase. 'We agreed trains were out if we wanted to fit Amy in too. So get in and stop waffling. If you don't want to drive I'll do it all myself.'

'No,' Celia said. 'Just get us out of London, then I'll take my turn.'

Traffic was still light as they threaded through the

London streets. 'It's so peaceful,' Joy said. 'Remember wartime? Dodging doodlebugs? It seems a million years ago.'

Celia sighed. 'It seems a long time ago sometimes. At others . . . And then there's the threat of it all happening again with Russia. I can't believe how things have changed. They were our allies – now we seem to hate and fear them.'

'Cheer up, Ceely.' Joy sounded sanguine as she looked out on the neat houses that bordered the road. 'Most of it's hot air.'

'I hope you're right.' Celia had been told privately that the Americans were getting ready to test an atom bomb in Nevada, which, if rumour was true, would be even more powerful than the bomb dropped on Hiroshima. The world was far from the safe place they had all been promised. And then her eye fell upon a tree covered in blossom and her lips parted in an exclamation of pleasure.

'Yes,' Joy said, slowing down the car momentarily. 'It's lovely, isn't it. Makes you feel quite bridal.'

Celia felt her cheeks flush. For some reason the blossom had reminded her of Aaron, of the fact that she was being driven away from him now. And, even though she knew that he was oblivious of her existence so near to him in London, the thought of the increasing distance between them was painful.

'Poor Peg,' Joy said, breaking the silence. 'She must remember her wedding day today. And none of us were there to share it with her.' There was silence then as they both thought of Peggy, whose problems were so much worse than their own.

It was Joy who spoke eventually. 'I'm glad we're back in touch. Let's not lose sight of one another again.'

'You know where I am.' Celia's eyes were still on the scenery but her voice was emphatic. 'I'm not likely to move and you're welcome any time. How long is your leave?'

'Just one more week.' Joy changed gear to negotiate a bend. 'It's lucky I was here when this happened to Peg . . . well, not lucky, you know what I mean. I'm glad I can be here for Peg. I rang Chuck last night and he sent condolences.'

'He sounds nice,' Celia said. 'Will you marry him, d'you think?'

'I expect so. Anything to get away from cruise ships.'

'Tell me about them,' Celia said. 'I've often wondered what they were like.' They talked then of their respective jobs as the city fell away and was replaced by something greener.

'We're making good time,' Celia said as they neared St Albans. 'Somehow I don't think we should turn up at Amy's before Geoffrey leaves. What time do you think that will be?'

'You know more about office hours,' Joy said, changing gear. 'But I'm not afraid of facing him, if that's what worries you.'

'Neither am I – in fact I'd almost enjoy it. But I

don't think it would be much fun for Amy. Let's see what it's like when we get there.'

'What are you hoping to get out of this – apart from seeing Amy, that is?'

'I want my mind put at rest,' Celia said firmly. 'Or my suspicions confirmed. One or the other.'

'What does Geoffrey actually do?' Joy asked. 'He was an accountant, wasn't he?'

'Yes. He qualified just as war broke out and he did quite well in the army, as you know. Rapid promotion, everyone's blue-eyed boy. He was going to go after a council treasurer's job. I don't think he could afford to go into private practice – or didn't want to. Anyway, just as he was about to take a job as deputy treasurer in the Midlands somewhere this new-town business started up. He got in on the ground floor and he's done well. I asked around yesterday and he's known as a rising star.'

'He's a fool!' Joy said bitterly.

'Why? Oh, I see what you mean. Yes, Amy was the ideal wife, wasn't she? Pretty, presentable and so good-natured. We don't know that it's all his fault, of course.'

'You're being a Civil Servant, Ceel. Cautious! He's obviously a bastard and has Amy frightened out of her wits.'

They drew up at a callbox on the outskirts of St Albans and rang Amy's number. 'If he answers hang up,' Joy hissed as the ringing tone began.

It was Amy who answered and Celia could tell by

her response that Geoffrey had already left the house. 'I'm here, Amy – well, five minutes away – and Joyce is with me. Yes, Joyce. We're coming round.'

A few moments later they were ringing the front doorbell of Amy's imposing detached house.

'I see what you mean about him doing well,' Joy said, and then the door was opening and Amy stood there. For a second there was silence. Amy looked bewildered, almost afraid. The other women were stunned at the sight of a gaunt, dishevelled woman in a dirty dressing gown which she clutched at the neck with a too-thin hand.

Celia recovered first. 'Amy,' she said. 'How lovely to see you.'

'Yes.' Joy lent support then, stepping over the threshold. 'How long is it? Too long anyway. Here, give me a hug.'

The feeling of someone's arms around her was too much for Amy. They led her down the hall towards what they could see was a kitchen. 'I'll put the kettle on,' Celia said, unbuttoning her coat. 'Sit her down, Joy. Here, give her this tea towel.' It was obvious from the volume of Amy's tears that a handkerchief would not do.

'There now,' Celia said when they were all seated and the tea poured. 'We can't stay for long, Amy, because as you know we're on our way to Peggy and the funeral is at two o'clock. Try to tell us what's wrong.'

'Yes.' Joyce put out a hand and squeezed her friend's

arm. 'And don't hold anything back, kid, because we can see things are not quite tickety-boo.'

It came out then, the horror of life with Geoffrey, but even as the facts emerged Amy made excuses. 'I can see his point. I am useless. We've moved around such a lot. Stevenage . . . that was the first one in 1946. And then I stayed here while Geoffrey went up to Newton Aycliffe. Newton Aycliffe . . .' She lapsed into a silence for a moment, remembering.

'So Geoffrey was moving to each new town as it was started up?' Celia said encouragingly.

Amy nodded. 'Until Harlow. Harlow was 1947, the same as Newton Aycliffe. Geoffrey got promotion then so he didn't have to move any more. He stayed at headquarters. That's when we bought this house. Peterlee was the next year – 1948 – but Geoffrey stayed put.' There was silence again until she looked up, almost defiantly. 'I drink too much.'

'We all drink too much,' Joy said, moving uncomfortably in her chair.

'No,' Amy said. 'I mean too much.'

'What does Geoffrey say about it?'

'He doesn't know, Celia. I don't tell him.'

'He must know,' Joy said vehemently and would have gone on if Celia had not flashed her a warning glance.

'It's not his fault . . .' Amy was weeping again. 'He does have too much to do and I don't back him up. Sometimes I get confused – I do what I think he wants but it's not . . . it's not what he meant. And the children. Adam is quite slow at school and Geoffrey says he isn't trying.'

'Isn't there anyone you can confide in?'

'Not since Mummy died. Daddy was never the same after losing Mummy. Things went wrong with the business . . . Geoffrey says Daddy brought it on himself. I don't know . . . I don't know anything any more.'

The last lingering hope of persuading her to accompany them to the funeral faded from both minds simultaneously. Celia looked nervously at the clock.

'We have to push on,' she said. 'Or we'll be late and let Peg down.'

'But we'll be back,' Joy said. 'Celia will keep in touch and when I get back next time we'll sort something out.'

But nothing they could say could banish the hopelessness from Amy's eyes. There was nothing to do but hug her fiercely and go.

'You can see what he does,' Celia said when they were out on the road and racing north. 'He makes her feel incompetent and so she *is* incompetent. But why is he doing it?'

'Steady on, Malcolm Campbell.' Joy sounded alarmed. 'You're over the speed limit.'

'Sorry.' Celia slowed the car's pace. 'It's just that I'm so upset for Amy.'

'It's obvious why he does it, Celia,' Joy said when the car was being driven at a more reasonable speed. 'He enjoys it. It's his way of relaxing after a hard day at the office. He beats up his wife and kids.'

'She never said he was violent,' Celia demurred.

'You're being pedantic, Celia. Is that the word I want? I mean you're nit-picking. He *is* being violent, mentally violent. You've seen her. If ever I saw a woman who'd been beaten up, she's it.'

'It is she,' Celia said absently. 'You're right of course. It's mental cruelty.'

'For which you can obtain a divorce, except her legs wouldn't carry her into the court. You've got to admit he's done a very good job on her. What are we going to do about it?'

'I don't know.' Outside the car window the green fields and wooded places looked pleasant in the sunshine. 'At least I don't know exactly. But first we're going to do something about that damned sale.'

'When is it? I go back to work next week.'

'You'll be gone,' Celia said, glancing in the mirror before moving out to overtake. 'I hope we're not going to be late. I hate going into church at the last minute.'

'At the rate you're driving,' Joy said drily, 'we'll be there yesterday.' She chuckled. 'You're an enigma, Ceel, do you know that? Calm as a millpond on top, a boiling cauldron underneath.'

'Don't be silly. And that sale is a fortnight on Friday, in Yorkshire – actually at the George.'

'It's amazing how things change.' Joy was suddenly subdued. 'We all envied Amy in the war. I mean, when did she ever suffer a shortage? Daddy supplied everything. And now . . . I suppose you could say she still has material things. That house was quite something. But I certainly don't envy her.'

They arrived at the church in the nick of time, slipping into seats at the back while the organ played softly. 'There's quite a good turn-out,' Joy whispered when they straightened up from their prayers.

'I'm glad.' Celia was already turning the pages of the hymn book to locate the hymns indicated on the board.

At that moment there was a rustle at the back of the church and the cortège entered. To Celia's relief Peggy was calm and dry-eyed, dressed from head to foot in black apart from a grey and white scarf tucked in her neck. She had a black hat on top of her wavy hair and her eyes were swollen but she looked dignified.

I'm proud of her, Celia thought, and felt her eyes fill with tears.

They sang 'O Love That Will Not Let Me Go' and then the vicar was talking about Jim, describing him as a hard worker, a man who had taken on the might of the pit and suffered for it as men had always suffered in the pursuit of coal. But he had been a good father, too, and a loving husband. 'This was a man in all senses of the word. He will be missed.'

Celia felt Joy shudder and when she looked carefully sideways she saw that Joy was crying. Hard-boiled Joy, who never showed her feelings! Was she crying for Andrew, who had never had the chance to be husband or father? Celia put out a hand but it was shrugged away. 'I'm OK,' Joy said and when they rose to sing 'Abide With Me' she blew her nose.

Around them the stained-glass windows glowed and winked like jewels in the sunlight. In the pews the congregation, more men that women, sang lustily. His fellow miners are bidding him farewell, Celia thought, and realised suddenly that this was a breed of whom she knew little. When Peggy had spoken of her home and her fiancé Celia had paid lip service to understanding mining, but it was only now that she realised how special the mining community was and how much they had come to terms with mortality.

As they filed out into sunlight she thought of how small an island Britons inhabited and yet there were so many divisions, creed and class, status and occupation. It will have to change, she thought, and then they were face to face with Peggy and could hug her briefly before she turned away for the walk to the churchyard.

They found Peggy's home easily enough by following the cortège on its return journey. Inside, the small terraced house heaved with activity. Women bustled about with huge teapots, obviously borrowed from the church hall or Scouts or Guides. A table was crammed with home-made pies, sandwiches, cakes – so different from the genteel mouthfuls Celia had seen at funeral repasts up till now.

'She's got a lot of friends,' Joy said.

'That's good.' But Celia knew that this was more than friendship. This was a community accustomed to death rallying round to give support. Each of the women who poured or served would be wondering if they would be the next widow. Perhaps some of them already were. She accepted a cup of tea and a piece of meat pie and resolved to learn a little more about her own country before she ventured abroad once more.

'How will you manage?' Joy asked, when at last they had Peggy to themselves.

'I don't know. There'll be compensation.' Peggy answered in tones that showed she didn't particularly care. She met their eyes and smiled ruefully. 'They keep talking at me about pensions and entitlements. I can't take it all in at the moment.' Her chin came up then. 'But I will manage. I'll have to, for the sake of the bairns.'

'We'll help. I don't know how,' Celia said, 'but we'll back you up. And we musn't lose touch again. It's been too long and . . .' She faltered and Peggy finished for her.

'And it took a funeral to bring us together. It's a pity Amy couldn't get here.'

Celia looked at Joy and saw her own question mirrored in Joy's eyes. Was Peggy too burdened with her own misery to hear of more or would she be helped by knowing that it was not indifference that had kept Amy away?

'Amy's got problems, Peg.' It was Joy who took the plunge. 'We won't go into details now but, believe me, she wanted to be here. She would've been if she could. But we'll all be together soon. Perhaps you could come south . . . or we'll come north.'

'And bring Amy with us,' Celia said. 'That's a promise.'

'We did intend to spend time with you. But' – Joy glanced through to a kitchen alive with helpers – 'it seems you've got enough company at the moment. We'll come in a week or two, when perhaps things have died down a little.'

'Yes,' Peg said. 'That would be nice. They're very good around here. They don't let you down. But there's always a fresh tragedy, another widow. You have to move on.' She smiled ruefully. 'We used to say there'd be no deaths after nationalisation. But it's just the same.'

They left the little house with its drawn curtains and odour of death and made for the AI. Originally they had intended to stay overnight near Durham. Now it seemed to make sense to retreat and regroup, to come back when they could be of more help to both their friends.

'Let's press on to York,' Celia said. 'We can stay there or near there and that'll make it an easier drive tomorrow.'

'Good idea,' Joy said. 'I'm enjoying this – or I would be enjoying it if we hadn't left so much sadness behind.'

They eventually came off the AI and found a hotel in Harrogate, the Majestic, whose name Celia remembered from childhood. 'It's a magnificent place,' Joy said. 'But can we afford it?'

'I feel – I know we shouldn't when you think of where we've been – but I feel as though we're on an adventure,' Celia said. 'The two of us travelling together, just as we did in the war.' They were walking through the huge and ornate lobby, their feet sinking into the thick pile of the carpet.

'You look like a guilty school girl absconding from Latin,' Joy quipped, and Celia grinned in agreement. They settled in the mirrored lounge, relaxing into deep armchairs.

'I must spend a penny,' Celia said when they had ordered apéritifs, and went in search of a cloakroom.

Joy took a compact out of her handbag and inspected her face. Not bad, considering she had not touched her make-up since 4 a.m. She powdered her nose and applied lipstick and, satisfied, put away her make-up. There was a table near her chair with a selection of newspapers on it. She reached for the top one and saw that it was the *Herald Tribune*. American! Of course – they would get tourists here. Harrogate was a famous spa.

She shook the paper out and saw the headline: REFUGEES FLOOD INTO WEST BERLIN FROM RUSSIAN SECTOR. Truly, Hitler had left Europe in chaos. Eight years after his death and still it was in a state of flux.

She had rifled through the pages and was about to discard them when she saw the small item low down on one of the back pages: SENATORIAL HOPEFUL TO MARRY COSTEX HEIRESS.

'Joy!' Celia was standing above her, a look of alarm on her face. 'Is something wrong?'

Joy folded the paper carefully before she replied. 'Not really,' she said. 'Unless you count learning that the man I believed I would marry one day is marrying someone else.'

26

Peggy

Peggy poured another cup of tea and then left it until it yellowed in the cup. On the mantelpiece the clock ticked remorselessly away. If she didn't get a move on she'd be too late and let everyone down. Wearily she pushed herself to her feet and carried the breakfast dishes to the sink. The children had eaten a decent breakfast, the first time they had done that since Jim died, and the sink was full, but there was no time to do the dishes now.

As she mounted the stairs to her bedroom she wondered if that was how she would date everything from now on, count it from Jim's death. The first decent breakfast, the first smile, the first moment without pain.

In the bedroom that she had shared with Jim she stood wondering just what you wore to an auction. She must have been mad to offer to go but it had seemed so obvious. Joyce and Celia were tied to their jobs – she was the one with time on her hands. And it had seemed such a long time ahead. So she had volunteered when they had spoken on the phone and heard their initial doubt turn to relief. Celia had sent her an alarmingly large cheque to cover expenses and to pay for whatever goods she could secure. 'It's her mother's things she wants, Peg. Personal things. She mentioned embroidery frames or something like that. Perhaps jewellery. I don't know. You'll just have to use your initiative. Her father is bankrupt so everything is being sold to pay his creditors. At knock-down prices, probably. That's what usually happens at these things.'

She had put Celia's cheque into the Trustees, along with the savings she and Jim had managed to put by. It had seemed a fortune then but now, as the auction loomed, she was suddenly afraid. What if she bid wrongly or too much? What if she meant pounds and they thought she meant hundreds? Now that it was only hours away she was convinced she couldn't manage.

In the end she put a white blouse under her black jacket and checked and rechecked her handbag. She made it to the station with twenty minutes to spare and a heart that was beating until it seemed it would burst from her chest.

Pull yourself together, she told herself sternly as the train came into view. She had travelled all over in the war without a thought. Why were her legs trembling now?

She calmed down a little on the train. It was only sixteen days since Jim's funeral. She was bound to be upset. How will I manage without him, she thought. She closed her eyes and put her head back against the carriage seat. Time would heal. It had to, because she couldn't go on feeling like this. Not for ever.

If she managed to get through today, especially if she did a good job, she would manage. In a little while, a few weeks, she would see about getting a job. Part-time probably, in a shop. Something inside school hours so that she was always there for the bairns. She would live for them. As long as she had them she could manage and she would have them for at least another ten years.

And then? What would it be like when they went off into the world, as they must do? She and Jim had talked about it so often, what they would do when there were just the two of them and money wasn't tight and they had all the time in the world. She cried silently into her handkerchief, until the train pulled into Darlington station and it was time to change for Barnard Castle.

She took a taxi to the George but as the hotel came into view she panicked again. 'Stop here,' she told the driver and paid him off thirty yards short of the hotel door.

There was already a crowd gathering. She could see the auctioneer's notices. 'To be sold by order of the Trustee in Bankruptcy,' they said. She walked towards the hotel, seeing the roses almost ready to bloom on the walls, the ivy-covered chimney stack, the low leaded windows. Through the glass she could see that the rooms were packed with people.

I can't do it, she thought. It's too much for me. After all, I've got the perfect excuse. Jim is dead. No one could expect me to do this – not so soon!

And then she remembered Celia's words. 'If you could do it for Amy . . .' By all accounts Amy's life was terrible. Peggy remembered the thousand small kindnesses Amy had done for her, for all of them, in those far-off days of war. And she remembered how sweet her own life with Jim had been. If Amy really was married to a brute she needed all the help she could get. She took a deep breath and elbowed her way into the room and towards the dais. Ten minutes later the bidding began.

The first thirty or so items were kitchen utensils and she let them go. By the time they got down to the more personal things she had relaxed a little. Lot 32 was a wicker work basket. 'Two and six . . . three shillings . . . three and six . . .' At four shillings Peggy entered the bidding. One and six more and the lot was hers. Someone sidled up to her and she whispered her name, as she had seen the other buyers do, and then turned her attention to Lot 33, a silver embroidery frame containing a half-worked traycloth and accompanied by a swatch of embroidery silks.

Three hours later, legs almost buckling with fatigue, she wrote a cheque with a trembling hand. Seventy-three pounds six shillings and sixpence for twenty-two items she hoped would mean something to Amy and twelve items she had bought for herself, or rather because she couldn't bear to see them knocked down for coppers. It was only the second time in her life she had written a cheque. Jim had always written the cheques. Now she must do it for herself.

She walked farther into Melmerby and found a teashop set up in the front room of someone's house. There were blue gingham cloths on the tables and small vases full of garden flowers set here and there. She ordered tea and toasted teacakes and then asked for pastries. Might as well be hanged for a sheep as a lamb.

While she sipped her tea she worked out what she had spent. Celia had given her seventy pounds, sixty to spend on goods and ten pounds to cover her expenses. In fact there would be some change for Celia and she and Joy had agreed to cut the costs three ways if Amy could not pay for anything.

The goods she had bought for herself were mostly from the hotel. Plated trays and teapots and jugs. A set of papier-mâché trays, two jug-and-basin sets, a brass fire screen. A bale of towels, brand new, a clothes horse and a brass coal scuttle and a set of three china ducks for hanging on the wall.

A sudden panic overtook her. Was she mad to spend money on things she didn't need when she had just been widowed? Was she losing all sense of herself? She had spent more than twenty pounds of her own money and she would have to pay some of the delivery charges. It couldn't all be left to Celia.

She was eating her last piece of teacake when she

realised that for the first time since Jim's death she could eat without the food sticking in her throat. Guilt was immediate. How could she be tucking into toasted teacake when Jim was dead? An impulse to run to the ladies' room and vomit up the offending food came and went as she remembered Jim, that last day, turning as he went, to smile and say 'Watch yourself'.

That's what she must do, watch out for herself so that she could care for his children, bring them up as Jim would have liked and make sure that they never, ever lacked for anything they needed. She poured a cup of tea for herself with a steady hand and when she had drunk it and settled the bill she went in search of a phone.

'Celia? It's Peg. I managed. Yes, quite a few things. I'm still in Yorkshire now. They're sending the things by road. It was very reasonable so it seemed best. No, what I got for Amy isn't bulky – except for a rocking chair. I thought that might have been her mother's and it was going cheap. I was amazed. And I bought some things for myself. What I'll do with them I don't know but I couldn't see them given away. Yes, you're right, I do sound as though I've enjoyed it. I was terrified at first but then . . . well, they make it easy for you. And there were such bargains. All right, I'll hang on to everything. Give Amy my love. Yes, I know. I'm OK, Celia. If I keep busy, I'm OK. It doesn't do to think too much.'

In the open air she wondered if she needed a cry and decided against it. Now was the time to get home and collect her children from her sister's. And then, when they were safe in bed, she would sit and make some plans. And if she felt up to it she would let herself remember how sweet, how very sweet, life with Jim had been.

27

Joy

Joy had drunk more than three-quarters of a bottle of red wine and still her misery was like a knife in her gut. From the moment she had read that brief notice in an American paper she had burned not only with humiliation but with fear of a future that seemed a void.

As day succeeded day she was able to acknowledge to herself that she had been, in part, the author of her own misfortune. She had refused to admit that what she was receiving from Chuck was the mere crumbs of his life. That if he had cared about her at all she would long since have been established in America, if not as his wife certainly as the woman in his life.

But she had been so unwilling to face a showdown that might end in loss that she had bought every lie, every evasion, believed that he was simply establishing himself on the bottom rung of the political ladder before he took to himself a foreign wife.

Looking at it now, she could see it for what it was, a farrago of lies and half-truths. But the ceaseless litany of political detail had been seductive. First the House of Representatives. When he had reached that milestone he was aiming for the Senate. After that the Congress and the Presidency. All he needed was a foot in the door and then he would proclaim her to the world.

And she had nodded and smiled and agreed that she should stay in the shadows until the time was ripe. Fool, fool, fool!

For seven years she had pinned every hope on Chuck, had sailed backwards and forwards across an ocean to catch brief interludes of love in what otherwise was a barren life. She had no friends, no hobbies, no settled home of her own and now she had no job, for the first thing she had done on her return to London was to give in her notice at the shipping company. Without the prospect of seeing Chuck there was no point in continuing in a job she didn't care for.

He had written to her twice since she returned from the north but she had thrown the letters unopened into a bureau. The phone had rung a few times but that too she had left unanswered.

Tonight, alone in her flat, she felt desolate. Outside, London was getting ready to crown a queen. The streets were already thronged with spectators, many of them Americans, all agog to see the fairy-tale Queen ride by in her golden coach pulled by eight grey horses and followed by kings and queens and princes, all in ornate carriages moving at walking pace.

She poured herself another glass and lifted it in an ironic toast to nothing in particular. Where had she gone wrong? She had thought herself so sophisticated, so worldly-wise, and all along she had been a dupe. Had Chuck ever loved her? Her brain fuddled by wine, she tried to work out how it had been in the beginning.

He had been attentive and respectful. That was what had attracted her in the first place, that he had treated her like someone who mattered. She smiled, remembering those early visits he had paid when she was staying with Edna.

She would open the door and he would be standing there, bearing gifts in one hand, twisting his service cap in the other, looking a mere boy. He had reminded her of that other boy shot down over Germany who would visit her no more.

At first she had used him to fill the void left by Andrew's death and then his eagerness, his youth, had overcome the barrier of her grief. The difference in their ages was slight – three years – but she had felt indulgent, almost maternal, towards him and his constant demands for love. For sex. He had made her feel wanted again and if sometimes she had wondered if there was any other dimension to their relationship she had put those doubts aside.

Now, though, the taste of rejection bitter in her mouth, she reviewed their relationship. He had been generous to her in those bleak early months of 1946, paying for that first decent flat, stocking her cupboards with goodies from the PX that were unobtainable in a Britain in the grip of austerity. There had been cinema visits and meals but the one constant had been bed. Always, no matter what they were doing, they had been working towards a sexual culmination. He wanted her for one thing only: sex. Her dreams of one day being his wife had been just that. Dreams! And now he was going to marry the rich, well-bred and undoubtedly virginal Costex heiress.

'Face it, kid,' she told her reflection in the window panc. 'You are definitely not wanted on voyage!'

And yet he had been so convincing! Intrigued, she fetched the letters from the bureau and opened them. Perhaps there had been a mistake. But now she was reading with a wary eye she could see his letters, the letters on which she had so depended, for just what they were. Camouflage!

Darling Joy,

As usual this place is a desert without you. If only you were here, with your funny English ways, to lighten the unrelieved gloom of Washington in mid-term. I talked with Mom and Pop the other day, suggested the possibility that I might marry one day. They seem fine about it so it's just one more step to telling them I have someone already in mind.

I miss you, Joyce. The time we have together is so damned short. Soon I'll take time out so we can be together for yonks.

There was more in the same vein, vague protestations of love and promises for the future but no real detail of his life. She turned to the second letter.

> No calls and no letters, Joycee. What's up? I'm hoping you're enjoying some idyllic rural holiday far from a post box. Anything, as long as you haven't tired of me. I know we've had to wait. Seven years! Who was that guy in the Bible who had to wait seven years to claim his bride? One day soon I'll be able to claim you . . .

She folded the diatribe and put it back into its envelope, too weary to read on.

She was preparing for an early bed when a knock came at her door. She opened it on the chain, wondering who could be calling. Visitors were rare but perhaps it was Celia, come with news of one of the others. It was not Celia: it was the woman from downstairs, nosy Miss Darrow who seemed to lurk constantly on landings.

'Miss Latham? Joyce . . . We've known one another long enough for Christian names, haven't we? I was just about to make my cocoa when I had a thought: I wonder if Joyce has fixed up anywhere to watch tomorrow.'

'Sorry?' For a moment Joyce was puzzled.

'The coronation?' There was a trill of laughter and a movement of Miss Darrow's patently false teeth. 'Well, not everyone has a set, do they. And I think I'm right in saying you haven't. So if you care to come and watch on mine you'll be welcome. There'll be one or two others of the neighbours and I've prepared some nibbles. Nothing alcoholic, I'm afraid, but we can toast Her Majesty in a good old cuppa, can't we?'

'Thank you very much,' Joy said weakly and then, when the door was closed and bolted, she gave way to a laughter that was more hysteria than mirth. So much for dreams of an American love nest. The reality was to be nibbles with Miss Darrow and a toast of teacups!

In bed she curled up, hugging her knees, crying until the pillow became wet and uncomfortable and she had to insert her hand between her cheek and the sodden cotton.

I must not cry! Inside her head she repeated the injunction of childhood, remembering how hiccups had followed a bad bout of crying, invoking her mother's rage or, worse still, her grandmother's.

When at last she dozed off it was on a resolve to stop skulking in the flat and make a new life for herself. Perhaps Celia was going to be alone tomorrow. Why had she left it to Celia to contact her? Why hadn't she telephoned Celia and made a date? She should have ceased to lick her own wounds and thought more of Peggy and Amy and in future she would! Perhaps they had been on the other end of her unanswered telephone, needing help and getting no reply. She would do better in future.

She woke to a soft knocking on her front door. A glance at the bedside clock showed her it was only seven forty-five. Too early for Miss Darrow, even on Coronation Day.

'Joyce.' She could see Chuck through the crack of the door but she made no move to take off the chain. For a moment she was dumbstruck then she rued that, for comfort, she had put on her oldest and most voluminous nightgown. But that emotion was only temporary. He wasn't getting in so what she was wearing was of little or no consequence.

'What are you doing here?'

He pushed at the door. 'Let me in, Joy. I can't talk from out here. Why haven't you answered my letters? And I've called you – I called to say I was coming but there was no answer. Why won't you let me in?'

She hesitated for a further moment and then she made to shut the door. Instantly his foot, clad in a neat plimsoll, blocked the opening. Joy sighed. 'Wait there,' she said and went in search of something more flattering than winceyette, knowing as she did so that she was going to capitulate in the end.

'Now,' he said, when he was in the tiny hallway and she was facing him. 'What gives?'

'You tell me!' He moved towards her and she backed away. 'You tell me what you're doing here without your future wife and I'll tell you why I haven't answered your letters.'

She had hoped with all of her heart that he would say, 'What on earth do you mean?' That he would say it was all a mistake, a lie made up by the newspapers. But in the second that his eyelids dropped she knew it was true, and by the time he had recovered himself she was turning away.

'How did you know?' he asked when he followed her into the kitchen. She lit a ring under the kettle and blew out the match. '*Herald Tribune* – not exactly front page, but I saw it.'

'The announcement – it's not what it looks, Joy. That's why I didn't tell you, because it didn't really matter.'

'Not matter?' For a moment she thought of the knives nestling in the drawer, knives that would penetrate the cotton of his sports shirt, break open his flesh, lacerate that calm and serious face that seemed to show such concern.

'Look,' he said. 'Sit down and I'll explain. What do you want, coffee or tea? I'll make it.'

She sat down at the table, placing her hands in front of her like a judge. 'Well,' she said. 'It had better be good.'

'You know the way it works. My best chance of the Senate is coming up at any moment. Gadsden can't last much longer. If I get it I'm in! And then I can please myself. I can tell the world exactly who I love and you know who that is. Virginia knows the game. You'd like her. She's tough and shrewd – not the spoiled little rich girl you might expect. And her father can swing it for me, Joycee. He has everyone in his pocket. But this . . . arrangement is only temporary. Virginia knows what's expected and she's willing to play along because her father is backing me. She knows it won't come to anything. So does he. I doubt I'd be his idea of a son-in-law anyway. It's a move, Joy. A political manoeuvre. You knew there'd be moves like this. I told you way back this was a dirty business. You don't get into Congress unless you're prepared to manoeuvre and pretend – yes, and cheat. But never, never could she take your place.'

On the stove the kettle let out a gush of steam but by that time Joy was in his arms and didn't care. She didn't care about anything because he loved her and it was going to be all right. She felt him let go of one arm as he reached behind him to turn out the gas and then they were on their way to bed.

'Why are you over here?' she asked as he removed the hastily donned négligé.

'For the coronation, of course, silly. Couldn't miss seeing Elizabeth riding to her coronation.'

But as the golden coach neared the abbey he was riding once more to climax in a bout of lovemaking that seemed destined to last well into the new Queen's reign.

28

Celia

Celia was relieved when the coronation was over and London came gradually back to normal. On the evening of the event she watched the fireworks whoosh into the sky from the Victoria Embankment, dazzle briefly, reflected in the moonlit Thames, and then fizzle out in the river.

Back at home she switched on her new television to see the Queen and the Duke appear once more on the balcony of Buckingham Palace. It was midnight but the palace was still surrounded by revellers. People were predicting a new Elizabethan age, a glorious epoch. She hoped they were right but for herself all she craved was a little peace.

She had been several times to Letchworth Street, hoping for a sight of Aaron Gotz, but she had always been relieved when he did not materialise. For one thing, if she came face to face with him she might find that it was not her Aaron Gotz at all but another. And she wanted it to be her Aaron, loved the feeling that he was near to her, part of the throbbing metropolis that was London. And in her most honest moments she admitted to herself that what she feared most was that it *would* be her Aaron Gotz and that he would look at her without a trace of recognition in his eyes.

She tried to put him out of her mind and concentrate on her work. Now she was to be made senior principal and moved to another post, still in London because staff were in short supply, but dealing with policy matters in the prison service. Once she might have welcomed a new challenge but not at this moment, when she had other problems.

She was deeply troubled about her friends. The sight of Joy's impassive face as she pointed out the item in the *Herald Tribune* had reminded Celia of the same emotionless face she had displayed when news came of Andrew's death. It was neither grief nor anger, just a frightening absence of feeling of any sort.

'He's dumped me, Celia,' Joyce had said when Celia lifted her eyes from the printed page. And she was smiling as she spoke, a reaction which chilled Celia. They had eaten dinner that night, making stilted conversation, Joy unable to be interested in anything but making a valiant effort, Celia terrified lest she say something tactless and increase her friend's distress.

They drove back to London the following morning in semi-silence and parted lovingly enough but with shared relief that they would no longer have to endure another's company.

Celia had contemplated contacting Joy and suggesting they spend Coronation Day together, perhaps try to find a vantage point along the route. But as the crowds flocked into London and people took up positions in advance of the event she put aside that idea. Once all this fuss was out of the way she would do something – about Joy, about Peggy, above all about Amy. None of her friends was in a fortunate position but Amy she envied least of all.

It was the eve of the great day when news came of the death of Celia's godfather. He had died quietly in his sleep in the greystone mansion to which he had retired. She took a week's leave and went to his funeral, but before she went she requested three files on recent entrants to Britain. Two of them were names picked at random. The third was Aaron David Gotz, now residing at 27 Letchworth Street, London W1.

It was strange to stay in Philip's greystone house without him there for companionship. She stood beside his bier in the study he had so lovingly created for himself, lined with his beloved books. His face was peaceful, the nose standing out sharply, the lips blue and thin but still recognisably the lips that had so often kissed her cheek.

She closed her eyes and prayed for the repose of his soul and she asked too that his influence might stay with her throughout a life that was obviously going to be a single life, as his had been.

In church she nodded agreement as the vicar outlined her godfather's virtues, and she sang out lustily during the hymns so carefully chosen by Philip in preparation for his death. She was dry-eyed at the graveside but grateful for the benign presence he had been in her life. She threw the first rosebud of summer into the grave and followed it with a handful of good, English earth.

Afterwards, as they ate smoked salmon and supped Chablis, Philip's friend and solicitor bent to whisper in her ear. 'I'll be in touch.' Celia smiled, embarrassed. She was sure Philip would have left her some memento but now was not the time to talk about it.

On an impulse Celia changed trains on the way home and went to St Albans. It was four fifteen when her cab drew up at Amy's door and she offered up a prayer that Geoffrey would not be at home.

As she rang the bell she heard a child crying somewhere inside the house, a subdued wailing that reeked of despair so that, for an instant, Celia was tempted to turn and run away from whatever lay behind the front door.

Eventually it opened and Amy stood there, a small girl clinging to her skirt. In the background a boy in grey short trousers and a white school shirt was standing. His tear-stained face told that he was the one who had been crying. 'Well,' Celia said, as cheerfully as she could. 'Aren't you going to ask me in?'

They settled in a kitchen that was unkempt, by any standards. Amy tried to clear some of the debris from the kitchen table but Celia stayed her. 'Sit down, Amy. I was hoping things would be better but they're obviously worse. I'm bringing you some good news – at least I hope it's good news. We managed to secure some of your mother's things for you. Peggy went to the sale, which was very brave of her considering . . .'

She had expected at least a smile of gratitude and pleasure. All she got was an outburst of tears. It was the little girl who supplied the reason. 'Daddy is sending Adam away to school. He doesn't want to go and Mummy says he's too little – but he's going.' The tone of her voice said her brother's departure would be inevitable because Daddy's word was law.

'I think we'll have some tea,' Celia said, rising to her feet. She was less in need of a beverage than of time to think. Her impulse was to summon a cab and take them all away, lock, stock and barrel, but reason prevailed. When they had sipped their tea she sent the children into the garden and took Amy's hands in hers. 'Now, Alexandra Mary Yeo,' she said. 'Tell me what you want me to do.'

'I don't know,' Amy said. 'I don't know what I want any more. Except peace.'

Celia sighed. 'I can't make decisions for you, Amy. All I know is that you're not the happy, sensible girl you were. I want to know why. And what can I do to bring you back to your old self. Is it your marriage? Is it because you haven't got your father now? I know what it's like to be without parents. Is that it?'

She already knew the answer but formalities had to be observed.

'It's me,' Amy said. 'I'm not up to being a wife and mother, Celia. Geoffrey says its Daddy's fault. He says I was spoiled and I was. Sometimes I think that's why he married me, to make me pay for all those years when I was indulged.'

'Why should he do that?' Celia asked, but she already knew the answer. He did it because wiping the smile from Amy's face was manna to his sick soul.

'What do you want to do?' she asked again, but without much hope of an answer.

In the train back to London Celia acknowledged that she had been foolish to expect Amy to make a decision. She had had seven years of a brainwashing as severe as anything people accused Stalin of having dished out to dissidents. The chances of her standing up for herself now were nil.

What is happening to us all? Celia asked herself as the suburbs of London reeled past. They had been so full of hope that night in London, their last night 'out on the town' together. They had been so full of plans in the lorry on the way back to camp, singing 'White Cliffs of Dover' and 'We'll Gather Lilacs' and Amy doing her Pat Kirkhouse impression and warbling 'I'm going to get lit up when the lights go up in London'.

Now Amy was a drunken wreck and Peggy a widow.

What was worse was that she and Joy were chasing moonbeams. But her own moonbeam, once admitted, refused to go away. For the last few minutes of the journey she closed her eyes and gave herself up to dreams of Aaron Gotz and a reunion that would have done credit to a Hollywood movie.

When she got back to Kingsway she banished thoughts of her own affairs. To her relief Joy answered the telephone almost at the first ring. 'You sound happy,' she said, taken by surprise at Joy's tone.

'I am. Don't ask why, I'll explain later. How are you?'

'Never mind me. We've got to do something about Amy. I don't know what but I won't be able to get her out of my mind now. I went to St Albans hoping to find things improved but, if anything, they're worse.'

When she put down the phone after arranging a meeting she took a piece of paper and made a list.

1. Discuss tactics with Joy.
2. Find out legal position re. Amy's children.
3. Ring Amy twice a day at appropriate times.
4. Check on Peggy.

And then, remembering Churchill, she added, 'Action this Day'. That was how she would deal with her own foolish yearning, turn her energies towards other people's problems.

29

Amy

The scarf was beautiful, shades of lavender and mauve with here and there a touch of iridescence. Amy held it against her, seeing herself in the mirrored column that supported the counter. At last she put it back, placing it carefully behind the pillar.

She moved away from it then, as though uninterested, looked at one or two others, then returned to the other side of the column and with her right hand reached for a scarf-hat hanging from a fitment. With her left she pulled the mauve scarf gently from behind the pillar, never looking in its direction until it was deep in the recesses of her shopping bag. She had used this manoeuvre before and it always worked.

She moved to gloves then, trying on and discarding several pairs, smoothing them over her fingers, all the while glancing casually round. No one stationary, no one watching her. She left the glove department and moved into jewellery.

When she left to go in search of coffee she had spent nothing but acquired a necklace of pearl beads and a scarf pin in the shape of a cherub. Somehow she felt the little Cupid with his fat tummy and pointed arrow would be lucky.

Something will turn up, she told herself as she drank coffee and nibbled Madeira cake. At the last minute something will happen to let Adam stay. But the knot of misery in her chest did not dissolve. She tried to think of the scarf and the necklace and the Cupid pin. She thought of the Muguet de Bois soap she meant to take from the display in pharmacy. She took off her engagement ring and twisted her gold wedding band round round and round but the only thing that brought comfort was to say 'Daddy . . . Daddy, darling Daddy' under her breath.

Guiltily she looked around but no one was staring at her. She relaxed and tried to think of something else, something pleasant. There were still coronation emblems on the menu cards, red, white and blue. The coronation had been lovely. Even Geoffrey had watched without criticism, had let them all sit together as a family and watch the new television. He had even smirked when Queen Salote of Tonga had gone past in an open carriage, rain streaming down her beaming face.

Queen Elizabeth's voice had been so girlish, high and light, when she had made her solemn oath of service to the people of Britain and the Commonwealth, and then the Duke of Edinburgh had placed his hands between his wife's hands in an act of homage, and Amy had looked up into Geoffrey's eyes and known exactly what he was thinking: that here was a husband with a wife to be proud of while his wife was nothing but a burden.

Taking the soap was easy. There was no one about and the long box containing three wrapped tablets fell into her holdall with a satisfying jolt. She was through the revolving door and out on the pavement before the hand fell upon her arm.

'Come back inside, please, madam.' The voice was soft but the hand on her arm was pincerlike. She tried to shake it away but the grip held.

'I don't understand.' She could see the faces of passers-by, eyes wide, mouths open. No one was helping her. The grip on her arm tightened and she felt a sudden shove. She staggered slightly and then she was being propelled through the doorway, back into the shop. 'Come now, madam, let's not have a scene.'

Her captor was a woman, tall and slim in a grey suit. Her head was bare and there were pearl earrings either side of mottled cheeks. 'Who are you?' Amy said. 'I can't come now. I have to be home for my children.'

'We should've thought of that before, madam.' And then they were through a door, a door she had not noticed before, and someone was forcing her up a flight of grey stone steps to a landing where a man was waiting, holding open a door so that she could be hustled through.

'Scarves,' the grey-suited woman was saying. 'Jewellery and I think gloves. I can't be sure about gloves but definitely jewellery.'

'Could you turn out your bag please, madam?' She heard herself begin to argue and then they were turning her bags out on to a desk, first the holdall, then her handbag.

'I don't know whose those are. They're not mine.'

'Alexandra Mary Harlow.' Someone was reading out her name from her driving licence. 'Is there someone you'd like us to contact, madam? The police'll be here directly so if you'd like someone – a solicitor, your husband perhaps?'

She couldn't answer, couldn't even nod or shake her head. The man spoke now. 'There's no point in denying it, you know. We've been on to you for weeks. At first I said, "No. Not dressed like that." But then there was that scarf pin last week. And the angora tam. You got away from us that time but we were on to you today from the moment you came through the doors. I don't understand you. A woman like you. That coat wasn't cheap, you've rings on your fingers and that's a gold watch. What are you, just plain greedy?'

'No!' She said it as vehemently as she could but then the light in the windowless room was narrowing to a pinpoint and she was falling into the very centre of the tiny flame.

When she came to, Geoffrey was there, holding

her hand solicitously so that no one would see his thumb pressing hard on the bones of her fingers so that she almost cried out with the pain. 'Lie still, darling,' he said. 'There's been a terrible mistake. I've telephoned Michael Ingram. He'll sort it out as soon as he gets here.'

She watched him, mesmerised by the quality of his acting and the depth of her own fear. He looked so kind, so solicitous, the perfect husband ready to stand by his wife. 'A model citizen,' she said aloud and then she was laughing and the room seemed suddenly full of uniforms.

She nodded dumbly when the policeman asked if her name was Alexandra Mary Harlow. Followed Geoffrey out to the waiting police car, glad that the cruel pressure on her hand had been replaced by the gentler arm of the law. Tried hard not to give way and fall, howling, to the floor.

An hour later she had been bailed to appear at the magistrates' court, obeying her solicitor's instruction to make no statement at this juncture.

Geoffrey did not speak on the drive home and when they entered the house he said nothing until the children had been reclaimed from the neighbour who had looked after them since their return from school.

When they were safely in, white-faced and round-eyed, he took up a position at the foot of the stairs. 'Your mother has done a dreadful thing,' he said.

'Geoffrey!' If it would have helped she would have gone down on her knees and begged but she knew it would make no difference. She saw Alice's face pucker, saw Adam frown and suck in his cheeks so that he too would not cry.

'She has done a dreadful thing,' Geoffrey said again. 'Something which will involve us all in disgrace and may mean she is sent to prison.'

'Please, Geoffrey . . .' She held out her arms to her children but his arm came between them.

'I think you should go up to bed now, both of you. I'll bring you a glass of milk by and by. After I have talked to your mother.' They would have moved to kiss her but he stayed them with a glance.

Their legs, where she could see them through the banisters, were small and pale and seemed to plod up the stairs. 'Let me go to them, Geoffrey. Please I'll do anything, say anything. Let me comfort them. They're afraid.'

'As well they might be.' He brought up a hand and placed his index finger against his lip, tapping slightly. 'I want you to go upstairs,' he said, 'and bring down everything you have taken. I know there's more. Bring it down here and don't speak to the children. I forbid you to speak to them until I give you permission.'

She would have moved to obey him but there was a sudden burning sensation behind her chest bone, a bulging in her throat. Her upraised hands were not quite quick enough to catch the vomit that spewed out and spattered the surface of the hall table. She looked at him, expecting to see revulsion, but all she saw reflected in his hazel eyes was satisfaction at her plight.

30

Joy

Chuck arrived at ten past nine, a faint coating of sweat on his upper lip after his jog in the park. Joy was already bathed and dressed for the trip up west he had promised her. 'It's my last day. We'll eat out and make plans.' But when he entered the flat she knew he had other things in mind. Two hours later they were still in a bed warmed by their exertions and the sunshine that flooded in at the open window.

He raised himself on his elbow and looked down on her, tracing first her lips, then her chin, with a lazy finger. 'Honey,' he said at last his finger traversing her throat and moving down to her breast, 'I came early because I have to leave early.'

He had explained to her that first day that he was over here on business, acting as guide for people who could be helpful to him in his political ambitions. 'They want to see the coronation and because I was over here they think I know the ropes. You know how it is. So I can't spend the time with you that I'd like. But they give me time off to work out in the morning. They're so decrepit it takes them half the day to gear up. So we can be together every morning.'

And so they had been. Seven mornings, which were to end today with lunch up town. 'Except there's a change of plan. It's a hell of a shame but they've decided to take an earlier flight. Still, now that we've got all the misunderstandings out of the way you'll be coming over again. We'll meet real soon and then, when I'm well enough in to be honest with everyone, things will be different, you'll see.'

She felt neither surprise nor disappointment. It was as though she had expected the planned lunch not to materialise. Inside her a tiny knot of unease had warned her from the start that there was trouble ahead.

She lay still as he moved, naked and brown, to the bathroom, wincing a little in mock pain because their lovemaking had been so strenuous. She watched as he pulled on the white underwear, the grey cotton jersey trousers and hooded top, laced up the white boots with their springy soles. She even smiled as she reflected that at least he looked the All-American Boy.

'Joy . . .' He was fumbling in the pocket that ran across his chest. 'I want you to have this.' The notes were new and crisp and numerous. 'Buy something nice. Something to make you happy until we can be together again.'

She shook her head. 'I don't need it.'

He sat down on the edge of the bed, his face full of concern. 'Listen to me. If I'd been up front with you about the arrangement with Virginia – if I'd told you what it meant – you'd never have given up your job. The least you can do is let me tide you over.' He reached for her and hugged her to him.

'God, I love you. I don't know why. It's that English voice of yours and that haughty look. She has class, I thought, that very first night.' She looked into his face and saw that his eyes were moist, his mouth trembling.

'Shut up,' she said, silencing him with a kiss. 'I'll come across as soon as I can – but no more surprises.' He kissed her again and then once more before he stood up and quit the room. As he shut the door she saw that his eyes were shining as though with unshed tears.

She leaped from the bed then and crossed to the window, anxious for one last sight of him to suffice her until they could be together once more. It was a moment or two before he emerged, crossing to the kerb and holding up a hand to a cruising taxi.

As the cab waited for the traffic to part and let it cross to him she saw Chuck square his shoulders and look up at the sky, letting the sun fall full on his face like a benediction. And then she saw him stretch and yawn and, as the yawn ended, she saw that he was smiling, the smile of a cat that had got the cream. A moment later he had stepped into the cab and was gone.

She sat on the edge of the bed for a while, her hands dangling between her knees, the money discarded on the coverlet. He had been in Britain for eight days and eight nights and in all that time they had been together for an hour or two each day. Was she being a fool, a poor, pathetic fool? She crossed to the telephone and reached for the directory. He had said he was staying at the Regent Palace but there was no Roche registered there. She dialled the Piccadilly and again drew a blank.

She was luckier at the Savoy. Yes, they had a Roche registered although he was leaving today. 'And Miss Mulholland?' Joy said, naming the Costex heiress as casually as she could. Yes, came the answer. Senator Mulholland and Miss Virginia Mulholland were also leaving today. In fact they were leaving in an hour. Did madam wish to be put through to their suite?

'No, thank you,' Joy said and put down the phone.

She had been suckered, well and truly suckered, but there was no need to feel guilty because the man who had suckered her was a past master at the game who might well make President before he was done.

She knew that if she took to her bed now she would never leave it. Instead she marched into the bathroom and turned on the taps. While the bath filled she pinned up her hair and when she stepped from the bath she dressed herself and applied a full make-up. Twenty minutes later she was out in the street and walking towards Bond Street and the emporium of Lavender et Cie.

The shop was not as she remembered it. The mahogany and brass exterior was much the same but inside there was no sign of the glass counters and no one spooning perfumed goo into pots. Instead all was discreet. Grey carpets, white walls, a pale pink ceiling and vendeuses in grey coat-dresses trimmed with pink. There were products displayed behind glass, wonderful products no doubt in equally wonderful pink and grey boxes.

'Can I help you?' One of the grey overalls glided forward as though on wheels.

'I'd like to see Mr Lavender. Mr Neville Lavender.'

'I'm afraid Mr Lavender doesn't see anyone without an appointment. Perhaps someone else could help?'

'No,' Joy said firmly. 'Please tell Mr Lavender I'm here. My name is Joyce Latham and I think you'll find he'll see me.' Her confidence left her as soon as the woman turned away. It was doubtful that Neville Lavender would remember her name. Her face, perhaps, but names evaporated with time. The woman would come back and humiliate her and it was all her own fault.

A moment later she was being ushered through the velvet drapes behind the counter and into an imposing office where Neville Lavender was limping from behind his desk to shake her hand.

'Miss Latham.' He indicated a seat and she sank into it gratefully.

'This is very kind of you,' she said as he resumed his seat.

'Not at all. It's always good to welcome back the people who've been part of Lavender's.'

'I was a very small and inglorious part,' she said. 'And it was a long time ago.'

'Not at all.' But he was grinning and Joy relaxed.

'Your uncle . . . ?'

'He died three years ago and he'd not taken an active part in the business for a while before that.'

'It's changed,' Joy said.

'Not as much as you might think. We've expanded but the products are much the same.'

'The same old goo . . .' Joy winced suddenly, wondering if she had gone too far, but again he was grinning.

'The same old goo – glycerine, petrolatum, zinc oxide, white vinegar, cetyl alcohol . . . oh, and perfume oil. Don't forget the perfume oil.' He put his fingertips together and rocked back slightly in his chair. 'I have a vivid memory of the way your nose used to wrinkle as you filled pots. We don't fill them by hand any more, by the way. We have machines to do it now.'

'Ah,' Joy said. 'That probably answers my question, then. I was wondering if you needed an experienced pot-filler.'

'No.' Joy felt tears prick her eyes as he spoke. Mustn't cry. Mustn't ever cry. Not until you were alone, where no one saw. 'No – but I might have an opening for someone with excellent experience of an international clientele.'

When Joy emerged from his sanctum, flushed with gratitude, she had a job.

31

Celia

Celia's morning paper was full of the news that Len Hutton was to captain the English cricket team, the first professional to do so. How Philip would have frowned at that. 'What is the world coming to?' he would have said. There was a fat envelope among her mail when she collected it from the mat. She saw the Durham postmark and knew it would be from Mary's, her college at Durham. She opened it and browsed through the information it contained as she drank her second cup of breakfast tea, longing to be part of the wonderful events it detailed and knowing it would not be possible.

On her way to work she thought about those far-off Durham days. Lying on the riverbank sharing dreams of a future that would be a great leap forward. And at night, in her haven far above the city rooftops, dreaming of all she would do and achieve when she graduated. What had she done? Not much. After those wonderful days at Mary's, absorbing wisdom and wider horizons, what had she done?

You fought in a war, her conscience said defensively. But she had not actively fought. She had done what she had always done, what she was doing now. She had done as she was told! Even in Paris she had obeyed orders. 'I have never trespassed,' she said aloud and then, when passers-by stared at her curiously, she sank her head between her shoulders and scurried on. What had happened to that girl that now she was a minor civil servant scurrying to work with nothing in front of her but retirement and a pension that would do? Even when the Gotz dossier had come, when she had seen details of his stay in Paris, seen her own initials on reports, she had done nothing. That's why her life was a wasteland, because she was a coward.

You're better off than Amy, the voice said. Peggy too. Count your blessings! Joy was another whose life was far from settled. You are the only one with security, said her conscience. Always be safe.

Once more she spoke aloud. 'I am sick and tired of safety.' She was ten yards from her office door but she turned abruptly and hailed a passing cab. 'Letchworth Street,' she said and settled back as they sped off into the traffic.

For a moment, as she waited for an answer to her knock, she wondered what she would do if someone else answered. A stranger who might be a father-in-law for all she knew. But it was not a father-in-law who stood revealed in the open doorway. It was Aaron, older and mercifully a little fatter, still with the unruly curls that had grown from his shaven head in Paris.

'Aaron?'

He looked at her for a moment, puzzled and wary. And then he smiled. 'It is Celia,' he said. 'It is Celia of "Stopping by Woods on a Snowy Evening".'

'So you remember Paris,' she said.

'I remember everything. I sometimes wish that I did not but I do remember. Now – are you going to come in or do you have big important business elsewhere?'

She felt such a wealth of emotion that it was difficult to find words, standing here looking at the face that had so preoccupied her over the years. It was all there, the pallor, the eyes dark and dark-ringed, like someone just cured of a fever. And his mouth, softer than she remembered and less defiant.

'Is it convenient to come in? If not there's a coffee shop around the corner. I saw it as I came by.'

He collected his hat from a stand in the hall and they walked to the coffee shop. She felt at ease with him now that he was older. Once, as they moved together, her fingers touched his fingers and the touch was electric. She made to pay for the coffees but he shook his head. 'My turn, Celia.' And she knew that he was remembering and was grateful.

'Now,' he said, when they were settled either side of a red-topped table. 'Tell me what you are doing here? I need time to recover from my astonishment.'

It was not a time for dissembling. Not when she had come this far. 'I came to find you,' she said. 'I saw your name on a list.'

A frown crossed his face. 'Lists. Always there are lists.'

'It wasn't anything really – just a renewal of your permit. The name was unusual so I thought it might be you and it would've been a pity to miss the chance of catching up on news. I try to keep in touch with people from those days.'

It was surprisingly easy to lie, she decided, seeing from his face that he was accepting what she said. She had never kept in touch with anyone, had never wanted to hear of anyone again except Aaron. At Christmas that first year, she had intended to find Glynn's whereabouts and send a card, but the intention had come to nothing. Only for Aaron would she have risked rejection like this.

'What are you doing over here?' she asked then. 'I thought you were going to Israel.' She knew from his records just where and when he had journeyed but it wouldn't do to say so.

'I did go to Israel.' He put out a hand to lift his cup and she saw that his nails were still bitten until they were red and sore. She wanted to reach out and take the thin hands into her own warm ones but a gesture like that might spoil things.

'So what went wrong?'

There was silence and Celia wondered if she should ease the tension with another question but, just as she was about to do so, Aaron sighed and began to speak.

'I came to England when I left Paris. I don't know what I expected – you had not been invaded, you had not seen your crops burned and your animals butchered. In England I was expecting peace and plenty, I suppose. And then London – scarred and jagged, great blocks in the East End razed to the ground, a skyline full of spaces and weeds springing up in the rubble.

'So I set my sights on Palestine, where the sun was always shining and the land brought forth plenty.' He shook his head in wry amusement before he continued. 'It was arranged for me. There were people who helped . . . Zionists. I am not a Zionist, Celia, I am a Jew. But to the authorities I was an "infiltree", someone who wanted to go somewhere else. I couldn't go back to Poland. I heard the stories from others – we were not welcome there. So I went to Vienna, because that was the best place to begin my journey.'

'What did you do for money?' Celia asked, unable to contain her curiosity. He had left Paris with little or nothing. Now he was crisscrossing Europe.

'It was all arranged by Haganah. In Vienna they told me to be ready to leave in twenty-four hours on a ship – on an illegal ship, dear Celia – that was leaving from a French port. I felt so excited. At last, after the camps, the hostels, the train journeys, I was on my way. Or thought I was. That ship fell through – and the next. Someone from Aliyah Beth gave me a raincoat and a beret so I looked like a Frenchman. I walked around the streets waiting for someone to challenge me. Sometimes I wondered if the war's end had been a dream and the Nazis were still out there, round every corner.'

'It must have been dreadful.' Celia put a hand to her mouth and he saw her distress.

'Not so dreadful. There was a ship eventually. I came to Eretz at last. And it was beautiful. But for some reason I could not share the dream. I wanted someone to build a great Jewish community in Palestine but not me. I didn't know what I wanted – I still don't know. But I knew I didn't want to settle, so I went to my cousin in Philadelphia. He sent on the money. We are flying Dutchmen, we survivors. We travel from place to place with our pieces of paper, never settling.'

'One day,' she said. 'One day you'll settle.'

It was he who put out a hand to her. 'Always the optimist. Do you know what we used to call you?'

She shook her head.

'We used to call you Madame Espoir – Madame Hopeful – because you were always telling us to be patient, all would be well.'

'Was I that bad? You make me sound like Pollyanna.' He raised his eyebrows and she explained. 'She was a horrid little prig who was always cheerful. I hated her when I was a child.'

'We didn't hate you, Celia. Sometimes . . .' He shook his head, unwilling to complete the sentence.

'I used to feel so helpless. You were all waiting to move on. You deserved it, you'd waited long enough. But it wasn't simple.'

Around them the café was filling up and he stood up abruptly. 'Come back with me,' he said. 'I have something to show you.'

They walked back to his home without speaking. The single room that was his was filled with the shabby furniture of a rented dwelling. Tables and chairs that did not match, curtains that ended an inch from the sill, an ancient gas fire with a frayed hose. She thought of her own carefully appointed place and was consumed with pity.

But he was gesturing proudly towards a bookcase. 'See,' he said. 'What I have is not much but I have books.' He was reaching for one book, the slim *Golden Staircase* that had been hers. Shabbier now from much use but still surviving. He opened it and read aloud: 'The woods are lovely, dark and deep, But I have promises to keep, And miles to go before I sleep, And miles to go before I sleep.'

He put the book down and turned to the rickety table that served as a desk. 'I do translations – German, Polish, sometimes Yiddish. And in between I write.'

'A novel?' Celia said. He shook his head and smiled.

'Not fiction. I write the truth. What it was like. You are in there, Madame Espoir.' He put an arm around her shoulder and drew her to the table to look down on the title page.

'*Wait for the Day*,' she said. 'I remember when you told me about that.' She turned to the first page and read aloud.

'The first thing I remember is the plum tree that

stood in our garden, its petals falling like snow and then the ripening fruit, which my mother would gather to make wine. In the summer my sisters and I swam in the lake and in winter we would skate upon the ice. In June we picked wild strawberries that grew in the woods and sometimes I took flowers home, for my mother to place in a jar.

'Once a week my father and his friends went to the Mikveh, the ritual bath, where they were soaped and scrubbed. Always they came home laughing. I promised myself that when I became bar mitzvah I too would laugh as I came home from the Mikveh. But when that time came the Germans were there and the laughter had ceased.'

She let the page go and turned to him. 'It's wonderful, Aaron.' It was natural to kiss him then, on his pale cheek, which was faintly stubbled and then again at the side of an eye that was suddenly wet with tears.

32

Peggy

Peggy moved around the market, buying her fruit here, her vegetables there, wherever she could get the best price. As far as she could make out she would have enough money to live on and give the kids the necessities but if they wanted extras – jam on the bread – she would have to find work. Especially when they were through school and ready for college. That had been Jim's dream, that no child of his would go down the pit and at least one of them would have letters after his or her name. If that was what Jim wanted, it was up to her to make sure it happened.

If she was going to see them off to college, with all that that entailed, a job was the only way to do it. She wouldn't be lucky like Celia and have a legacy left to her by an uncle. How had Celia put it in this morning's letter? 'An awfully large amount'.

As Peggy queued for fish she tried to estimate what would be 'an awfully large amount' to Celia. Still, she had loved her Uncle Philip and spoken of him often when they were together in the war. 'Three cod tails,' she said aloud. 'And keep them small.'

When she had finished her purchases she had a small glow of virtue at shopping well done. She would have liked to treat herself to a cup of coffee but folks were so funny with her since Jim's death, full of sympathy if they were trapped face to face and had to speak but scurrying out of the way to avoid her if it could possibly be managed. If she went in the coffee shop a blight would fall on the conversation and then the hurt would start up in her chest and her eyes were still sore from last night. She decided to give the coffee shop a miss and turned for home.

As she walked she thought about Celia and her money. Perhaps she would see a bit of life now, travel, meet a nice man. If there was a wedding and she got an invitation she would go, no matter where she got the money. It was funny, that. When they'd been demobbed she hadn't really felt the missing of them. Now she felt almost as if they were family, which made what was happening to Amy all the worse. Celia's letter had been vague but frightening. 'I simply can't describe how she looks, Peg, except to say you would hardly recognise her. I don't know what I can do but I must do something. Whatever happens, I'll keep you up to date.'

Peggy realised she was smiling. Good old Ceely,

keeping everyone in touch, worrying about everyone, just like the old days. She looked around guiltily in case she had been seen smiling. She was outside the second-hand shop and she paused for a look. They had a jug-and-basin set like the one she had bought at the George and it was marked £2.10.0d. She had paid sixteen shillings for hers. She searched the window, noting and marvelling at prices, and then she saw the handwritten sign scrawled on a shoebox lid: CLOSING DOWN. EVERYTHING MUST GO.

She had half thought of offering some of the things she had bought at auction to the man who ran the shop but he wouldn't want them now. Not when he was giving up. She pressed down the catch and put her head inside as the shop bell gave a vigorous chime.

'You're closing down then? I might have some things to get rid of.'

'I'm not taking stock in at the moment, pet.' He moved uneasily in his chair. 'This arthritis is getting me down, otherwise I wouldn't be giving up. Little goldmine, this place is. Lovely flat up top and all.'

'Well,' Peggy said. 'I'll wait till you've got it sold, see if I can sell them to the next owner.'

She backed out to another vigorous jangling of the doorbell.

She had a pork dip at dinnertime and a pot of tea and then picked a bunch of flowers from Jim's garden. She cried as she plucked orange marigolds and white marguerites but somehow they were good tears.

I was lucky, she thought, remembering love that,

although it would never come again, had been very sweet. 'Oh Jim,' she said aloud as she closed the gate, 'you were a lovely chap.' And then she smiled, imagining his embarrassed face if he could hear her.

'Steady on, now, Peggy,' he would have said. 'No need to go too far.' But he would have liked hearing it just the same. She knew because she had so often told him and seen his reaction.

There was no one about in the cemetery as she walked between the neat rows of headstones. It comforted her to see flowers here and there at the graves of people who had died long years before. People didn't forget. There were marigolds in a jam jar on Billy Farrow's grave and his wife had been married again for five years or more.

Could I remarry? She thought. The question was shocking. How could I even think such a thing? She scurried on to where the earth was still brown and raw. She had ordered a headstone with an inscription from Jim's favourite hymn, 'Life That Shall Endless Be'. She had put five pounds down and the rest would be paid at ten shillings a month. She plucked a weed here and there and tidied some stray scraps of paper and wrappers that were lying around, and then she sat down on a nearby bench and tried to clear her mind.

People died and life went on but she couldn't grasp that. Not yet. I'm hurting, she thought. As though something has been wrenched out of me. She put up a hand to her chest, half expecting to feel a hole there, or at least a jagged edge. And yet she could walk about now and smile and nod and control her crying. She had not been able to do any of those things at the beginning and it was only seven weeks and five days.

She stood up and looked once more at the six feet of earth that held all that was left of her love. 'I'm going to manage, Jim,' she said quietly. 'But for the life of me I can't think how.'

She dawdled on her way back so that she would arrive at the school as the children came out. Margaret came first and then Peter behind her. She saw them glance towards her, their faces uncertain. Poor little souls, she thought. They don't know how they're on with me.

She waited until they were almost up to her and then she held out her hands. 'Come on,' she said. 'We're going home to tea and tonight, as it's Friday, we're going to the pictures. There's a Walt Disney on at the Grand.'

She squeezed their hands as they slipped them into her own. 'I'm in a good mood today so we might have ice cream an all.' She thought of all the times Jim had bought ice cream for them, holding four cornets in his big hands, taking a quick lick at any that threatened to run. He had been the best father in the world. 'I've been thinking,' she said as they walked towards home. 'What we need in our house is a dog.'

Two faces stared up at her in shared amazement. Peter spoke first. 'You wouldn't let us have a dog. Dad used to ask and you'd say, "Over my dead body".'

He stopped suddenly, realising he had mentioned the unmentionable.

'I never said that,' Peggy said. 'Did I, Meg?' Her daughter's eyes widened with anxiety. Should she lie or should she tell the truth? 'Never mind,' Peggy said. 'If I did say that I was daft. Now let's get a move on or we'll miss the B picture.'

33

Amy

They sat in an oak-panelled antechamber. The solicitor and his clerk sat together, murmuring over papers. Geoffrey stood looking out of the window, his back turned to her.

I am an outcast, Amy thought.

For some strange reason this struck her as funny and she emitted a nervous giggle. She smiled weakly, by way of apology, and they looked away again. She wondered what would happen if she began to hum – or whistle. Anything to break this awful, unnatural stillness.

'What do you think will happen to me?' she asked suddenly. The solicitor looked up and cleared his throat.

'I don't think we should speculate,' he said. 'Once they have heard the medical evidence I'm hopeful . . . one is always hopeful but this time I think we can reasonably expect . . . well, not much longer now. Mr

Lewis should be here very shortly. I suggest we leave it to him.'

The barrister appeared one minute before they were due in court. 'Now,' he said, running his eye over the brief. 'Hmm, yes . . . hmm . . .' His eyes met hers only once and then he smiled briefly. 'Try not to worry. We should be all right.'

He moved to the window then and he and Geoffrey spoke in low tones. Amy strained to hear but it was useless. They were talking about her as though she didn't exist. As though she was ill. That was what people did at sick beds, talked out of earshot. She wanted to ask what would happen to the children if she was sent to prison but she already knew the answer to that because Geoffrey had told her more than once. 'They would be better off without a mother than with the pathetic apology of a mother they have at the moment.'

Amy dug her nails into her palm, enjoying the pain, until she felt the nail of her ring finger break under the pressure. She couldn't even hurt herself properly. I want a drink, she thought. More than anything else in the world I want a drink. And then someone in a black robe appeared and someone was holding her elbow and guiding her forward.

'Up the steps, that's right. Don't sit down till he tells you.' And Amy was looking at a sea of faces. Hostile faces. She gripped the ledge in front of her, feeling her stomach tilt and lurch. If she was sick here Geoffrey would say she had done it deliberately.

She could hear her name: 'Alexandra Mary Harlow.' But that was not her name. She was Alexandra Mary Yeo, beloved daughter of the landlord of the George and in a moment someone would explain and she could go home.

But no one did allow her to go home. Instead, there was a procession of people into the witness box to describe how her activities had been watched and noted for days before the day of her arrest.

'She was clever,' the grey-suited woman testified. 'Very clever, one of the best I've come across. I formed the opinion she was a practised thief so it was difficult to be sure at first. My colleague observed too but it was only on the last occasion that we could be certain.'

So they had known all along. In her mind Amy saw her progress between the counters, remembered the heady feeling of excitement, the terror that was at once terrible and wonderful. And all the time their eyes had been on her.

She was about to sink to the floor when one face sprang out of the crowd, pale and determined, but with the mouth uplifted in a smile of encouragement. *Celia*? She couldn't have spoken aloud for no one had turned round.

'Alexandra Mary Harlow. Is that your name?'

'Yes.' How had they told her to address him? 'Yes, sir,' she said and lifted her chin for whatever came next.

It went over her head, most of it, but there was no

avoiding the final speech for it was directed at her as though it were shot from a gun.

'We have given due weight to the medical evidence presented by your able counsel and to the fact that your husband is a man of great standing in the community. Nevertheless, it is impossible to ignore the severity of an offence committed, not by someone in need, but by a woman who I am given to understand has her every whim indulged by a perhaps too-tolerant husband. It is because of the hurt that a custodial sentence would cause your husband and children that we have decided, on this occasion, to take a lenient view . . .'

She was not going to prison. In a moment she was going home. Everyone was looking at her as though she should be grateful, which filled her with a terrible wry amusement. And then she looked to where Celia sat and saw the calm eyes of a friend. Once more she lifted her chin. 'Thank you,' she said and turned to leave the dock.

She had hoped that Celia would come to her in the court and act as a buffer between her and the rest. But when she came out into a sunlight that smote her eyes until she had to close them, there was no sign of her friend. Only Geoffrey, pincerlike on her arm, holding the door of the car and closing it behind her.

'I hope you realise what you have done,' he began as the car moved off. 'Thank God I decided to send Adam away. Alice must go, too, of course. I'm going to contact a school on Monday.'

'Please don't. She's too young – she's only six.'

'I have to do it, Alexandra. For their own sake I have to get them away.' In the rear-view mirror his eyes were bright with something suspiciously like enjoyment, flicking up constantly to watch her.

Please God, help me, she thought, except that there was no God, no help, no way out at all.

Amy was taking off her coat in the hall when the bell rang. She heard Geoffrey coming in from the garage, putting the keys on the kitchen table. The bell rang again and she moved to the door.

'Don't do that.' He was there behind her but it was too late. She had opened the door and the next moment Celia's arms were around her.

'It's all right, Amy. I'm here now. There, there – don't get upset. Is there somewhere we can sit down?'

'I'm sorry but my wife doesn't want to see anyone at the moment. She's been through a gruelling experience today.' Amy could almost sense the chill of his presence behind them.

'Just today?' Amy felt Celia tense and then pull gently away so that she could turn to confront Geoffrey. 'Just today? As I look at her I think her gruelling experience has lasted a little longer than that.'

'I'm afraid I don't intend to discuss my wife's affairs with an outsider.'

'I think it may be impossible to avoid it as I don't intend to leave until you do.'

Amy felt her mouth go dry. Geoffrey wouldn't take this. 'Please . . .' she said.

'It's all right, Amy.' Celia's arm had come round her once more. 'Why don't you go and make some tea? I expect you could do with some.'

She went obediently enough but once in the kitchen she made no move to fill the kettle or assemble cups. Instead she put her ear to the crack of the door and listened, half in terror, half in wonderment.

'There's no point in this. As you can see, my wife is ill. I appreciate that you mean well but it really would be better if you were to leave.'

'Don't go,' Amy mouthed, but she knew that it would make no difference. Celia would have to go because this was Geoffrey's house and she, Amy, would have to stay because she was Geoffrey's wife, 'till death us do part'. She moved to the sink and turned on the hot tap. By the time she withdrew her hands Celia would be gone and events could take their course.

But Celia had no intention of leaving. 'I want you to let Amy go,' she said quietly. 'Yes, you smile because the very idea seems ridiculous. And unpalatable, I'm sure. Why should you part with something which gives you so much entertainment. I'll tell you why. If you can't realise that Amy is near the edge—'

'My wife's name is Alexandra!'

'If you can't realise that Alexandra is near the edge you're a fool. I don't think you are a fool – you're something much worse. I won't call it a vice, I'll call it a foible – you enjoy inflicting pain. Oh, not the physical kind. That's not your style, although I suspect it might be easier for . . . *Alexandra* to bear. If I'm right, and she is near complete breakdown, I intend to apply to the Official Solicitor to have a protection order made on the grounds that she is not in command of herself and that you are contributing to her breakdown.'

'You'd never get away with it.' Through the crack in the door Amy could see that he was pale now, with an even paler line of fury around his lips.

'Probably not, but I would achieve a quite massive amount of publicity. I'd employ excellent counsel – I have Philip Warburton in mind. He's frightfully expensive; I'm frightfully rich all of a sudden. By the time I'm finished you may have your wife but you won't have your reputation, nor, I feel fairly sure, your feet on that ladder you're so intent on climbing. You have a choice. You can be the man whose wife left him – a sad but dignified figure – or you can be an object of revulsion. Martyr or monster, Geoffrey. The choice is yours.

'I don't want an answer now. But while you ponder I think it might be in your interests to go easy on your wife. Because if any harm befalls her I will brandish your part in it from one end of this country to another.'

'You can't prove anything,' he said. 'Because there is nothing to prove.'

'Then I'll lie,' Celia said cheerfully. 'And I'll be believed. And if you think I wouldn't stoop to lying, hear this. In a good cause I would do anything! Anything, Geoffrey.' There was a light in her eyes that left no doubt she meant what she said.

They both turned as Amy appeared in the doorway. 'I can't go without the children,' she said. 'He'll never let me take the children.'

'Hush, Amy. Let me deal with this. The children go with their mother, Geoffrey. You can smile like that but think about it. Think of living with the consequences of being a household name. And you are just far enough up that so-important ladder of yours to make the papers. You see, I've checked you out. You can have your rosy future or you can have your peculiar perversity. You can't have both because I won't let you.'

'You're bluffing.'

'Try me.'

'Why are you doing this? What gives you the right to interfere?' She had him winded. That was a good sign.

'I'm doing it because I'm against blood sports, Geoffrey. Whatever form they take. Now, I'm going to have a cup of tea. This . . .' She took a cardcase from her handbag. 'This is my card. Ring me and tell me how we are going to play this. I'm going to have a cup of tea with Amy and then I'll be gone. But only for the moment.'

In the kitchen the women looked at each other. 'He won't let me go,' Amy said.

Celia reached out and gripped her friend's arms. 'Amy, you have to help me. I can make this happen but only if you help me. You do want to leave him, don't you?'

'If I can take the children – I must take the children.' Amy was twisting her hands in a washing motion until Celia stilled them.

'You must be strong, Amy – and you mustn't drink. No, let's not pretend that you don't. You know you do and you musn't. For the children's sake. You have to be strong. Now, where's that tea?'

'Where would I go? I have nowhere to go, Celia! There's only this house – Geoffrey's house. Not for me, it's the children – they must have a home!'

'And they will. Trust me – I know what I'm doing. But you must pull your weight, Amy. I can't do this on my own. Now, will you stand fast?'

There was a long silence and Celia's lips parted in despair until . . . 'Yes,' Amy said. 'Yes, Celia. I will stand fast. He doesn't think I'm capable of it but he's wrong.' She paused. 'How did you know about it? About court, I mean.'

Celia sighed. 'I came today to see you. Just to see you, because I was concerned about you. Your neighbour told me what was happening, where you were. And then, in court, I realised just how far things have gone. You can't go on like this, Amy. If you do you're going to wind up . . .' She faltered, unwilling to be too unkind. It was Amy who finished the sentence.

'In a mental home? That's where he wants me to be, isn't it?'

'We musn't let him win, Amy. For the children's sake you must be strong.'

'Yes,' Amy said. 'I see that now. I must do it for the children.'

34

Peggy

As she smoothed down the clean sheets and plumped up the pillows Peggy was in turmoil. Where would all this wind up? In an hour or less she was taking a woman, two children and a cat into her home, a home that barely accommodated her own family.

'I'd never have believed he'd let them go, Peggy,' Celia had said when she had rung Peggy. 'But he has, and I want to get them away before he changes his mind. So far my bluff has worked but bluff is all it is. I have to work fast. I'd bring them back here but, to be frank, Amy's in no fit state to be left and I'm out all day, and she isn't really up to coping on her own at the moment. It's not fair on the children.'

So Peggy had agreed they could come here, even the cat when she heard that Amy had offered to have it put down if it would be 'inconvenient' and the children were crying at the prospect. It had seemed the only thing she could do at the time. Now, she was not so sure.

What if it didn't work? How would she get them out? And just what did 'in no fit state' mean? Once again Peggy experienced a feeling of vulnerability sweep over her. I'm not up to this, she thought. Not yet. Not without Jim.

At first she had hoped it would fizzle out. Husband-and-wife tiffs often did, except that Celia's tone suggested it was far worse than a tiff, and if half of what they had said at the funeral was true it was more of a hell than a marriage. But court! What had Amy done to land in court?

She had given Amy and her daughter her own double bed. Amy's boy could share with her own son and she and Meg would sleep on the put-you-up in the living room. It was far from an ideal arrangement and couldn't go on for long. Peter and Margaret were doing well at school and needed their sleep, which would be a good excuse if she had to put an end to it.

She checked the stew simmering gently on the stove. Plenty for seven but there would have to be some arrangement about housekeeping.

I don't want them here, she acknowledged to herself. I want to help and I suppose I sympathise but I want my house to myself.

To quell her agitation she put on her coat and let herself out of the back door.

She could cut down the backstreet and be through

the cut and in open country in five minutes. As she walked she remembered those first heady days of her homecoming, she and Jim alone together in the dark, terrified of their new closeness and yet exulting in it. She cried a little, tears of release. She could remember now and almost enjoy it. Perhaps the healing process had begun.

She climbed the low hill that was Belgate's western boundary and looked down on the village. Narrow rows of terraced houses thrown up by the coal owners to stable their colliers. Train lines crisscrossing as though thrown down by a petulant child and over it all the shadow of the pit wheel.

Durham had been built on coal. The people of Durham had lived by the hewing of it. And some had died in the pursuit of it. It was six years since nationalisation but the dream of total safety had not materialised. And if rumours of pit closures were true the idea of security was another dream that would never be realised. There were fewer faces in the pit nowadays and mechanisation meant fewer men to a face. Any pit deemed uneconomic was doomed. It was not what they had been led to expect. She took one last look at her beloved Belgate and began her descent from the hill. Celia had said they would arrive at two o'clock and Celia's times were always precise.

As Peggy walked between hedges of meadowsweet she thought about Celia. Had she ever been in love? Perhaps there had been someone in Paris. And yet Celia had never bothered with boys in all those years of war, when other girls had been clustered round the mirror, night after night, keen to go out on the hunt.

I had Jim, she thought. All the time I knew he was waiting. She cried a little then, remembering how sweet her homecoming had been. Sometimes now, at night, she let herself imagine that he was there, warm and loving in the bed beside her, and sometimes, in dreams, she felt his weight press down upon her as they loved, and she woke to find he was not there.

She turned when she came to the end of the wheat field and made her way home, hurrying the last quarter-mile in case the pan had boiled dry and she was left with seven hungry mouths and no means of feeding them. She would have to make sure that enough was put by for Peter and Meg when they came in from school. You couldn't buy best shin beef and not give it to your own.

By the time she heard the car at the door her heart was pounding. It was seven years since she had seen Amy. They had got on well enough in the old days but that was it: they were old days and long gone. She looked at herself in the mirror above the mantelpiece. She had aged in the last seven years. Had Amy changed too?

But the change in Amy was so evident and so dreadful that any doubt was immediately banished from Peggy's mind. Whoever this thin, gaunt woman with the tremulous hands and fear-filled eyes was, she was a creature in need of comfort.

As for the two children behind her, the boy clutching

a frantic cat, both of them bewildered and looking like refugees, they too were shocking to behold. She thought of her own two, sturdy and confident, and was consumed with pity.

'Get yourselves in here,' she said. 'And sit yourselves down. I'm so glad to see you.' For a moment the two women looked into each other's face, remembering and regretting the girls they had been, and then Peggy held out her arms and enveloped Amy, while behind them Celia let out a long, slow sigh of relief.

They sat round the table to eat, the visitors only toying with their food. The children seemed to huddle together. Amy ate obediently like one who knows she is on probation. 'Would you like to go outside and play?' Peggy said when the pudding had been eaten and she was brewing tea. But the children shook their heads and moved closer to their mother. 'All right,' Peggy said. 'My lot'll be in directly and you can go upstairs to play.'

'You're a brick to be doing this,' Celia said when they found themselves alone in the kitchen. 'I'll make other arrangements as soon as I can. Perhaps Joy can think of something. You knew she'd gone back to her old job at Lavender's?'

'I thought she was going to America.'

'That seems to be off. I haven't pried. You know Joy, she'll tell me when she's ready. But she's left the cruise ships. That's definite.'

'What about you?' Peggy asked as she waited for the kettle to boil. 'You look blooming. It's not romance, is it?'

'Don't be silly,' Celia said. 'I've troubles enough without that.'

Peter and Meg came home at four and declined their stew until later. They looked curiously at the newcomers and then elected to take them upstairs. 'Can you play Monopoly?' Meg asked and received a nod from Amy's Adam by way of assent. There was silence above and below for a while and then the sound of childish chatter percolated down the stairs and the three women relaxed. It's going to be all right, Peggy thought, and was glad.

'It's good of you to put us up,' Amy ventured.

Peggy shook her head. 'It's not good at all, Amy. It's only what you would've done for me and I dare say we'll manage for a bit. I'll be quite glad of the company, to tell you the truth.' For a moment the old glad-eyed Amy who had believed in happiness looked out from Amy's eyes – but only for a moment.

'She looks awful,' Peggy said as she saw Celia back into the car for the journey home. 'And those bairns – funny, solemn little creatures. La-di-da but not like children. Still, leave them to me!'

'It's not over yet,' Celia said. 'The least little thing and she'll go back, Peg. It's all she knows, you see, with her father gone.'

'You leave her to me,' Peggy said again, shutting the car door. Celia looked out at the stout arm in its blue cardigan.

'I couldn't leave her in better hands,' she said and let out the clutch.

'Drive carefully,' Peggy called. Behind her Amy appeared in the doorway, suddenly woebegone, but even as Celia's eyes flared alarm Peggy gathered Amy to her and lifted her free arm in farewell.

'Now,' Peggy said, as the car gathered speed. 'I don't know about you, Amy Yeo, but I could do with another cup of tea.'

'Will Celia be all right?' Amy asked as they went back into the house. 'It's a long drive.' Upstairs there was still the sound of laughter.

'You leave Celia to Celia,' Peggy said. 'You know how sensible she is. If it's too far for her she'll stop off somewhere. I've been thinking about tonight. Shall we bunk in together and put the kids in two and two? Then we can talk about old times. And the future. There's plenty to talk about there.'

But if she had hoped for a spark of interest from Amy she hoped in vain. All she got was a weak smile and an offer to help with the tea.

35

Celia

On the way back to London Celia felt overcome with fatigue. It was not just the driving, wearisome though that had been. Her own mind was in turmoil, a turmoil she had had to subdue for Peggy's sake but which now threatened to overwhelm her.

At York she pulled into the car park of a hotel and went inside. She asked for sherry and carried her glass to a window seat. Outside, in the gathering dusk, the English countryside stretched gentle and green and she felt peace overcome her. She looked around at the others in the lounge, wondering if they were looking at her and if so did they guess her secret?

A month ago she had been a civil servant, discreet and tipped for promotion, thinking of nothing else but getting home at night to her cat and her eyrie above Kingsway. Now – she looked down at her glass trying to sum up her present state – now she felt like a girl again and all for the sake of a man whom she hardly knew and who was obviously in conflict with himself.

She remembered what Aaron had said to her the last time they had talked. 'Why did it happen, Celia? Why did people let it happen? Why didn't they stop it before it grew and took hold of the world? Is there a devil in all of us, waiting to come out? After we were liberated I looked at people, the camp guards even, and all I saw were ordinary men and women. They laughed, they cried, they even begged for mercy. Mercy from us, who they had tortured and would have killed.

'In Poland, if a Jew hid from the Nazis his fellow citizens betrayed him. Even priests turned their backs on Jews. And if you stand by while evil flourishes, are you not evil? I weep for them, Celia. I weep for myself but even more I weep for them.'

At half-past seven she took to the road again, bracing herself for the hours of driving ahead, thinking only of the fact that each mile brought her nearer to Aaron.

It will make you unhappy, she told herself. Sooner or later it will end in tears. But when reason told her she should find an inn for the night she kept on driving, because all she wanted to do was to get back to the place where he might be.

It was one o'clock in the morning when she let herself into the silent building. There were two messages, one from Joy and one from Aaron. She put his aside as the greater treat and read what Joy had to say. 'Hope the

Wolseley didn't let you down. Edna's Bill will collect it Monday night. Hope all went well. Ring when you can. Yours to a cinder, Joy.'

Aaron's letter was longer.

> I walked in the park today and thought of you on your crusade to help a friend. And then I went home and worked on my book because I knew it would please you, dear Celia, that I do not waste time. But it is so strange that London is not the same without you when it is only a few short weeks since I knew you were near.
>
> Today I write about my time on the ship as I journeyed to Palestine. Soon my book will be ended.
>
> So I hope that when you read this you are safely home. Know that this is important to me.
>
> Until we meet,
>
> Aaron.

She sat down at the kitchen table, too tired to take off her outer clothes, able only to see that phrase 'important to me'. For the first time in her life she was important to someone. She had been loved before – by her aunts, by Philip certainly – but now she was important, which meant, please God, that she was also loved.

When at last she had washed and changed into her sensible pyjamas and dutifully cleaned her teeth, she kneeled down by her bed and tried to pray. She had not prayed since schooldays. The habit had fallen away in the barracks where everyone who did it was regarded as weird. Now, though, there were so many things to think about. Peggy and what was to be done about Amy – and Aaron. Aaron above all.

She tried to pray formally but her mind was too jumbled with fatigue and joy so that in the end all she did was give thanks for this wonder that had come upon her.

It was half-past eight when she woke and she sprang from the bed, aghast that however much she hurried she would be late for the office. She was buttoning her jacket when Aaron knocked at the door.

'You're back,' he said and smiled so broadly that all thought of duty fell away from her. 'Are you going to your work?'

'Not today,' she said firmly. 'Today I am free as a bird.'

They took a cab to the Embankment and walked in the sunshine. 'London is healed, I think,' he said as they looked down the river. 'When first I came here this city was wounded. Now it has licked its wounds. It is beautiful once more.'

Celia wanted to tell him that he too was beautiful in her sight but she was afraid of betraying too much. Instead she smiled and took his arm to urge him in the direction of the pier, where they could board a boat to explore the mighty River Thames.

There was a breeze on the river. They stood at the prow of the boat as it cut its way through the swirling waters, past Traitor's Gate and on towards Greenwich, their shoulders and arms touching until at last their fingers sought and twined.

'How is your book going?' she asked and saw his brow cloud.

'Soon I will finish it, Celia. I used to think of nothing else. Bring it to an end, I thought. That is all that matters, the reason for living is to write it all down. Now that it is almost done, I wonder . . . what comes after?'

A seabird swooped above then and they turned to watch its flight, for neither of them had an answer to Aaron's question.

36

Joy

'You wanted to speak to me?' Joy stood in the doorway of Neville Lavender's office. She had seen the room before, with its imposing desk and panelled walls. Now he stood up and gestured to her to come in.

'Yes. Thank you for coming. Shall we sit here?' Joy's heart sank as she subsided on to one of the brocade sofas and Neville sat down opposite her. This felt distinctly like a parting of the ways. And yet he had seemed pleased with the way she had carried out her duties as a senior assistant.

He cleared his throat. 'I wanted to speak to you . . .' He cleared his throat again and this time she knew for certain that her days at Lavender's were numbered. 'I wondered if . . .' He stood up abruptly and went over to his desk, returning with a bulging Manila folder. 'I feel the pattern of business is changing,' he said. 'There's rising prosperity now and I want Lavender's to take advantage of it.'

'Very wise,' Joy said, nonplussed at the way the conversation was going.

'Since my uncle's death I've concentrated on the business side of things but as perhaps you know my interest has always been in the products.' He moved slightly as though to accommodate his leg and Joy's lips moved in sympathy. Suddenly he grinned and Joy realised that when he was not frowning he was a handsome man. What a fool his wife was to jeopardise her marriage.

'It's a long time since the war,' he said, 'but I fear it is ever with me.'

'You manage very well,' Joy said. 'I'd forgotten you were wounded . . . that you lost a leg.'

'I wish I could,' he said ruefully. 'Still, others fared worse. Now, as I was saying, I want to expand. We're doing well here but the clientele is changing. The face of wealth in this country is different now. People travel. They see foreign products and they think they must be better because they're strange – exotic, if you like. So I want to launch a new range and I'd like you to give me an opinion.'

'Why me?' Joy could not prevent herself uttering the question. She had prepared herself for the sack and now she was being treated as a consultant.

'You've travelled,' he said. 'I remember you aboard the *Marmora* and all your wealthy clients.'

Joy smiled. 'Yes, I remember. How is your wife?'

He looked at her and she saw his face had flushed slightly. 'My wife is no longer with me. It was an amicable parting. We had come to the end of the road.'

'Ah,' Joy said. She was about to add, 'I know the feeling', but it wouldn't have been true. She had not parted from Chuck 'amicably'. He had simply walked out on her. For now she knew the five hundred pounds had been a parting gift, a pay-off. Instead she said, 'I'm sorry. These things happen.' And then he was spreading the contents of the folder before her and she was approving or disapproving, giving an honest opinion of what she thought would please the type of customer he was seeking.

She heard the other assistants preparing to leave but Lavender did not suggest she should go and she had no wish to. At last someone came to deliver the keys and they were alone.

'So you think it would work?' he asked at last.

'Yes. You'd need to spend money on packaging, create an identity. Lavender products look good but I think you need something more. If women are to spend money they like to have something to hold in their hand, to feel they've bought something precious.'

The money Chuck had given her was still in her jewel box. Five hundred pounds, a small enough pay-off for seven years of her life. She had gone out to spend it several times and come back empty-handed. There was nothing she wanted enough to buy.

'Exactly. That's the feeling I want to create. We give

them an excellent product, one that really works, but we make them feel cherished too.' Neville Lavender levered himself to his feet. 'I've made you late. Are you rushing off somewhere?'

Joy shook her head. 'No, not really.'

'Then perhaps I could buy you dinner and we can carry on this conversation. But you must stop me if I bore you.' He smiled again and she thought that he should smile more often. 'My wife thought me obsessive about my work so don't be afraid to call a halt.'

They went to the bistro around the corner. He suggested walking and when Joy looked dubious he patted his false leg. 'It's a trusty servant . . . it'll see me to Ambrose Street, never fear.'

The bistro was dimly lit and comfortable. They settled in a booth at the back, Neville being welcomed as an old and valued client. 'Now,' Neville said, when they had ordered and were sipping an apéritif, 'tell me what has happened to you in the last few years.'

'Oh . . .' Joy said taken aback. 'There's not that much to tell.' How could she tell him that she had been a gullible fool for years? 'I went to work in a beauty salon when I left Lavender's. And then in 1948 I went on to cruise ships. The trade was picking up again. People wanted to relax and there was money about. Since then I've gone back and forth across the Atlantic. And that's about it.'

He was smiling quizzically. 'It ought to have been a pretty good life but your voice says something different.'

Joy's shoulders slumped and she bit her lower lip.

'You're too perceptive for my liking. There was a man. An American. It didn't work out.'

'And that was the reason for crisscrossing the Atlantic?'

'Yes. He was in Washington but he came to New York when he could.'

'And it's over?'

'Yes,' Joy said. 'That is the one certainty. It's over.' She wanted to ask if his marriage was definitely over but it wouldn't have done. Instead the conversation turned first to the war and then to the new armistice in Korea and their hopes that the peace would last. On a lighter note, they discussed Neville's great passion, cricket, and the appointment of his hero, Len Hutton, to the England captaincy.

'He's a good man,' Neville said. 'Our fortunes will pick up, you'll see.'

'Did you play?' Joy asked and saw him smile, as though remembering.

'Oh yes. I played. Bowled better than batted, but I suppose I was a bit of an all-rounder. I captained the first eleven at school and played briefly for my county – and then the war and that was the end of cricket.' He spoke cheerfully enough but Joy was suddenly sharply aware of what the war had cost him, the end of a side of his life that had obviously meant a great deal to him.

She changed the subject then, deliberately introducing his new plan for Lavender's, and they talked animatedly about their business future until it was time to go home.

As they waited for the taxi that would take her home he said, 'Would you work with me on this? We'd renegotiate what we pay you, of course, but I'd value your input.'

'I'll be glad to,' Joy said, on an impulse putting out her hand. He shook and then held it for a moment. 'I'm glad you came back,' he said. The next moment he had hailed a cab. 'The least I can do is send you home in style.' He spoke to the cabbie and parted with a note. 'See you in the morning.'

On the way home Joy willed herself not to think. What had happened was good but a little scary. It was a long time since she had been wined and dined by anyone except Chuck. She had always turned down invitations from other men, believing herself to be already promised. What a fool she had been. What a stupid, blinkered fool. Tonight Neville Lavender had made her feel . . . special. Important. He had listened to her opinions, laughed at her jokes, encouraged her to talk about herself and her life.

He had talked of his own life too, its rewards and its difficulties. He had spoken of youthful hopes and adult disillusionment. I like him, she thought. Either he has changed or I have. Perhaps years ago I was too stupid to realise what he is really like.

When she got home she dialled Celia's number. 'How did it go yesterday?' She listened as Celia told her about Amy's move. 'What are they going to do?' she said. 'Unless Peggy's house is huge they can't bunk in together for ever.'

She listened again as Celia offered alternatives. 'Well,' she said at last, 'I have a spare five hundred pounds. If I give it to you will you pass it on? It's not much but it'll help a bit. And, by the way, Ceely . . . before you ring off, why do you sound so happy?'

37

Celia

Aaron came at eleven o'clock, by invitation. There was a significance about this meeting that neither understood but both recognised. There was a moment of unease, a mental circling of each other, and then Celia smiled and Aaron smiled back and the ice was broken. But even as his body relaxed his jaw tightened. 'I need to talk to you, Celia.' He had a bulky parcel under his arm. Now he placed it on the table and put both his hands, palms down, on top of it.

'You've finished the book,' she said, recognising what lay inside the brown paper.

He nodded. 'Three hours ago.'

'Then you haven't slept.' She was alarmed.

'I don't need sleep, Celia. I need you to read my book and then tell me what we should do with it.'

'We'. She savoured that word for a moment. 'What

we should do with it'. He wanted her in his life. She was reaching for the manuscript when he stayed her hand.

'Not now. Today let us just be happy. Tonight . . . tomorrow . . . when I am gone, you can read it. Now . . .' He was grinning and rubbing his hands together. 'I am hungry, Celia.'

She scrambled eggs for him and brewed coffee, fluttering around him like a handmaiden until he begged her to sit opposite him. 'This is good, Celia. Better than Paris.'

'Do you remember the food there?' Celia said, screwing up her nose as she subsided into a chair.

'Soup, always soup,' he said. 'And dreadful bread.'

'Food was so short.' Celia was remembering the shortages, the anxieties that they would not manage to feed boys who had been starved for years.

'It wasn't so bad.' Aaron was holding his coffee cup in both hands, looking into space as he reminisced. 'When you have eaten nothing, when you have seen men starve to death beside you, even watery soup is good.'

'It *was* watery,' Celia said but she too was smiling now.

'When I was hungry, in the camp – and sometimes afterwards – I used to dream about food. And daydream, too. Of *challah* and *lokshen kugl* and *gefilte* fish and my mother kindling the sabbath light.'

'*Challah* is egg bread, isn't it, shaped into a plait?'

'Yes.' He was still smiling so it was all right to let him remember. 'My mother would make it into a plait or, if I had been a good boy, she would make me a special shape, an animal or a little man with raisins for eyes. And always . . . always she would throw a little piece of dough into the fire as an offering and bless it with a prayer.'

'You must have had a happy childhood,' Celia said. 'My parents were dead. I envy you that.' She stopped then, remembering what had followed his happy childhood. Nothing to envy there.

They carried their coffee into the window seat and sat high above Kingsway in the round window. 'This is an eyrie,' he said and she smiled because his concept mirrored her own. 'Or a tower,' he continued. 'You are like the lady in the tower who lets down her hair . . .'

'Rapunzel,' Celia said. 'Rapunzel, Rapunzel, let down your hair.' She put her cup into her saucer then because she knew what would happen next, knew that Aaron's hand would come out to her, would touch her hair and then her face.

She put up her own hand and covered his and for what seemed like a long moment they sat there, in the sunlit window, until it seemed right to move closer. His kiss, when his mouth touched hers, was tentative and soft, as she had always known it would be.

'Celia?' He was uncertain.

'It's all right,' she said and moved until her arms were around him.

It seemed they stayed like that for a long time, content to kiss, to move their limbs occasionally for ease, oblivious of the life of London that existed outside their ken. Sometimes one or the other would speak but, strangely, neither of them spoke of what each knew was happening between them.

He spoke of a plane moving steadily across the sky until it was lost to sight behind the window frame. She reminded him that in Paris his hair had been short and had curled fiercely as it grew. Now it was soft to her touch and went obediently behind his ears when she stroked it.

There is a moment when the fierce heat of a July day trembles and turns, preparing for night. The sunlight softens on the edges of buildings, and birds cease flying far, as though they know the day has reached its point of no return.

When that moment came they rose from the window seat and walked, hands touching but not holding, towards Celia's bedroom, there to undress back to back with hands that trembled on buttons and fumbled with shoes, until at last they were both safe beneath the covers and could turn to each other once more.

This is what I have waited for, Celia thought. This is what love is. Perfect happiness and complete fulfilment. But even as Aaron's breathing quickened she sensed the fear in him, a fear that mounted until she put him gently away from her.

'Don't be afraid,' she said. 'It feels strange for me, too. Strange but right. I know this is right.'

He kissed her eyes then, gently, her forehead, her temples, the tops of her fingers, the base of her throat.

'I love you, Aaron.' She felt him tremble and realised he was crying. 'Don't cry,' she said. 'Don't cry.' They lay together, naked and touching, but when she would have begun to love him she felt him withdraw. 'It doesn't matter,' she said at last. 'It doesn't matter at all.'

She lay for a while, trying hard not to give way to tears at her own inadequacy. I love him and I don't know how to help him, she thought. Did he want to make love? Perhaps if she had been more experienced? But in her heart of hearts she knew it was more than that. His need was greater than a mere physical expression of love.

In the end she turned on her side and put an arm around him. They lay for a while and then he spoke, his breath soft against her face.

'I'm tired, Celia,' he said. 'I am tired of travelling.' An hour later he gently extricated himself from her embrace and, in a bedroom now lit only by moonlight, he put on his clothes, kissed her gently and let himself out of the flat.

'Take care,' she called softly. 'Take care.'

And he was gone.

38

Peggy

There were letters on the mat as they shepherded the children out of the door. Peggy scooped them up and put them on the window ledge. 'I'll open them when we get back.' There was tension in the air and she wanted to get the little group out of the house and down the path as soon as possible.

Her own children gambolled ahead happily enough. Amy's two followed on behind on less willing legs, turning occasionally to look at Peggy and their mother for reassurance. Peggy smiled back. That Amy was too preoccupied with her own fears to be of much use was painfully apparent. The last week had not been easy, partly because Amy was suffering from the withdrawal of alcohol.

'How much were you drinking?' Peggy had asked one night, when Amy's trembling hand could barely lift a cup to her lips. The answer had been an unknowing shake of the head. 'Where did you get it from? I mean, booze is expensive.'

Just for a second the old Amy had flashed forth. 'I had money, Peggy. I was never short of money. And there was drink in the house. We had a cabinet . . . it was just there.'

Peggy had kept her own counsel then, disapproving, first of a man who saw his wife become a drunkard and still kept a well-stocked bar, and secondly of a woman living amid plenty, who was foolish enough not to put a bit by for a rainy day. For Amy had nothing. Only coppers in her purse and a ten-shilling note discovered in the back of her diary. Her father's estate had been bankrupt. She would not receive a penny from it. And it was no use looking to Geoffrey for help now.

If it had not been for the thirty pounds Celia had left 'to tide things over' it would have been difficult to put food on the table for the six of them. It couldn't go on. Amy was increasingly fearful of the future and, besides, it wasn't fair to Peter or Margaret to have their home taken over. Not for ever. All the same, it would be a harder heart than hers that could hold the door and say 'Go'.

She had suggested temporary entry into the local school partly to stem Amy's fears that her children would fall behind and partly to free herself from the worrying prospect of two bored and bewildered children sitting around all day. The headmistress had been willing enough to take them and today was their first day.

They went over the threshold with one tremulous backward glance and the teacher's firm hands on their shoulder. 'Leave them to me,' she said and received a grateful smile from Peggy in return. Amy almost ran from the school yard and as Peggy hurried after her she could see that Amy's shoulders were shaking with sobs. For one tiny second satisfaction gripped her. Amy had always had everything. Now she was getting her share of the reality of life. But the mean thought was gone as quickly as it came.

'Come on,' she said, linking her friend's arm. 'They'll enjoy it. It's a good school – and it's the start of a normal life for them, Amy. That's a beginning.'

She put on the kettle when they got back and then fetched the post from the hallway. 'There's one for you,' she said, pushing a buff envelope towards Amy. She was reading her gas bill when she heard Amy's swift intake of breath. 'What is it?'

Amy kept on reading, her face becoming more and more horrified as she continued. 'Well?' Peggy insisted. Without a word Amy handed her the letter. It came from a firm of solicitors in St Albans and was couched in official language.

> We write to notify you that it is the intention of our client, Geoffrey Elliot Harlow, to take proceedings against you on the basis that you have given grounds for divorce by reason of your desertion. The matter

of custody of his children, Adam and Alice Harlow, will also be entered into the suit.

'I knew he wouldn't let me go,' Amy said when Peggy finished reading and looked up.

'But he is. He's divorcing you.'

Amy shook her head. 'No, Peggy. You don't understand Geoffrey. That letter is to tell me that if I don't come back he'll take the children. So I'll have to go back.'

'Rubbish!' Peggy leaned across the table. 'I don't know much, Amy pet, but I know you can't go back there because if you do you won't last five minutes. You look a hundred as it is . . . I'm not being nasty, I'm just stating facts. And where will your bairns be then with you dead and only him left?'

She waited for a reaction and got only a despairing shake of the head. 'Well?' she said at last. 'I'm not going to argue. We need Celia in on this. I'll ring her later on. Now, get your coat on. We're going down the shops to get the dinner. Those bairns'll be famished when they get back.'

They bought best end of neck. 'We'll stew it with barley,' Peggy said. At the greengrocer's they bought spring cabbage and carrots and a pound of Bramley apples for a pie. 'You can make the pastry,' Peggy said. It wasn't that she wanted help. She hated sharing her kitchen. But the only way to take Amy's mind off her problems was to keep her busy.

On the way home they passed the second-hand shop.

The 'For Sale' sign was still up but the window was half empty. 'Did Celia tell you I went to the sale at the George?' She had been afraid to mention it before for fear of reviving painful memories of home but for once Amy perked up.

'Yes,' she said. 'She did say.'

'No need to sound so astonished. I do get away from Belgate occasionally, you know. Celia gave me some money – and I bought one or two things we thought you'd like. I had to guess so I hope I guessed right. Anyway, we'll have a look when we get back and you can tell me.'

The way home led them near the school. The sound of children enjoying themselves echoed clearly across the distance. 'It's playtime,' Peggy said, glancing at her watch. 'We'll cut down here and have a peep.'

The minute she suggested it she regretted it, seeing a vivid mental picture of Amy's two with their backs to the wall and terror on their faces as ebullient Belgate erupted around them.

The reality was better. Amy's son was dodging around in a game of tag. Her daughter did indeed have her back to the wall but Peggy's daughter stood protectively beside her and there was an expression of relaxed interest on both faces. 'See,' Peggy said. 'I told you it'd be all right.'

'I'm glad,' Amy said almost tearfully, 'but what's the use of them settling in when they'll only be there for five minutes.'

There was nothing Peggy could say. They couldn't

go on as they were, that was certain. She contented herself with giving Amy's arm a tug and turned her homeward.

Over coffee they looked at the auction lots, brought out from under the stairs.

'Oh, Peggy,' Amy said as she handled her mother's half-completed embroidery. But she did not cry until she sat in the rocking chair, rocking as her mother had done in those far-off happy days.

'There now,' Peggy said, when the weeping was over and they could go on with examining what she had bought. 'I did my best but I had to guess what would matter the most.'

'You got it exactly right,' Amy said. 'I didn't care about expensive things. We had everything in Geoffrey's house. I wanted the things my mother had handled. And Dad's pipe rack. I'm glad you got that.'

'Geoffrey's house?' Peg couldn't refrain from comment. 'You said "Geoffrey's house" not "my house" or "our house".'

'It was never mine, Peg. Not from the first day. I had such rosy dreams of building a home. We both did. But my dream came to nothing. You're the one who built a home.' She gestured around her. 'You were the lucky one.'

Peggy shook her head but in her heart she knew Amy was right. Better to have and lose than never have at all.

'I bought a few other things,' she said diffidently.

'Some teapot-and-jug sets, a wash-stand set . . . you can have any of them you want. They were going cheap. I couldn't resist them – but they're yours if you want them.'

'No,' Amy said. 'You keep them. I don't know how I'm going to pay Celia for the things I do have.'

'You'll get a job,' Peggy said. 'We'll both have to get jobs eventually. And we will! We didn't beat Hitler to give in now!'

That brought a faint smile to Amy's face. 'We didn't beat Hitler, Peg. When I look back . . . what did we do?'

'We wore passion-killers and slept on biscuits. We huddled round the stove in a ruddy awful Nissen hut . . .'

'We cleaned out the ablutions and answered to numbers and saluted some very stupid officers.'

'We had fun, though. When I look back I think of the laughter.'

'Remember the face-packs? We all put them on one night. Yeast-Pac, I think that was the name. Then the siren went and Celia said we should wash them off but we knew better. "The raid won't last long," we said. Five hours! Longest raid of the war.'

'I chipped mine off with nail scissors in the end. I do remember that.'

The reminiscence did them both good and they ended up laughing. At last Amy reached out and squeezed Peg's arm. 'You are brave, Peggy, the way you laugh when you must be sad. I wish I was brave like you.'

'There's no point in anything else is there?' Peg said. 'You've just got to get on with it. Which reminds me, get those tatties peeled. I'll go and give Celia a ring while the kids are out of the way.'

39

Joy

Joy was getting ready for a Sunday out in the country with Neville when Celia telephoned.

'So you were right,' Joy said when Celia had related the contents of Peggy's call to her. 'He's not going to let go. Why does he want to hang on to her, Ceely? Obviously, he doesn't love her and it's hard to believe a man who's achieving the recognition in his professional life that you say he's achieving would behave like that at home. I'm not doubting it's true – I've seen the results of it, haven't I? It's just so incomprehensible.'

She put down the phone when they had arranged to meet and hold a council of war, Celia's final words ringing in her ears: 'He's an outside saint and an inside devil, Joyce. I've heard of them before; this is the first time I've encountered one.'

While she waited for Neville Lavender to collect

her, Joy sat at the window of her flat, looking out on the rooftops. They were at last going to discuss her new role at Lavender's, the last week or so having been quite hectic. 'Might as well do it somewhere pleasant,' Neville had said. 'Besides, there are too many interruptions here.' So they were driving out towards Richmond, to find a quiet country pub and have lunch. By the time she came back she would know exactly what he had in mind.

If she was going to get a decent pay rise, she might be able to move from here. What she would give to have somewhere with a bit of green. Even a window box, although a tree would be heaven. No chance of a garden, not at London prices. She was planning a pocket-hanky garden in a back yard when Neville's dark-blue Rover pulled up in the street below and it was time to go running down to meet him.

He was out of the car when she came through the door and, in spite of her waving him back in, he insisted on coming round to fold her into the passenger seat. He is so nice, she thought, and I could have him if I made the effort. But there's no spark there. I couldn't like him more but that's not enough. Besides, he's still married.

There were occasional calls from his wife which, although they did not distress, certainly irritated him. And the staff were gossiping now. Sooner or later he would have to make things official. Or go back to her. One or the other.

She settled back as the car wove through the London

suburbs and resolved to enjoy herself today. Tomorrow, when she met Celia, she would have to pull her weight and come up with some ideas. It couldn't all be left to Celia and Peggy.

'Penny for them?' She saw that Neville was making occasional glances to his left, trying to catch her eye.

'They're not worth it.'

'You looked very serious for a moment. Almost fierce. That's not your usual expression.'

She laughed aloud. 'What *is* my usual expression?' His hands on the wheel were large and capable. Nice hands with blond hairs on the back of the fingers.

'You want the truth?' He was keeping his eyes on the road but she knew the question was meaningful.

'Wouldn't want anything else.'

'Well, the first time I saw you I thought you were immensely sad. I knew why, of course. I'd expected it but the depth of your sadness was a shock. And then, when you were trying to convince my uncle to give you a job, there was a kind of cheeky despair about you that I found very moving. As though you were making your last throw.'

Joy shook her head. 'You're making me out to be a much deeper character than I am. I don't think that deeply . . . well, I don't think I do. I just . . . live . . . get on with living, I suppose.'

'So why the frown a few moments ago?'

'That was for a friend. I was thinking then, because I've got to try to help a friend in a hole. And two other friends who are trying to get her out of it. We were together in the war, the four of us. I've got to do my share.'

'The Four Musketeers,' he said. 'One for all and all for one. I like that.' He operated the automatic clutch and the car speeded up. 'Tell me all about it over lunch and we'll see what we can do about it.'

They settled at a window table in an inn that was built out into the river. Beyond the glass the river was fringed with wild flowers and mother ducks led flocks of ducklings up and down the smooth water. Far-off smoke drifted up from a chimney hidden amid woods and an angler on the opposite bank flung a languid cast into the water whenever he took time off from puffing on his pipe.

'I could stay here for ever,' Joy said, feeling the peace of it seep into her bones as she sipped an apéritif of dry sherry. They ordered shrimps and then rack of lamb and drank a fine Chablis.

'Tell me about your friends,' he said as they ate their dessert.

'We came to talk business.'

'And we will. Over coffee. We have the whole afternoon – unless you have to dash back?'

'No.' Joy thought of how lonely the flat was. 'No, I've nothing else on today.'

'Good. We can see something of the countryside, then, and come back here for dinner if you like. We can turn Lavender's on its head in that time, surely. Now, what is your friend's problem?'

She launched into her story of Geoffrey's ill-treatment

of his wife and saw Neville's lips tighten. 'She mustn't go back to him,' he said at last. 'That much at least is clear.'

'That's what Celia says. You'd like Celia. She's a civil servant.'

'And what makes you think I like civil servants?' His eyes were twinkling and she found herself twinkling back.

'You'd like this one. She looks like Celia Johnson, and her eyes are the size of saucers.'

'Then I must meet her, mustn't I? Now, to return to your unfortunate friend, I know an awfully clever man. We served together in the war. His name is Jeremy Julius and he's a lawyer. He seems to specialise in matrimonial law, usually for very rich people, but he's a decent chap. He might be just the person to sort out your Amy and her problems.'

Joyce accepted his offer to speak to Jeremy and then, both remembering, they talked about the war and the comradeship they had found in it. 'I used to think the friendships would end with victory,' Joyce said. 'I liked them but not enough to make an effort once we had peace. And if I'm honest, I probably wouldn't have done if it hadn't been for Celia. She kept us all in touch and in the end I came to like the idea. That's why I must help her now.'

'And you will,' he said. 'Now, before we go out to explore, let's talk about our plans.'

Our plans, Joy thought. It was a nice phrase and boded well for her future at Lavender's. She gave herself up to thinking about the new products, which they had decided to call L'Elégance, and did not give another thought to her friends until she got home.

Miss Froud had pushed her Sunday paper through Joy's letterbox, something she did most weekends, when she had finished with it herself. Joyce leafed through it as she sat at the kitchen table, sipping a nightcap and winding down from the day. She must introduce Celia to Neville. They would make the perfect couple. There was much talk of peace in Korea but she would believe that in six months' time if it had lasted. Once more they were arguing over whether or not Timothy Evans had been hanged for a murder he did not commit. She found it hard to believe that there had been two murders in the Rillington Place house and it was proved beyond doubt that Christie had murdered four times. It stood to reason he had murdered Evans's wife and baby too.

She was closing the paper, ready to discard it, when she saw the headline low down on the back page. TRAGEDY IN LONDON SUBURB – ANOTHER VICTIM OF THE HOLOCAUST. She read on, to learn of the suicide of a survivor of the concentration camps, one Aaron Gotz, a young man who had survived Nazi terror only to hang himself in his room in Kensington. Aaron Gotz! It had to be Celia's Aaron. Too great a coincidence otherwise. She looked at her watch. Ten fifteen. She reached for the coat she had just shed. If Celia didn't know she must be told. If she did know she would be in sore need of comfort now.

40

Amy

Downstairs the radio was burbling away. Amy could hear Peggy's voice and the children, squabbling good-naturedly over breakfast. She knew she ought to get up and take her share of caring for the children but the impulse to turn over, cower down beneath the covers and close her eyes was almost overwhelming.

She would have to go back to Geoffrey. In her heart of hearts she had known there was no escape. People like Geoffrey were invincible. He would win because he had everything on his side. If her parents had been alive she would probably have left Geoffrey early on but she had stayed and now there were two children to consider. If she had had to think only of herself she would have slept on the streets rather than go back, but she had no choice, had never had a choice, really, since her wedding day.

The memory of that first night made her cringe even now, turning on her face, drawing up her legs, curling as far as she could into the foetal position. 'You're hurting me, Geoffrey.' And then, as it got worse, 'Please Geoffrey . . .' And then his reply, measured and cold: 'For goodness' sake keep still and let's get it over.' And days later, when she had begun to realise that a descent into hell had begun, she had asked the vital question. 'Don't you love me, Geoffrey?' He had smiled, a smile half pity, half contempt. 'Whatever love is. I suppose I must. I married you, Alexandra. That should be enough.'

'Amy?' Peggy was calling. Her children were waiting. She wasn't Daddy's little girl any more and the George, where everything had been easy and sweet, was no longer there for her. It had been broken up and dispersed, the landmarks of her childhood scattered to the four winds.

'Coming.' Wearily she threw back the covers and lowered her feet to the floor. Her body ached intolerably and yet she used it less and less. Even the effort of getting out of bed left her breathless. Geoffrey had always told her she was useless. Perhaps he had been right all along.

To assuage her guilt she volunteered to walk the children to school and relieve Peggy of the chore. Their route lay along a busy main road with coal lorries racing back and forth from the pit. She walked on the outside of the curve, feeling the rush of air as each lorry raced past. The children walked ahead of her, two by two, chattering away. That was the one redeeming feature, that Adam and Alice were settling. Except that they couldn't trespass on Peggy's good nature much longer and there was nowhere else she could go. She had no close family, only cousins and an elderly aunt of her father's who lived in a house in Halifax. All she had were her children. For their sake, she must go back – Geoffrey had told her more than once what happened to wives who deserted. They were left destitute, deprived of their children, outcasts. And he was already beginning to carry out his threat. The solicitor's letter had been only the beginning.

'Careful!' A woman had seized her elbow. 'You want to watch it swaying about like that. You'll be under one of them lorries, if you're not careful.' She tried to stammer her thanks but the woman was looking at her strangely as she hurried away.

She stood at the school railings until the last child filed from sight and then she made her way home, keeping as far from the kerb as she could.

Peggy was standing in the doorway, an open letter in her hand. 'I've just brewed. Get a cup. This letter's from Joy – good news and bad. Now, don't look like that. It's good as far as you're concerned. Poor Celia's the one with the problem.'

'Celia?' Amy put a hand to her chest. If she lost Celia . . . 'What's happened to Celia?'

'Get your tea and sit down,' Peggy said. 'And then I'll tell you.' They sat either side of the table. 'Well,' Peggy said. 'Joy's got a friend who knows a solicitor. A top-class divorce lawyer. She's spoken to him . . . well, her friend has, and he says he'll act for you.'

'Divorce?' She had never contemplated seeking a divorce. Divorce was what happened to other people. Irresponsible people, not people like her. That's why the letter from Geoffrey's solicitor had made her so afraid. There was no way she could stand up to Geoffrey, not when all the cards were in his hand.

'Well . . . that's in the future.' Peggy was choosing her words carefully. 'But your right to get something from Geoffrey, for keeping the children, at least, you must do something about that. Besides, you haven't got much choice, Amy. Either you divorce him or he'll divorce you. And if it's him that does it it could affect your rights over the children. You've got to watch your back. Joy's sending the money for you to go down there. I'll keep the bairns and you'll have her and Celia at the other end so don't go to pieces.'

'I'll have to go back,' Amy said. 'There's no other way, Peg.'

'Rubbish! I'm not going to argue now, Amy. But you can't go back. For the kids' sake as well as your own you must talk to someone who understands these things. Joy's got it all arranged. Besides, there was something else in the letter.'

The tone of her voice told Amy that something awful was coming. 'What is it? she said.

'There was a man, someone Celia met after the war. A survivor of one of the camps. Apparently they were very friendly.'

'Do you mean—'

'I don't know. I never knew anything about him until now. I thought there might be someone but with Celia you could never tell. Joy knew, apparently. Well, it reads as though she did. It's very sad. He's hung himself. No one knows why. There'll be an inquest and Joy says she'll let us know. But neither of them wants it to stop you going down.' And then, as Amy's eyes filled at news of this fresh disaster, Peggy said, 'Remember, Amy, this is terrible for Celia. We'll have to be strong for her.'

41

Celia

The letter came the day after Aaron's death. Celia recognised the writing on the envelope, remembering it from Paris and from the scribbled notations in the margins of his manuscript. She sat at the table for a long while before she opened it, knowing what it must contain but unwilling to see it in black and white. She had lain dry-eyed through a long night, Joy sleeping next to her for comfort, only one question on her mind. Why? she asked herself again and again. Why now?

The answer was there on the scrawled pages:

Dearest Celia,

How do I tell you that I am too tired to go on? Perhaps a part of me died a long time ago, perhaps in the camp, perhaps before that, when I realised that there were people who could hate me for no other reason than that I was born a Jew. I have tried to bring this part of me to life again and since you came back into my life I have thought it might be possible. But there is a lack in me, Celia. Something is gone that should be there. I cannot forget that in Auschwitz they could gas 10,000 Jews a day. Always, as I waited for the day of liberation, I knew there was a reason to survive, to live so that the truth might be told. Now that it is written I have done with it. Be happy for me, Celia. I have struggled and now I have peace. Shalom.

Aaron.

As she folded the letter and put it back in the envelope she willed herself to feel nothing. If she allowed herself feeling, the pain would surely kill her. She went to his house then but there was no welcome for her there, only blank faces and a refusal to admit she could play any part in their grieving. So she went to the coroner's officer and was given brief details of the manner of Aaron's death. In return she must testify at the inquest. 'We're not getting much from his friends,' the policeman admitted. 'Maybe you can throw some light on his mood.'

But what did she really know of what had been in Aaron Gotz's mind? As she sat in the courtroom she tried to work out what his thought processes had been. He had loved her that night – she had sensed it, felt it and if he could not bring that love to fruition it did not diminish it. But if he had loved her why had he left her? If it had not been for the comforting pressure of Joy's arm against hers she could not have borne the sombre atmosphere of the coroner's court with its fumed-oak panelling and whirring ceiling fan, which sent dust motes whirling round and round in sunlight filtering through coloured glass.

'Not much longer,' Joy whispered comfortingly but the evidence seemed to go on and on. A bearded Jew gave evidence of identity. Aaron Gotz had been a survivor of Auschwitz who had been unable to settle in the post-war world. He had lived in America and Israel and latterly in London. He had not been noticeably depressed of late but he did brood upon the past.

It was the turn of the pathologist then. He had examined the body of Aaron Gotz and found it to be the body of a man of twenty-seven years, in moderately good health. There was a set of numbers tattooed on the wrist, believed to be a tattoo inflicted when the deceased was incarcerated in a wartime concentration camp.

The body had been discovered at approximately nine o'clock on the morning of 3 August 1953. The pathologist had made a preliminary examination two hours later. At that time he estimated death to have occurred some twelve hours previously. Death had been, in his opinion, self-inflicted. A post-mortem examination showed that death had occurred from strangulation caused by a noose made of cotton sheeting. The hyoid bone had been fractured and there was bruising around the neck.

The coroner thanked the pathologist and then called the next witness. 'It's you, Celia.' Joyce was shaking her arm and then she was stumbling towards the witness box.

She gave her name and was gripping the edge of the box in an effort to concentrate when a face sprang out from the seated assembly. A calm face from out of the past, smiling acknowledgement and encouragement at one and the same time. The last time she had seen Glynn Chambers she had been leaving the hostel in Paris. He had carried her bags to the car and kissed her on both cheeks. And now he had come to her, from out of the past.

She did not dare to smile but she felt a sudden confidence. She must tell the truth. That was all. Her chin came up and she fixed her eyes on the coroner. At his behest she gave her name and address.

'What was your relationship to the deceased?'

'We were friends. We met in Paris just after the end of the war. And then again a few weeks ago.'

She told of that last day and his parting words and the coroner referred to the manuscript, which lay on the table in front of him. 'It is a sad testimony to man's inhumanity to man,' he said. And then, referring to documents, he noted that the deceased had willed the manuscript to Miss Blake in the hope that she would find a way to have it published.

Celia held tight to the balustrade as she descended

from the box, kept her head high as she resumed her seat, and then let her whole body tremble. 'It's over now,' Joy said. 'We'll soon be able to go home.'

Glynn was waiting when they came out on to the step. 'Death by his own hand' the coroner had said and pinned the blame firmly on the effects of war and the gypsy life the deceased had led since then. Celia would have sought out the Jewish men who had sat huddled together during the inquest but they melted from the court as though they were smoke, just as they had done when she had sought them out on the day after Aaron's death.

'Let's get out of here,' Glynn said. He looked at Joy. 'I'm Glynn Chambers. I knew Celia – and Aaron – in Paris at the end of the war.'

'I'm sorry.' Celia had collected herself. 'I should have introduced you. Joyce Latham, Glynn Chambers.' They turned and began to walk towards the main road until Glynn could hail a cruising cab and bundle the women into it. 'Just drive,' he said to the cabbie. 'I'll give you a destination in a moment.' He turned to Joyce when he sat back. 'I'd like to take you both somewhere for lunch. Somewhere quiet. The Athenaeum, perhaps.'

'That's very kind of you,' Joyce said apologetically. 'I'm afraid I have to get back to work. But Celia could go.' She turned to Celia. 'It would do you good. There's nothing to go home for. I'll come round as soon as I can get away from work.'

'I should go home,' Celia said uncertainly.

'Please.' Glynn put out a hand to hers. 'I'd so much

like to hear what's been happening to you. I've often wondered . . .'

'Well.' Celia half smiled. 'I suppose we could go somewhere.'

They dropped Joyce off at Bond street and went on to a quiet restaurant in Piccadilly. 'Now,' Glynn said, when quails' eggs in a delicate sauce had been placed before them. 'Begin at the beginning. You left Paris in the summer of 1947. Tell me what happened after that.'

She recounted her story then, the hard work, the promotion, the flat high above Kingsway. 'And then, one day, I saw Aaron's name on a list.'

'And you sought him out?'

She should have been ashamed to admit it but she was not. 'I went to him,' she said. 'And for a few weeks we were happy. He was writing the account of his life. He'd just finished it.'

'I expect that was important to him,' Glynn said. 'A kind of catharsis.'

Celia nodded. 'He'd been to so many different countries and never managed to find a place he could settle in. Once he said to me that he felt like the Flying Dutchman, condemned to sail the world for ever and ever.'

'What happened to Aaron and his like wasn't fair,' Glynn said and held out a handkerchief when Celia cried.

'Now,' she said, when she had recovered her composure. 'Tell me about you.'

'Nothing sensational, I'm afraid. I went back to schoolmastering when it was all over. My old school, Allingborough. It's on the south coast. I've a house there . . . I mean I'm a house master. I enjoy it. It's a good school with a good pedigree. Oh, sometimes I hanker after the excitement of the resettlement days but, all in all, I'm content. Perhaps you'll come and see me there one day.'

He took her back to her flat in a cab, promising to ring the next day. His kiss on her temple was warm and firm and not unpleasant, but she was relieved when at last she was alone and safe in her flat. She would have liked to curl up with Aaron's manuscript but it had not been returned to her. 'A few days,' the coroner's officer had said. Instead, she lay in a chair by the open window, letting the warm August air drift over her as she remembered the Tuilleries Gardens and the River Thames and a dark young face smiling into hers. That was how she must remember Aaron, smiling, because he was glad they were together.

42

Amy

Joy's heart sank to her boots when she first caught sight of Amy coming through the barrier at King's Cross. Wisely she chose not to mention her friend's downcast expression. Instead, she took Amy's arm and hurried her towards the taxi rank. 'Come on, Amy. We're going straight to Lavender's. Neville is letting us meet in his office. I thought you'd prefer that to the solicitor's offices. But you'll like Jeremy Julius. He's nice. Very human.'

Amy's first impression of the solicitor was that he was young. Solicitors should be elderly or at least middle-aged. But he seemed to know what he was talking about and when his gentle questioning brought forth details of Amy's ordeal over the years he nodded sympathetically, as though he understood.

'I'm sure we can sort this out,' he said at last. 'I

think you should apply for a legal separation at this juncture, custody of the children to reside with you. Our best bet is to present the other side with such a solid case that they decide not to contest. I'll need detailed statements from you and from anyone else who can bear witness. Your friend, Celia Blake, has already offered to testify.'

As she sat in Neville Lavender's office, it all sounded perfectly feasible, but when they were out in the street Amy's old doubts returned. 'He'll find a way, Joy. You don't know Geoffrey. He won't accept this. I know him.'

'Then you know you can't go back.' Joy turned into the doorway of a coffee shop and ordered two cups of cappuccino as soon as they were seated. 'You have to work this out because it's the only choice you have.'

'Perhaps this has scared him,' Amy said. 'Perhaps he'll be different . . .'

'And perhaps he won't.' Joy was adamant and Amy was puzzled by her vehemence until she explained. 'I've just come out of a relationship, Amy. I know how scary it is to be alone, how much you want to stay inside, where it's safe. But a bad relationship isn't safe, Amy. In the end it devours you, eats up your life. I've spent seven years telling myself tomorrow will be different. Tomorrow he'll be better. Tomorrow it will all come right. But it never does, Amy. It simply gets worse. Don't make my mistake. Get out now and see what it's like to be free. And you won't be alone. We'll be behind you, all three of us.'

It was the same story when she went to Celia's, where she was to spend the night. Celia was pale and her eyes were red with weeping, but she was composed and her arms around Amy were welcoming.

'You must make your own decisions, Amy. I'll back you, whatever you do. But remember what was happening to your children. Forget yourself and think of them. I don't think they're permanently damaged, but you must see for yourself that they're unhappy. Or were! According to Peg they're almost back to normal now.'

They moved to a small Italian restaurant, the three of them at a corner table, each with her own agenda but trying very hard to cooperate.

'Are you all right?' Amy asked, aware that she had been preoccupied with her own pain.

'I'm fine.' Celia's smile was watery but there just the same. 'I'm going to be all right, Amy. And so are you.'

'I'll drink to that.' Joy raised her glass. 'Here's to the Musketeers. All for one and one for all. Now drink up for heaven's sake and we'll order another bottle.'

'No, thank you,' Amy said firmly. 'If I'm going to see this through I'll need all my wits about me. I enjoyed that glass but enough is enough.'

43

Peggy

As she stood on the platform, waiting for Amy's train to arrive, Peggy realised that she had come to this station only twice in the last eight years, since the war's end, in fact. And yet, during those years of war, she had hopped on and off trains, sat on her kitbag in corridors, been hauled aboard already-moving trains by willing hands, sat up all night on deserted stations in the hope of a connection. And now, on the tiny platform of her own home station, her heart was beating uncomfortably with the worry of meeting a train. It was amazing how quickly you got into a rut.

She looked at her watch. A few minutes more and the train should come into sight. She was standing in the middle of the platform so that she could scan the departing passengers to left and right. Hopefully, when she caught sight of Amy she would look better than she had when she departed. 'You look like someone on their way to be hung,' Peggy had said, her patience finally exhausted.

Amy's reply had been succinct. 'That's what I feel like.' She had stuck her head out of the window when Peggy slammed the door and continued in the same vein. 'I know they mean well – you all do and I'm grateful. I'll never be able to repay you. But there's no way out, Peg. Not if I want to keep the children. The cards are stacked against women in a situation like this, you know they are. Only men have rights – unless they've been cruel or committed adultery.'

'He was cruel,' Peggy said. 'And he will be again if you go back. I know you're worried to death now but you still look better than you did. And you're not . . .' She had paused, not wanting to be hurtful.

'Not drinking?' Amy managed a half-hearted smile. 'Well, not up to now but if I can get up the courage to go into the buffet at the other end it might be a different story.' She smiled more broadly at the sight of Peggy's aghast expression. 'Don't worry. I'm not likely to spend Celia's money on gin and I haven't a farthing of my own – unless you count the threepenny bit in my suspender.'

'You got that idea from Joy,' Peggy said. 'She always kept up her stockings with threepenny bits.'

And then the whistle had blown and the train gushed steam and Amy had been carried away, still at the window, still anxious.

There was a hoot down the line now and a hiss

of steam and then the train was chugging towards her and coming to a halt. Amy got out of the second carriage from the rear, looking, to Peggy's relief, more like her old self. 'Come on then,' Peggy said, when they had passed the ticket barrier. 'What's happened? We haven't much time before the kids land and I'm dying to hear. How's Celia?'

Amy's face clouded. 'Well, you know what she's like. No hysterics. But she's grieving, Peg. Joy's being a brick but you can see she's worried. She had a nice chap with her, by the way. Joy, I mean. Neville Lavender. He's her boss but he's ever so friendly. He was the one who got me the solicitor.'

'What happened with him then?' Peggy said. 'It's like drawing teeth getting you to the point.' They were passing the Half Moon and Amy looked at her watch. 'No,' Peggy said firmly. 'I've got half a bottle of sherry at home if you're desperate but I'm not going in a pub without a man.'

'I was only checking the time,' Amy said. 'I haven't had a drink all day and I don't want one.' They walked on. 'Well,' Amy offered as Peggy was about to burst, 'he says I could go for constructive desertion. That means that I left because Geoffrey made it impossible for me to stay. Or we could say Geoffrey's behaviour amounted to mental cruelty. I'd have less chance with that and not much chance with either of them, if we're being honest. If a woman wants out of her marriage it's assumed she's in the wrong. You're supposed to stay and take it, whatever it is.'

'So? You're looking pretty cheerful so I know there's something else.'

'Well . . . Geoffrey being who he is and with the reputation he's built up working on the New Towns, Mr Julius thinks that he won't want a court case at all.'

'I see. So what he wants is to frighten you into going back.'

'Exactly!' Amy was positively triumphant now. 'He can't afford it all coming out in court so if I stand up to him, he'll back down.'

'And will you?' They had reached the front door and turned to face each other.

'I'll try. With you three behind me I think I can but if he gets to me – you haven't seen him when he starts, Peg – well, I don't know what might happen. But with you and Celia and Joy to back me up . . . I've thought about it all the way home and I think I can do it.'

'We will.' Peggy turned the key and opened the door. 'At least, I will. And I know it's not easy, but you can stay here as long as it takes you to get turned round. I heard about my compen today . . .' She saw Amy's look of incomprehension. 'I'll be compensated by the Coal Board for Jim's death. I'll need to see to the kids and their future but at least I'll have something behind me. We'll manage somehow, the six of us. At least we won't starve.'

They were in the hall now, the door closed behind them. Amy put up a hand to her eyes and then reached out to enfold Peg in her arms. 'Oh Peggy, Peggy . . . I shouldn't feel sorry for myself when I have friends like you. It's lovely of you to say we can stay here and I'm grateful but it might not come to that. Mr Julius thinks he can get me a settlement or maintenance for Adam and Alice. Not a fortune because we don't want to push Geoffrey too far. But I'll have something and if I can get a job I should be all right. In the meantime' – she opened her bag and took out a bulky envelope – 'Joy's made me take this: five hundred pounds. She says she doesn't want it back but I will pay it back, of course. For now it means I can rent somewhere – somewhere near you, hopefully.'

'I'll put the kettle on and then we'll get down to things,' Peggy said practically, but as she assembled the tea things Amy could see she was in a brown study.

'I've more to tell you about Joy and her boss,' Amy said when the tea was poured. 'I think he's keen on her, Peggy. She doesn't seem interested but he's ever so nice. She says she's going to throw him and Celia together when Celia's over all the trouble.'

'Hold on,' Peggy said. 'Before we go on to that, I've been thinking. You need a flat, well a flat or a house. But a flat would do to start with.'

'I don't think I could afford a house,' Amy said doubtfully. 'Not for ages.'

'No,' Peggy agreed. 'But you need a home.' She stood up suddenly and rummaged behind the clock. 'I found this the other day. I cut it out of the *Daily Mirror* not that long after I joined up.' She passed the tattered news clipping to Amy, who read it aloud. '*Home's not a place. It's a combination of people you know, doing jobs you know, places that look the same, familiar faces, familiar food, familiar laws and so on. And now what's happened? Even those remarkable few who live in the same house find it another world. S and K pie isn't every Wednesday any longer. There's a hole in the ground where the Snoaks lived. The Grey Lion got blown up. Laura's in the WAAF and George is over Genoa in a Lancaster . . .*'

'It's true, isn't it?' Peg said when Amy had finished. 'We were all upheaved. No wonder things don't work out for some people.'

'It wasn't all bad. We saw places and made friends we'd never have seen or made if it hadn't been for the war. All the same, this harking back isn't finding me a roof over my head.'

'There's a flat above the second-hand shop.'

'It's not for rent, Peg.' Amy's cup had paused halfway to her mouth.

'I know. It's for sale. One thousand five hundred pounds. Every time I've passed that shop I've wished I had one thousand five hundred pounds.'

'What for?' Amy had put her cup back in the saucer and her eyes were round.

'To run, silly. I fancy running a second-hand shop. Ever since that auction I've been thinking I'd like to do it.'

'Could you make it work?'

'I don't know. But he did. He's giving it up because

of his arthritis. Otherwise, it's a goldmine. And I'm as good as any man. If you were in the flat you could mind the shop while I was out buying. I'd pay you for it – not a fortune, but something.'

'Oh Peg.' Amy's eyes had gone round in a face that grew paler by the minute. 'It sounds ideal, but could we make a go of it?'

'We won't know till we try. I'd need your five hundred pounds as a down payment – my compen's coming, but it could take a while.'

'You've got it. And Celia said I only had to ask . . .'

'With my compen I could get a mortgage. Or maybe Sid would let me pay over time. Anyway, Amy, are you game to have a try?'

In answer, Amy raised her cup as though in a toast. 'Here's to us, Peggy. Harlow and Dobson. Or Dobson and Harlow?'

Peggy clinked her cup with her friends. 'Not Harlow and Dobson. Peg and Amy's?' Amy wrinkled her nose in disapproval. 'Second Best?' Peggy offered.

'No,' Amy said firmly. 'Second Best sounds second-class and we'd be selling really nice things.'

'That's it,' Peg said. '"Nice things." I like that.'

'"Nice things" it is then,' Amy said. 'Now, what will we call the next shop?'

'Let's not talk of a chain till we've got this one going. Still, if we work hard, Amy, we can make it work. I know we can. There are places where you can buy seconds, brand-new goods with just a little flaw in them. We can sell those too.'

'And china.' Amy's eyes were shining. 'I love nice china. And that's something people are always wanting.'

'You can be in charge of china,' Peggy said. 'Now let's go and meet the kids. We can talk on the way.'

Amy reached out suddenly and touched her friend's arm. 'If it hadn't been for the war we'd never have met, Peg.' Her brow clouded. 'But then I'd never have met Geoffrey, either. I suppose it's swings and roundabouts.'

'You wouldn't be without your bairns.' Peg was ever practical. 'Still, it does make you think. If it hadn't been for Hitler . . .' She raised her cup in a toast but they spoke in unison.

'To Churchill.'

There was a moment of silence before Amy spoke.

'Would you ever marry again, Peg?'

'Chance'd be a fine thing. I might, if I got the chance. But I'll cross that bridge when I come to it, if you don't mind. You'll marry though. Oh, you can shake your head in horror and I understand why. But some nice man'll snap you up. Just don't do it till we're out of debt, that's all I ask.'

'Not till we've made the first million.' It was Amy's turn to raise her cup and toast the vow.

44

Celia

Celia had elected to travel to Allingborough by train. They would be quiet on a Saturday, without the press of workers travelling in and out of London. Besides, she didn't feel up to driving, especially not the borrowed Wolsely with its surging engine.

Since the inquest she had felt unreal. Bereft without the rights of the bereaved. She had been shut out of the funeral arrangements and, if it had not been for the zeal of the coroner's officer, she would have been excluded from the inquest too. And yet she felt responsible. If they had not met again would Aaron be alive? She had read and reread the MS in search of a clue, but who was she to know the workings of Aaron Gotz's mind? On her own admission, she had hardly known him.

Now she leaned her head against the train window

and watched Kent rolling by. It was a week since the inquest, but she felt no better.

Glynn telephoned the next day and he was comforting. 'Aaron wanted you to understand his motives, Celia. I think he felt he'd come as far as he could go. Perhaps it was completing his book that made him feel like that, I don't know. And perhaps there's a clue in there – at the end – towards what he was feeling. If you'd like me to, I'll read it.' She had posted it to him the next day, together with a note.

'I must get it published if I can, Glynn. It's the least I can do for him. I wanted to pay for his funeral but they wouldn't let me. They didn't like my involvement, so they're hardly likely to welcome my doing anything with his written work, but I feel I must try.'

His letter came two days later.

> I have the MS and at first glance it's good, even brilliant. Let me read it, then we'll decide what to do with it. In the meantime, don't worry. Perhaps that's what I love about you, that you get involved. But if the book is a story worth telling – worth publishing – the overriding right surely is Aaron's. He wanted his story told. That's why he wrote it, why he gave it to you.

So she was going to Allingborough today, to see the school and to talk to Glynn. And somehow the thought that he would be there, waiting for her at journey's end, was a comfort.

She saw him, bareheaded on the platform, as the train swooped into the station. 'Celia.' He bent to kiss her cheek, and she smelled the odours of soap and tweed and newly barbered skin. 'I thought we'd look over the school this morning. Then lunch. After that we can talk and perhaps see a little of the coast. If you'll stay, and I hope you will, we'll have an early dinner before I put you on the train.'

His car was an open sports. 'A Triumph,' he said. 'My one extravagance.' They drove between hedges filled with meadowsweet and campion to the imposing school building. 'Erected in the time of Queen Anne,' Glynn said, and Celia smiled at the pride in his voice.

They visited the buildings grouped around the quad, examined the wooden panelling in the tea pavilion, where the names of past cricket teams were listed, and wound up in the quiet of the chapel. The roof was adorned with carved wooden bosses emblazoned with coats of arms, and in the sanctuary was a memorial, erected to commemorate the dead of World War One, now bearing the names of those who had died in World War Two.

'So many young lives cut short,' Celia said. But it was not the bearers of the names listed in gold of whom she was thinking.

They drove into a nearby village for lunch, eating in a raftered dining room and chuckling over the wide menu because it reminded them of Paris and shortages.

'Not soup, I think,' Glynn said.

'Nor potatoes.' Celia wrinkled her nose. 'It was years before I could face soup and potatoes.'

They took their coffee into the lounge, sitting in deep chintz armchairs that had seen better days but were comfort personified. Glynn asked her permission to smoke his pipe and when she agreed he puffed gently for a moment or two. 'Now, to this book,' he said. The hand that held the pipe was square and blunt-fingered but it would be a kind hand if it touched you, Celia thought, and was confused by the idea. Why should she think such a thing? She tried to concentrate on what he was saying.

'I think he's written something important. It's raw, he's pulled no punches. At times even I – and I thought I'd heard it all – I was brought up short by the horror. The details of life in a concentration camp are mind-blowing. And what he says about illegal entry into Israel and the politics of the thing . . . well, it's eminently readable and, I'm inclined to think, rather important.'

'Will you take care of it?'

He leaned towards her across the table. 'Stop frowning. You know I'll take care of it. Now, drink up that coffee and I'll take you to the seaside.'

The breeze ruffled her hair as they drove and she put up a hand to wipe tresses from her eyes. 'Do you want me to put up the hood?' he asked, concerned.

Celia shook her head. 'That's the last thing I want. It's heaven to feel the sun – in London I'm an indoor creature.'

'High up in your eyrie?'

She was taken aback by his words. 'You've never been to my flat!'

'No, but I've built up a picture. You told me it was high above Kingsway – and quiet – and you are a very private person, Celia. I can imagine where you'd be happy and you have been happy there.'

Have I? she thought. Have I ever been happy except when Aaron was with me? And then they were walking down to a shingle beach and Glynn was taking her hand to help her down the slope, letting go as soon as they were on level ground.

They walked for quite a long way, the sun warm on their backs, the waves petering out a few feet from them.

'The tide is just on the turn,' Glynn said, and so it was.

Celia noticed the flowers first, white petals tinged with green, fragile and sea-drenched but still beautiful. '*Galtonia candicans*,' Glynn said. 'The summer hyacinth.' There was a further spray a yard away and then sprigs of mimosa and the small white trumpets of lilies, all lying along the tideline.

'How did you know that Latin name?'

'I love my garden – I'll show it to you when we get back.' He spoke absently and she saw that he was puzzled. 'It's bizarre,' he said. 'Hothouse flowers out here – washed in by the sea.' But Celia had looked ahead and seen the padded circle of wire with its sodden ribbon.

'It's been a wreath,' she said. 'Someone's thrown a wreath into the sea and it's broken apart.'

They turned and looked back. The remnants of leaf and blossom were there in a straight line – in disarray but still together on the tideline. 'It's like the diaspora.' Celia was looking out towards the horizon 'Scattered on the wide sea but always trying to return, to be part of one another again.'

'Now then,' Glynn said as Celia bowed her head. His arm round her shoulder was a bastion and she leaned against it. 'Cry for yourself,' he said. 'But don't cry for Aaron. He lived to taste freedom and if he couldn't come to terms with it he still had it. Don't underestimate the importance of that fact.'

'His life was ruined.'

'Yes. But not wasted. We remember him and if we can do something with his writing he will live on in other people's memories too.'

They turned away from the sea then, leaving behind the lilies and the mimosa, soon to be moving once more on the turn of the tide. 'And miles to go,' Celia said, half under her breath.

As if he could read her mind Glynn took up the quotation. 'The woods are lovely, dark and deep, But I have promises to keep, And miles to go before I sleep.' He smiled down at her. 'Robert Frost?'

She would have cried again but he took her hand firmly in his. 'Aaron kept his promises as far as he could, Celia. He travelled those miles. He told his story. Now, let him sleep.'

As they trudged up the beach he kept hold of her hand, drawing in into the crook of his arm so that she was close to him. Once, she would have shied away from such contact but this felt right. When they reached the cliff top he turned and smiled down at her. 'All right?' he said and was content when she nodded in reply.

Epilogue

1955

It is twelve noon on a summer's day. In London crowds flock to see *The Seven Year Itch* and goggle at posters of Marilyn Monroe, skirts foaming around her thighs as she stands above a New York air vent.

In spite of protests, another woman, Ruth Ellis, is hanged for the murder of her lover while in Germany. The Bundestag authorises a new German army. It will be called Bundeswehr and led by Hitler's operations chief, Lieutenant-General Heusinger. The war that ravaged half the world has been consigned to history but on both sides of the Atlantic Aaron Gotz's *Wait for the Day*, which tells the truth about the Holocaust, is selling well.

In a small country church Joy sits, eyes fixed on the sunlit altar. She is thinking of war, of dugouts and doodlebugs and comradeship that stands the test of time.

Outside two women are parking a Ford van. It is new and shiny and they park it carefully, one alighting to assist the other into the narrow space. When it is done to their satisfaction they move towards the church doorway. 'I'm going to enjoy this,' Peggy says, shifting her leather handbag to her other arm. Amy looks at the new watch on her slender wrist and wonders if the bride will arrive on time.

They greet Joy with kisses and move into the pew beside her. 'Isn't this nice?' Peg says and reaches for the Order of Service and the glasses the doctor has just told her she must wear for reading.

'I hope everything's all right.' Amy glances apprehensively at the church door and Peggy remembers the old, confident Amy who was always sure good things would happen. She is sad at the change in her friend but only for a moment. Things are going well and Amy, if not the girl she once was, is a bonny woman once more. Only last night she paused, tea towel in hand, and said in a voice full of wonderment, 'Do you know, Peg, I hardly ever think of Geoffrey now. It's hard to credit, isn't it, when once I was so afraid of him?'

Now Amy bends to whisper in Peggy's ear. 'Do you remember that night we went to London? The night they lit Big Ben and we saw the prefab? Weren't we young then?'

'Young and daft!' Peggy has a faraway look in her eyes. 'By, I fancied one of those prefabs. Everything built in.'

The organ swells suddenly and they turn to see the

bride. Peg and Amy ooh with delight at the sight of Celia in Brussels lace. Joy looks at the man who escorts her, proud and erect in spite of his limp. And she thinks that Neville, her husband, is not only the most handsome man in the world but also the kindest.

For a moment, as she comes down the aisle, Celia remembers Paris and flowers strung necklace-like along a tideline, but the memory is fleeting. She smiles into the faces of her friends as she passes and then moves on, to where Glynn and the future are waiting.